DEATH CRUISE

Depth Force Thrillers
Book Nine

Irving A Greenfield

SAPERE
BOOKS

DEATH CRUISE

Published by Sapere Books.

24 Trafalgar Road, Ilkley, LS29 8HH,
United Kingdom

saperebooks.com

ISBN: 978-1-80055-919-6

*The author wishes to thank Mr. Michael Bergman, whose editorial and
technical assistance has been extremely helpful in the writing this book.*

"BRING US DOWN TO ONE FIVE ZERO!" BOXER ORDERED.

Boxer reached toward the klaxon button and braced against the bulkhead as the Halsey *blew some forward ballast and nosed downward.*

"Skipper, multiple targets closing fast on our tail," sonar reported. "Speed seven zero knots. Four fish, Skipper!"

Boxer pressed the klaxon button twice, "Dive... Dive!"

Almost immediately, the ballast tanks blew, and the Halsey *went down and to the right, hit bottom hard and rolled onto her port side. "Damage Control Officer!" Boxer shouted. "Report!"*

Suddenly immediately an explosion rocked the Halsey *and threw Boxer to the deck. As he tried to pull himself up a second explosion rolled over the hull, and the lights went out.*

CHAPTER 1

From the sail's bridge, Admiral Jack Boxer watched the mushroom cloud rise and spread over what was once the Ice Castle, a Soviet base station carved from an iceberg that the Russians had towed out into the Southern Ocean. He checked the silver-dollar-shaped radiation indicator that he and all of his crew wore on their coveralls. The level was getting dangerously high. Boxer keyed the crippled Russian sub *Sea Dragon.* "Comrade Admiral, we've got to get the hell out of here. Fast."

"Roger that, Comrade Admiral. My technicians report extremely high radiation levels."

Boxer nodded to his Exec, Captain Mark Clemens. "Borodine affirms our findings. We've got to get out of here now, or we're in deep shit."

Boxer's radio cackled. "Comrade Admiral Boxer, the *Sea Dragon* has about four or five hours left before I'll have to abandon her."

Boxer rubbed his salt-and-pepper beard, as he stared at the brilliant fire against the night sky that once was the Ice Castle. "Can you still dive?"

"Negative. We've taken too much damage in the forward torpedo room. The *Sea Dragon* is taking water. To dive now is to certain death."

"Roger that," Boxer answered. "We've only got fifteen to twenty hours more life out of this old sub. Our main propulsion system is losing pressure fast. Our only hope of survival is to join forces aboard the *Tiny Tim* and try to make it to the Ross Ice Shelf. With luck, we may make it overland to the American base at McMurdo Sound, or we can hope to be picked up by one of our ships, or yours."

"It's the best chance we've got," Borodine said.

"It's the only chance any of us has," Boxer answered. "I'll have my navigator relay our coordinates to you. You should be able to rendezvous with us in about thirty minutes."

"Ten four," Borodine replied. "Thirty minutes." He hung the speaker onto its cradle and hit the klaxon three times. "Now here this ... now here this. This is the captain speaking. All hands prepare to abandon ship. We will attempt to rendezvous with the American submarine *Tiny Tim*."

Boxer checked his NAVCLOCK. It was twenty-three hundred hours when the *Sea Dragon* pulled along the port side of the *Tiny Tim*. Both ships rode on the surface. Boxer said to his EXO Clemens, "Get a deck detail topside. I want that Russian sub."

"Aye, aye, Skipper." Clemens keyed his orders below and at once a crew dressed in heavy Arctic gear clambered onto the freezing deck. It was covered with ice, and footing was treacherous. The men tossed lines to crewmen on the *Sea Dragon*, where they were cleated off.

One by one, the Russian crewmen were helped aboard the *Tiny Tim* by the American deck detail. Most were thoroughly drenched and freezing.

Boxer ordered Clemens to go below to help. "See that those men get into something warm and dry."

"Aye, aye, Skipper."

Soon the mess area was crammed with Russian seamen drinking hot coffee, tea, or soup.

Both ships rolled and pitched in the heavy seas, and several of the Russians lost their grips and were drowned in the freezing ocean.

Borodine shouted to his EXO, "Get the men off quickly. We're settling at the bow very fast."

When the last of the enlisted men and officers was taken aboard the *Tiny Tim*, Borodine followed his EXO Viktor Korzenko across to the *Tiny Tim*. Eight-to-ten-foot waves washed over them, drenching them to the skin with freezing water.

The *Tiny Tim* rolled onto its port side.

Borodine and Viktor were submerged and had to fight to pull themselves up to keep from drowning.

Boxer climbed down to the deck and shouted to his deck crew, "Get those men out fast."

Two divers clad in heavy scuba gear kicked themselves off into the churning sea and rescued the two Russians.

"Get them below, and into warm, dry clothing, now," Boxer yelled.

Borodine paused for a moment as Viktor was helped below. He said to Boxer, "Thank you, comrade. You have saved our lives. The *Sea Dragon* is settling quickly, now. She'll go down in a few minutes."

Boxer ordered the deck detail to chop away the lines. Within minutes, the *Sea Dragon* nosed into the sea. He put his arm around Borodine's shoulder and ushered him below to join his men. As Boxer took over the CONN from his EXO, he said, "We got them out just in time."

"Not a minute to spare," replied Clemens. "Now we're really in bed with the Russians, Skipper. We'll have to work with the Russians, or die with them."

Boxer put his hand on his exec's shoulder. "We've done it before, Clem. Comrade Admiral Borodine and I have saved each other's asses on a number of occasions. He'd do the same for me if our situation were reversed. Out at sea, we have only each other to look after ourselves. But right now, we've got to get the hell out of here."

"Aye, aye, Skipper."

Boxer keyed his helmsman. "Mahony, make one seven five degrees."

"Making one seven five degrees, Skipper."

"DO, take us down to one zero zero feet."

"One zero zero feet," the diving officer replied.

To Clemens he said, "That should give us some stability, and hopefully reduce our radiation intake level."

Clemens nodded.

Boxer keyed his engineering officer. "What's our status?" he asked.

"The reactor's down, now, Skipper. The main propulsion system is out. We're running on our emergency batteries. In several hours we'll no longer be able to dive. Then it's just a matter of time till we're dead in the water."

"Give me your best estimate of how much time we've got left."

EO replied, "If we keep her down to six knots, I figure maybe ten, twelve more hours at most."

Boxer turned to Clemens. "Our maximum distance is only sixty to seventy more miles. We're at least two hundred miles from the ice shelf."

"We'll have to abandon ship and take to the inflatable landing craft."

Boxer shook his head. "We'll never make it. Our only hope is to contact another ship in the vicinity."

Clemens scratched his head. "One of ours?"

"Ours…" Boxer motioned with his head toward the Russians crowded into the mess area. "Theirs… All that matters is that we're picked up. We'll deal with the consequences when the time comes."

Boxer picked up the MC mike. "Communications, send out a Mayday. There may be a research vessel or a supply ship out there that can help us. I'll have your counterpart from the *Sea Dragon* standing by to monitor any Russian traffic."

"Aye, aye, Skipper."

Boxer said, "Clem, take over the CONN. I'm going to have a chat with Admiral Borodine."

"Aye, aye, Skipper." Clemens slid into the captain's swivel chair behind the main COMCOMP console as Boxer made his way to the galley.

Boxer helped himself to a cup of black coffee from the urn, and fixed a strong tea with lots of sugar. Then he made his way to where Borodine was standing with the surviving officers of the *Sea Dragon*. He handed the cup of tea to Borodine.

"Thank you, Comrade Admiral Boxer, from myself and all of my crew."

"I trust they are being treated well?"

"Yes, of course. Your men have been very helpful."

"Good. Mind if we have a chat in my quarters? I'd like to discuss our current status with you."

"Certainly."

"I'd also appreciate it if you'd send your communications officer to assist mine. Morrison understands and speaks a little Russian, but if he picks up a Soviet ship he could use an interpreter."

Borodine called to one of his men and gave an order. The man saluted, and headed to the bridge, escorted by one of the *Tiny Tim*'s crewmen.

Boxer motioned to a small curtained-off cubicle behind the galley. "My quarters, Igor."

It was only when Borodine stood there in the captain's quarters sipping his tea and holding his blanket around himself that Boxer realized that the man was naked except for his hat and rubber boots. "Why didn't you mention that you needed a change of clothing?"

Borodine shrugged his shoulders. "My men needed them more than me."

Boxer took his spare blue overalls from a hook over his bunk and tossed them to Borodine. "They may not fit you well, but you're welcome to them." Borodine was built thicker than Boxer, but not quite as tall. While the Russian dressed, Boxer sipped his coffee and said, "We'll have to abandon ship in about ten hours at most."

Borodine zipped up the overalls, slipped back into his rubber sea-boots and looked at Boxer. He rubbed his graying beard. His expression was very grim. "We were monitoring a severe storm headed our way before the *Sea Dragon* went down. It won't help our situation."

"I've got ten inflatables aboard, with a normal capacity of ten men. They'll have to handle almost double that."

Borodine shook his head. "If we don't raise a rescue vessel before this ship gives out, I volunteer my men and I to go down with her. It wouldn't be fair to jeopardize your crew's chances of survival."

Boxer smiled. "Igor, my friend, we're all in this together. We'll just do the best we can."

The speaker next to Boxer's MINICOMCOMP interrupted them. "Skipper, an American supply ship answered our Mayday."

Boxer slapped Borodine on the shoulder, and broke out into a broad smile. "That's good news." He spoke into the MC, "Good work. What's the ID on that ship?"

"It's the U.S.S. *Polar King*. It was on its way home from a supply run to our research station on the peninsula. She'll divert to rendezvous with us. She has our position."

Boxer asked, "What's our ETA?"

"Eighteen hours, Skipper."

The smile left Boxer's face. He said to Borodine, "Not good. We'll be forced to abandon the *Tiny Tim* and await the transfer in the inflatables for six hours. I don't like the odds."

Borodine exhaled deeply. "As you said, Jack, we'll just have to do the best we can."

Boxer keyed the COMMO. "See if they can step it up. We may not make it for eighteen hours."

"Aye, aye, Skipper." In a few moments, COMMO keyed Boxer back. "The captain of the *Polar King* said negative, Skipper. He doesn't want to jeopardize his ship in the heavy seas. He says there's a major storm heading across his approach."

"That jackass. Doesn't he realize my men will be sitting out that storm in rubber rafts? Who's the CO of the *Polar King*?"

"Captain Andrew Axelrod, Skipper."

"Andy Axelrod? That wimp. He would pull a stunt like this."

Borodine was surprised by Boxer's outburst. "You obviously know this captain well."

Boxer screwed up his face in disgust. "Axelrod was a year ahead of me at the Academy. He was a coward then, and he still is now. He harassed the first year plebes unmercifully. One day he went too far with a friend of mine and I broke his nose. Several of the upperclassmen came to my defense, and I was given a reprimand instead of being expelled from the Academy."

Borodine chuckled, "If I had done what you did in my country..." Borodine made a slitting motion across his throat with his forefinger.

Boxer continued. "Axelrod was reprimanded, too, for his part. I've never forgiven him, and flatly refused to serve with him since graduation fifteen years ago."

Borodine shook his head. He put his hand on Boxer's shoulder. "Not the man you would want to head up your rescue."

"He'd be the last. But right now, he's all we've got."

"You outrank him. Can't you order him to get here faster?"

"Not likely. He's going to go by the books and cover his ass, no matter who else gets hurt. Or killed. The best we can do now is continue on our course as long as we can, and prepare to abandon the *Tiny Tim*. We'll head for the ice shelf in the inflatables. We'd better set up a chain of command, and prepare for the worst."

Borodine nodded. "To prepare for an Antarctic storm at sea is to prepare for the worst."

At 0930 hours the EO reported in to Boxer. "Skipper, the batteries are nearly dead. Recommend we surface now while we still can."

"Thanks," Boxer watched the lights on the emergency propulsion system part of the COMCOMP turn from green to amber. He keyed the diving officer. "Set the diving planes at zero five degrees... Blow the forward ballast tanks nice and easy. I want to take her up gently."

"Aye, aye, Skipper. Zero five degrees on the diving planes."

"Clem, get an ice chopping detail topside as soon as we surface. The hull will freeze in minutes."

"Aye, aye, Skipper," Clem answered and he gave an order to a CPO. A crew of five men slipped into Arctic weather suits and grabbed ice axes. The *Tiny Tim* angled upward at the bow.

Boxer watched the Time To Surface clock tick down and the lights change from green through amber to red. A klaxon sounded. "Surface... Surface... Deck crew stand by to exit," Boxer said into the PA system.

The chief of the watch threw open the forward hatch and a blast of frigid Antarctic air filled the ship. Five men climbed onto the deck to clear off the ice as it formed.

Borodine approached Boxer and cleared his throat. "Comrade Admiral Boxer. My men and I wish to help with the ice chopping detail."

Boxer smiled. "Comrade Admiral Borodine, I gladly accept. However, I'd appreciate it if you'd join me on the outside bridge. The quartermaster will outfit a crew of men to help us with the ice."

Borodine saluted. He gave a command to Viktor, and five Russian sailors dressed and followed the American crew on deck.

Boxer said, "We'll send a new crew out every fifteen minutes, so the men don't exhaust themselves." He turned to his EXO. "Clem, take the CONN for now. I'm transferring command to the sail."

"Aye, aye, Skipper."

Boxer undogged the hatch on the sail and climbed up into the bridge, followed by Borodine. It was just 1100 hours and the sun rose for its four-hour late-autumn display. Boxer said, "Next month there'll be no sun at all until the spring."

"Four months of total darkness. It's a very cruel land, this Antarctic."

"Cruel or not, it's our only hope right now."

Just then the intercom squawked, and the EO interrupted their conversation. "We're out of juice, Skipper. That's all she wrote."

"Roger that." Boxer keyed the DCO. "How much longer can we stay afloat, DCO?"

"Almost none, skipper. We're taking in water in the forward torpedo compartment, and in the main gear box of the propulsion system. More important, the reactor's kicking up. The radiation level is code amber, now."

Boxer turned to Borodine. "Well, my friend, it's time to abandon ship. We'll put ten of your men with ten of mine in each inflatable. And then we'll head for the Ross Ice Shelf."

"My offer still stands, Jack. My men and I will go down with the ship. You and your crew save yourselves."

"Negative, Igor. Either we make it to safety together, or we'll die together. I'm not about to abandon anyone out here."

Borodine smiled. "Then good luck to us all. And if we don't make it, I'll be glad to die alongside you."

Boxer clapped him on the shoulder. Then he keyed the MC. "Mr. Clemens, take the CONN. We're coming below."

Boxer and Borodine assigned their men in groups of ten each per life raft. They took whatever protective clothing and equipment they could carry aboard. COMMO took along an old hand-crank-generated radio set. Mahony took a sextant, chart, and navigational tools.

Boxer, Borodine, and their execs studied the charts and took a last dead reckoning. Boxer keyed COMMO. "Try to raise the *Polar King* again. Tell the captain that we are forced to abandon ship and will try to make the ice shelf in rafts. Tell him that if we make it, we'll stick close to the edge of the shelf and head for the McMurdo Ice Station. Give him our coordinates and have him pick us up at sea or on the ice shelf."

"Aye, aye, Skipper."

In about ten minutes COMMO reported to the bridge. "Captain Axelrod says he'll do the best he can, Skipper."

Boxer inhaled deeply and let it gush out in frustration. "His best may not be good enough."

Borodine put a consoling hand on his shoulder and said, "Let us hope that it is, my friend."

Boxer turned to his men. "Gentlemen, if we don't survive this ordeal, I just want to let you know that you're the finest crew any captain could hope to command." He let that sink in a moment. He could see the men's faces fill with pride. "All right, men. Let's move out."

CHAPTER 2

The deck detail broke open one of the rugged molded cases attached to the aft section of the *Tiny Tim*'s deck. The first of the inflatable landing crafts popped open within ten seconds, accompanied by the hissing sound from the automatic compressed air canisters. Boxer shouted down into the sub, "Mahony, you're team leader on LC-1. Move your crew out."

As Mahony led his group of ten Russian sailors and ten Americans into the first life raft, Boxer noted to Borodine, "If anyone can guide us safely to the ice shelf, it's my helmsman, Mahony."

Borodine nodded his head. "Yes. And my navigator, Fyodorovich, is with him. We will be in good hands."

The deck detail gently shoved the raft into the sea.

The engineering officer and a Russian counterpart stepped into the second inflatable, followed by their team, twenty men in all. The officers carried charts and whatever tools of their trade they could salvage. LC-2 was shoved off, and rode low in the water, weighted down by the excessive crew aboard, and the fifty horsepower outboard at the stern. The engine kicked in, and the tiny craft purred after Mahony in LC-1.

One by one, Boxer called out his officers to lead a twenty-man team in the life rafts. Borodine summoned the Russian crew leaders.

"You're in LC-3," he said to his diving officer.

"Aye, aye, Skipper."

Twenty more sailors moved out, and then twenty more, until there were two rafts left.

Boxer called his EXO, "Clem, please follow me below. We've got some unfinished business." Boxer turned to Borodine. "Igor, you and Viktor please wait for us on deck. I've got to get some things."

Borodine nodded, and Boxer and Clemens went below. Boxer gave Clemens an order, and the EXO made his way toward the stern. Boxer removed the sealed black box that contained the ship's log, and a .45 automatic handgun which he wrapped in a waterproof pouch and tucked inside his coveralls. He made a final inspection of the bridge, and then lugged a heavy sack into the forward torpedo room.

Ten minutes later, he met Clemens at the forward hatch. "Ready?"

"Ready, Skipper."

"Okay, let's go."

The two men climbed on deck. Boxer turned to Borodine. "Igor, Clem will ride with you on LC-9. Viktor, you come with me, please."

"My pleasure, Comrade Admiral Boxer," Viktor smiled.

Boxer said, "Clem, you and Admiral Borodine shove off. I'll be right behind you."

"Are you sure, Skipper? I can take care of things for you. Why don't you shove off and I'll follow you?"

"I'm sure, Clem. We'll do this my way. Now move out."

"Aye, aye, Skipper."

With Borodine and Clemens away in LC-9, Boxer told Viktor to heave to alongside the *Tiny Tim* for a moment.

"Excuse me, Comrade Admiral, but what is the problem? Can I help you with anything?"

"Negative, Viktor. Just stand by."

Boxer produced a device about the size of a cigar box, and fiddled with some dials and switches on one edge. He tossed the box down into the hatch and braced himself to jump into the raft.

Boxer leaped across the three-foot gap from the awash deck to the inflatable. A swell lifted up LC-10 as Boxer came down. His jump fell short. He cracked his head against the wooden stern supporting the outboard and fell into the sea.

"He's hit his head," someone shouted. "Grab him."

Several sailors reached over the side, vainly trying to grab onto Boxer's body. "Can't reach," someone replied.

Boxer bobbed under the swell. When his head broke the surface, he gasped, and sucked in a lungful of air. "Save yourselves. Get the hell out of here. The sub is set to blow in ten minutes."

Without hesitation, Viktor threw off his coat and jumped into the icy sea. He made his way out to Boxer and grabbed a handful of clothing. "Come. We can make it."

"Leave me. Save yourself."

"I owe you my life. I will not abandon you."

LC-10 inched closer to the two struggling men, and several pairs of strong hands reached over and pulled Boxer and Viktor aboard. Boxer was wheezing, out of breath, and bleeding from a scalp wound. Viktor began to shudder from the cold. Their clothes and hair and Boxer's beard were icing up already.

Borodine and Clemens maneuvered their craft alongside the other. Borodine quickly assessed the situation. "Get them stripped and into something warm, immediately. They'll freeze to death."

Boxer looked up at Borodine. "Igor, get everyone the hell out of here. I've set the *Tiny Tim* to blow up in minutes."

"Yes, Comrade," he answered; then to the two men at the outboards, he said, "Let's get going. You heard Comrade

Admiral Boxer. And you other men, get them out of those wet clothes and into something warm and dry. Let's move it."

The American sailor on Borodine's raft gunned the engine and they moved off in the direction of the other vessels. The Russian helmsman on LC-10 saluted Borodine and did the same. Boxer and Viktor's clothes were stripped off and they were wrapped in warm blankets. Some of the men scrounged for extra clothing.

Boxer and Viktor dressed in the spare coveralls. Boxer tucked the .45 into an inner pocket of his foul weather parka. A Russian sailor handed over a hip flask of vodka. "For you, Comrade Admiral. Drink, it will warm your insides."

Boxer took the container and looked at the man.

"I was saving it for when we safely reached shore. But you take it. It will make you feel better."

Boxer raised the flask in salute and took a sip. He smiled. It was good Russian vodka.

"To your health," a Russian seaman called out.

The rest of the landing craft's crew chorused in, "To your health."

Boxer raised the flask again. "To the brave men of the *Sea Dragon* and the *Tiny Tim.*"

The crew cheered.

"And to the bravest of us all, Comrade Viktor Korzenko."

Someone slapped Viktor on the back and the men cheered again.

Suddenly there were the rumblings of four undersea explosions in rapid succession. Geysers of water shot upward from where the *Tiny Tim* had settled beneath the sea.

A fifth, much greater explosion followed. A mighty surge of water leaped toward the heavens, sending spray up to several miles away. A fiery glow bathed the area, and a cover of steam blanketed the sight of the *Tiny Tim*'s death. The waves caused by the blast hit the tiny rafts and tossed them dangerously about. Boxer shouted, "Let's get the hell out of here."

Borodine shouted to Boxer across the widening gap between the two life rafts, "The storm is almost upon us."

Boxer looked behind. The skies were thickening with clouds. A huge thunderhead loomed on the horizon, its anvil shape pointing in their direction. "Have the men lash themselves in so they're not swept overboard."

Borodine gave the thumbs-up sign. His craft picked up speed and headed southeast in the wake of LC-8.

Boxer followed, bringing up the rear. He clutched a handheld transmitter/receiver, his lifeline to the rest of his crew.

The storm overtook them ten miles off the Ross Ice Shelf, a glacier that filled much of McMurdo Sound, and landlocked the American geophysical ice station on Ross Island. Boxer keyed his transmitter. "LC-9, this is Admiral Boxer on LC-10. Can you read me?"

"Roger that, Skipper." Clemens's voice was accompanied by static squawk. "Over."

"Clem, institute radio check every ten minutes, down the chain to LC-1. Make sure the men are battened down. Report back to me with any problems."

"Aye, aye, Skipper. Out."

"Ten four," Boxer replied. He crouched low against the gun'ales of the raft, protecting the walkie-talkie inside his parka.

Boxer's order was passed on to LC-8, first in English, then in Russian. It was then relayed to each raft in succession down the line, due to the very short frequency range of the transmitters. All craft were accounted for and battened down.

The westerly blew the frigid Antarctic cold across the continent and drove it at the ten tiny craft at over sixty knots. The sea rose to ten to twelve feet. The life rafts rose and fell with the swell. Icy spray washed over the men, who huddled together to keep warm.

The inflatables pushed on through pack ice that had broken off the glacier. The sea water had turned to slush from the banging and smashing of these ice floes against each other. Boxer had trouble keeping the preceding raft in sight, only catching glimpses of LC-9 as his own craft rose up on a swell. He spoke into Viktor's ear.

Viktor shouted a command in Russian to the Soviet seaman at the outboard controls. The sailor gunned the motor and LC-10 closed the gap between the two vessels.

Boxer keyed his transmitter. "LC-9 … this is LC-10. LC-9 … this is LC-10. Do you read me?"

Silence.

"LC-9 … this is LC-10. Boxer here. Do you read me? Come in, please."

Static. Then faintly, "LC-10 … this is LC-9. Clem here, Skipper. Reading you very faintly. Over."

"Roger that, LC-9. Start a radio check. Repeat… Start a radio check."

"Aye, aye, Skipper. Starting radio check. And Skipper…"

Boxer picked up static squawk. "Repeat message. We do not read you. Repeat message."

"Skipper. Admiral Borodine looks ill. Appears suffering from hypothermia."

"Roger that, Clem. Have the men huddle close to him. Warm him up, Clem. And start the radio check."

"Roger that, Skipper. Ten four."

"Out," Boxer replied, and tucked the transmitter back under his parka.

Viktor looked at Boxer, wondering what was wrong.

Boxer shook his head, and spoke close to Viktor's ear. "Comrade Admiral Borodine is suffering from hypothermia. I've ordered the men to warm him up."

Viktor nodded his head. He could see several of the seamen on his raft suffering the early signs of hypothermia as well. "We've got to reach shore soon. The men can't take much more of this."

Boxer pulled a pair of field glasses from a coat pocket and trained them in the direction they were heading. He could barely make out the hulking mass of Mount Erebus, the twelve-thousand-foot snow-covered active volcano that looms over Ross Island. "About another hour. Less if this storm blows by us."

Viktor followed Boxer's gaze, then did a three-sixty check of the horizon. "Maybe the supply ship…?"

Boxer put the glasses back in his parka. He nodded. "Let's give it another try." He produced the transmitter and pressed the send key. "LC-9 … this is LC-10. LC-9 … this is LC-10. Boxer here. Do you read me?"

After the brief interval of static, "LC-9 here. This is LC-9. Skipper, it's Clem. The Admiral doesn't look so good."

"Keep trying to warm him up, Clem. And pass on a message to Morrison, on LC-3. He's got the radio."

The rain whipped Clemens's face. He turned his back to the storm and spoke into the transmitter. "Having trouble receiving you, Skipper. Say again."

The swell lifted Boxer's raft. He signaled the helmsman to gun the motor, and they raced down the wave like a roller coaster ride toward Clemens's raft. "LC-9. Tell COMMO on

LC-3 to try to reach the *Polar King* again. Tell them our position is desperate."

Clemens waved across the narrowing gap between them. "Roger that, Skipper. Wait a minute."

Boxer keyed the transmitter. "Repeat, please. Over."

"Holy shit, Skipper. The chain is broken beyond LC-7. They can't reach number six."

"Damn," Boxer spit. "Have them speed up and try to connect with LC-5."

"They already tried, Skipper. LC-5 doesn't respond, either."

Just then, an ice floe drove hard against the stern. The helmsman was jarred from his perch. "Help me," he yelled in Russian just as he was hurled overboard.

The raft spun out of control. Boxer shouted. "Save him." Several men rushed to the stem and grabbed for the man. He floated beyond their grasp.

Viktor leapt for the controls. "Man overboard," he yelled, and swung the raft around.

The helmsman was washed by a wave. He went down. When he bobbed to the surface, he floated face down.

Viktor pushed the raft closer. Hands reached out over the gun'ales to grab the man. The raft rose out of reach. Two chunks of the pack ice closed on the Russian sailor, crushing him, and driving him under. This time, he didn't come up.

Viktor was frantic. "Josef... Josef," he shouted at the spot where the man went down. Viktor circled the area. Still, his crewman stayed submerged.

Boxer inched toward the stern and put a consoling hand on Viktor's shoulder. "Sorry, Viktor. He's gone."

Viktor stared at the pack ice a moment longer, then looked at Boxer. He swallowed, and regained his composure. "Yes. You're right. We must go now."

The storm abated just as the last light of afternoon began to fade. Boxer spotted a string of life rafts ahead beyond LC-9. He shouted to Viktor, "Can you take us to the lead raft? I need to get closer."

Viktor nodded, "Roger that," and sped off ahead.

Boxer approached the lead inflatable and keyed his transmitter. "This is LC-10. This is LC-10. Can you read me?"

Very faintly, "LC-7 here. This is LC-7. I read you, Skipper. Go ahead."

"Have you regained contact with the others?"

"Roger that, Skipper. LC-3 has reported that Mahony has reached the ice shelf on LC-1. He's trying to find a low enough place for the men to scale."

Boxer gave a sigh of relief. "What about the rafts in between? LC-7 lost contact with the others."

"Negative on that. Sorry, Skipper. I saw LC-4 being flipped over by a wave. All hands were lost."

"Damn." Boxer's face was somber. "Let's hope the others make it safely." He hoped he was correct, but in his heart he knew that all three craft had been lost.

As night set in, a series of red-and-white lights flickered up ahead. "Good work, Mahony," Boxer said aloud. He switched on the transmitter. "Now hear this ... this is Admiral Boxer speaking. All life rafts head for the beacons. We're almost at the ice shelf."

The weary faces of the men gave way to smiles of relief. Boxer headed for the back of the chain of rafts and shepherded his crew safely ashore. Mahony and his crew had climbed the ice face and let down lines for the others to traverse. When the last of the men had pulled himself to the surface of the ice shelf, Boxer and Viktor climbed to the top. Boxer sat there, lungs heaving from the workout. He looked around him at the survivors, one hundred and thirty out of the two hundred that set out on the rafts. "Good work, men. We made it."

But at what cost, he reflected. At what terrible cost.

CHAPTER 3

Boxer sat there on the edge of the ice shelf, catching his breath from the exhausting climb. He turned to face inland, and took in the bleak surroundings. In the last rays of sunshine, the view all the way to the hulk of Mount Erebus at the horizon was a desolate, flat, endless plain of orange snow, dotted occasionally with clusters of ridges several feet high. Boxer had the thought that this would be an excellent place for Dante's gates of hell.

Clemens hurried over to Boxer's side. "Skipper," Clemens was puffing from exertion. "Admiral Borodine's ailing. He's having trouble breathing, and he's very weak. I'm afraid he may have pneumonia."

Boxer looked up at his EXO. "Well, have the MO take a look at him."

Clemens looked down at his boots.

"What the hell's the matter, Clem? Get the ship's medical officer to check him over."

"The MO didn't make it, Skipper!"

"What?"

Clemens said, "He was on one of the rafts that capsized."

"What about the medical kit?"

"Gone, too."

"Damn." Boxer stood up. "Put two good men with Borodine at all times. One of ours, and one of the Russians. And make sure he has enough warm clothing. And Clem … keep an eye on him. He's too good a man to lose this way."

Clemens nodded. "Damn good man, Skipper. I'll keep him with me."

Boxer put his gloved hand on the EXO's shoulder. "Thanks, Clem. I really appreciate it."

"Roger that, Skipper."

"Let's see if we can keep moving. We'll stick to the edge of the shelf, and try to keep Mount Erebus in sight."

Clemens offered his hand to help Boxer to his feet. Boxer waved him off. "I'm fine, Clem. Thanks." He got up and looked around at the ragged clusters of men huddled together in groups of ten to twenty, trying to keep warm by sharing their body heat. "Let's stretch them out in groups of no more than five or six men each, Clem. Head in the direction of the ice station."

Clemens watched the men pressing together. "Wouldn't they keep warmer as they are?"

Boxer said, "Sure. But you can't trust the firmness of the ice shelf underfoot. There are deep chasms in the ice that are filled in by snow. The weight of a group that size could break through the surface and send them all to hell. They would be safer in smaller groups."

"Aye, aye, Skipper. I didn't realize…"

"Let's get the men moving."

Clemens turned and headed toward where the men were congregated.

Boxer sought out the communications officer and when he spotted a figure with a heavy pack on his back, and a tall antenna reaching high overhead, he called to him. "Morrison, I want you to try again to contact the *Polar King*. Then we're going to try for the ice station. We'll never make it out here overnight without shelter."

The COMMO slipped an arm free from the pack containing the radio, and Boxer helped him set it on the frozen ground. Together, they attached the antenna. Then, Boxer watched the

COMMO work his magic on the radio, adjusting the many switches and dials until he was satisfied.

"I'll need some help cranking this old baby up, Skipper. You'd think that with today's technology, they'd have put a modern back-up radio aboard the *Tiny Tim*."

"Here, let me give you a hand with that."

"If you'd just hold it steady, like this," Morrison said and showed Boxer how to hold it just so, with one hand on either side. "I'll get one of the enlisted men to help us crank it up."

Morrison motioned to a radioman, and the fellow came and knelt in front of the device. He pulled a handle out from the body of the unit and cranked for all he was worth. Nothing but static came out of the speaker.

"Keep trying," Morrison said, and played with the dials until the squawking subsided.

Boxer said, "Okay, give it a try. Send the following message: URGENT... US SUBMARINE *TINY TIM* ABANDONED... give him the coordinates again... FORCE EVACUATED TO ROSS ICE SHELF... REQUEST RESCUE IMMEDIATELY... ADMIRAL JACK BOXER... OVER."

The COMMO repeated Boxer's message several times.

There was no reply.

"Damn. Try it one more time. Then we've got to get the hell out of here."

"Aye, aye, Skipper." Morrison repeated the message again. This time they were answered by an ear-splitting squeal, followed by a mumble of static squawk.

"That's it, I'm afraid, Chief."

Boxer put his hand on Morrison's shoulder. "Let's hope that all that noise means that our message was received by the *Polar King*."

"Hope so, Skipper," Morrison said, as he packed the radio back into his pack.

Boxer detached the antenna and helped Morrison slip the pack over his shoulders. "Stay close to me on the march to McMurdo. Hopefully, as we get closer, they'll be able to monitor our signals from the station."

"Sure thing, Skipper. I'll be right behind you if you need me."

Boxer made his way down the line of men until he came to Clemens and Borodine. Boxer looked inquisitively at Clemens, who shook his head. He walked over to Borodine and put an arm around him. "Igor, how are you holding up?"

Borodine forced his head up so he could face Boxer. "Not as well as could be, my friend. But don't worry yourself about me. You've got more important things to do than play nursemaid to an old Russian sailor."

"Look, Igor…"

Borodine placed a finger to his lips. "I'll be okay, Jack. But you must look after the others. They are depending on you to get them to safety. My men, as well as yours." He motioned with his head toward Clemens and the two other seamen assigned to him. "I appreciate your help, Jack. I really do. But if I don't make it, just leave me here and save the others."

Boxer looked at Borodine's face. It was pale and gaunt, with dark circled underscoring red rheumy eyes. The man had aged twenty years in the last few days. Boxer placed a hand on Borodine's shoulder. "Comrade Admiral Borodine," he smiled. "You're staying with me if I have to haul your ass home on my back."

Borodine smiled back. "All right, my friend. You win. How can I argue with a man who is obviously crazy. This climate does such things to a man, I understand. We'd better be going, now."

Boxer saluted and made his way toward the head of the procession. He paused to see that there was at least one officer in each small group. He also issued the walkie-talkies and whatever lights and flares he could salvage from the inflatable landing craft. Then he took his place near the front. He took a final look back at his entourage as the orange glow settled beyond the horizon, and it became pitch black. "All right, men," he said. "Let's move out."

Boxer and his men started the arduous trek across the ice as the temperature dropped to near zero degrees. The flashlights carried by each group appeared like fireflies in the black sky. In a half hour, Boxer let the lead group go on ahead without him, and he turned back to check on the procession behind him. The dots of light headed back in an almost straight line, varying only where the men had to make their way around an area of four-foot-high ice ridges in their path. Suddenly, there was a scream ahead, followed by men shouting: there were no longer any lights up ahead.

He grabbed the leader of the group behind him. "Hold it up. Pass it on back for the men to halt." Then he said, "A few of you men come with me. Bring some lights. And some rope."

Boxer took an electric flashlight and ran up ahead to the shouting men. They were clustered along the ridge of a crevasse. He turned one of the men around. "What happened?"

The man was shaking uncontrollably.

Boxer shook him by the shoulders. "Calm yourself, man. Tell me what happened."

The man hyperventilated for a minute, his chest heaving and his breathing creating puffs of vapor. "They fell through the ice."

"What?"

"They fell through the ice, Skipper. There were six of us. We were marching along, bitching about the cold, joking about what we were going to do when we got back home, and … they fell through."

Boxer realized that the men broke through a crust of snow covering a chasm in the ice floor. "Who's down there?"

The man shuddered. "O'Brien, Merle, Wayne, and Jackson. They dropped out of sight right in front of me. I started to sink … but Mahony grabbed my coat and pulled me out."

Boxer shouted to the crowd gathering behind him. "Get some lights, and some lines over here. We've got some men down in there."

Flashlights were beamed into the opening in the snow. The lights glowed against the walls of a crevasse a dozen feet across and possibly a hundred feet deep. The bottom of the pit was in darkness. Boxer shouted, "Mahony."

"Here, Chief. I don't think there's much hope for those men, Skipper."

"There might be a chance that some or all of them are still alive down there. Get me some lines. I'm going down."

"Then I'm going with you."

Boxer and Mahony outfitted themselves with flashlights and ice axes and extra line, and rappelled down the ice wall of the crevasse. Down about fifty feet, Boxer shouted, "Ahoy, can anybody down there hear me? Captain Boxer here."

There was nothing but silence in the pitch-black pit below. "Hello. This is Captain Boxer. Can you hear me?"

Again nothing.

The two men climbed down another thirty feet. They played their flashlights on the walls and floor of the chasm.

Mahony spotted something protruding from the snow at the bottom. "There, Skipper. Something red."

"A parka. Damn, it's one of our foul weather parkas. Follow me down. Careful, now. Don't want to loosen any more snow onto them."

With his boots planted firmly against the ice wall, braced tightly against his lifeline, Boxer grabbed a handful of red cloth and tugged. "Give me a hand, Mahony."

Together, the two of them pulled a semiconscious figure from the grip of the snow pile. "It's O'Brien. Hand me the extra line."

Boxer tied a double bowline around O'Brien's chest. "Mahony, go up with him. Have someone try CPR on him. Try to bring him around."

"Roger, Skipper."

"Then come back down. I'm going after the others."

"But, Skipper, they're buried. You'll never…"

"Get moving. Now."

"Yes, sir." Mahony snapped. He signaled to be pulled out of the pit, and walked up the wall with the aid of the life line. Then he helped the men get O'Brien out. They stretched the man out on his back, and a two-man team began breathing into O'Brien's mouth and pumping his chest.

Boxer hung head down in the hole, frantically digging at the snow, flailing it aside furiously, searching for more bodies. It was futile.

He was startled by a hand on his back. Mahony had rejoined him in the pit. He asked, "O'Brien?"

"I think he'll make it, Skipper. We got him breathing again. He's a bit shaken up, though."

"Who wouldn't be?"

Mahony shone his light all around the bottom of the hole. "Anything else?"

Boxer shook his head. He clapped Mahony on the shoulder. "We'd better go."

Two tugs on the lifelines signaled the crew on the top to begin hauling Boxer and Mahony out of the chasm. They walked over to O'Brien, who was now sitting up on his own.

"How you doing, son?" Boxer asked.

"Fine, Skipper. Feels good to be alive, thanks to you and Mr. Mahony."

Boxer smiled. "Let me know when you're ready to move on."

"Thanks again, Skipper."

Boxer and Mahony sought out Clemens and Viktor. Boxer told them, "I want as many of the men as possible tied together in single file. Especially those in front. At least that way they'll stand a chance if anyone falls through the surface snow."

All of them agreed that it was a good idea, and soon the procession started off again, led my Mahony, then Boxer. The first thirty men were tied together with about twenty feet of slack separating each of them.

Boxer said, "We've got to keep moving, or we'll die here."

Mahony nodded. "Between you and me, Skipper, if the *Polar King* doesn't get to us real soon, most of these men aren't going to make it."

Boxer took a look behind him and back at Mahony. He didn't say anything. The look on his face said it all. "Let's go."

Mahony kept to the edge of the ice sheet, to keep from wandering off, and to enable the crew of the supply ship to spot their flashlights.

They covered approximately two miles when they began to hear a groaning sound seeming to come from underfoot. The groaning was punctuated by occasional creaking noises. Boxer tugged twice on the line connecting him to Mahony. He shouted to him, "Let's move inland a bit. I don't like the sound of this."

Mahony gave a thumbs-up. Boxer turned around and motioned for the men following him to move away from the face of the ice. Just then, a deafening crack resounded, and Mahony screamed. Boxer turned back to face him.

A giant chunk of ice calved off from the sea wall. Boxer watched Mahony fall off the edge in an arc toward him, and then he was tugged off his feet before he realized what had happened. Boxer had the presence of mind to yell, "Get back," to the man behind him, as he catapulted over the edge.

The third man was swept off the ice sheet, and slammed hard against the sea wall. The line held firm behind him.

Boxer swung back against the ice face, and took the shock with the soles of his boots.

Mahony plummeted to within a few feet of the sea before he was jerked to a stop by his lifeline.

The newly formed iceberg glided into the ocean, leaving only a tenth of its bulk above the surface, and moved out to sea.

The lifeline was crushing against Boxer's chest. He felt as if he'd broken a few ribs. Below him, Mahony dangled like a broken puppet. Boxer summoned up all his strength and slowly began pulling Mahony up to him. His arms felt like they were being ripped from their sockets.

Then he in turn felt himself moving up to the surface of the ice shelf. He wrapped Mahony's lifeline around his arms and just held on. As he was pulled to safety he said, "Get Mahony up. He's hurt."

Viktor and the engineering officer, Van Doren, took the heavy line from Boxer's hands and pulled Mahony to the surface. Blood flowed from a nasty gash in the man's forehead. The *Tiny Tim*'s quartermaster tore a spare shirt into strips and bandaged Mahony's head. "That will have to do for now, Skipper. We have no antiseptics or medicine of any kind."

Boxer nodded. "Someone stay with him. He's been through a lot today."

Clemens joined the little group. "Are you okay, Skipper?"

"Yeah, I'm okay," Boxer lied. He turned to look at a man stretched out on the ground, and felt a stabbing pain in his chest wall. He winced, and stifled himself from crying out, and betraying his battered condition. "Who's that?"

Viktor replied, "One of our men. He was behind you on line. He was smashed against the face of the ice wall, and broke his neck. He must have died instantly."

Boxer took a deep breath. "I'm sorry."

Viktor nodded. "Are you able to continue on, or would you rather stay here for a while?"

Boxer forced himself to his feet, fighting off the pain in his ribs. "Let's move on."

"You are a brave man, Comrade Admiral Boxer. You would make a fine Russian officer."

Boxer looked at Viktor, caught the broad grin on his face, and broke up. "Speaking of fine Russian officers, how's Igor holding up?"

Viktor's face turned solemn. "I'm afraid if we don't get him some medical attention soon, he may not survive."

"Then we'd better get going. McMurdo Station's that way," Boxer said. He pointed ahead of them.

Clemens said, "I sent a scouting party up ahead, Skipper. The ice sheet thins out up ahead. It slopes down to about twenty feet above sea level."

"Let's head for it."

As the men trudged forward, the breeze picked up, and the temperature dropped well below zero. As they descended the slope and neared the thinner ice, the wind started to kick up the dry snow layer around their feet.

Boxer turned to Viktor and called for Clemens to join them. "Try to keep the men close together, now. The wind's picking up and blowing the snow around. I don't want to lose anyone else."

Viktor saluted, and went off to warn his men. Clemens notified the Americans. Then they moved on.

Before long, wind was whipping up the snow at forty knots, whirling it around the men. It felt like a blizzard, but there was no precipitation. Boxer shouted to Clemens, "Stay close. We're in a whiteout."

The snow blanketed the exhausted crew, obliterating their view of the others even a few feet away. The men dropped to the ground and huddled against the howling wind and blinding snow.

An hour passed until the whiteout abated. Boxer brushed the snow from himself. "Clem?"

A weak voice answered, "Here, Skipper."

"We'd better dig out, Clem. You okay?"

"I think so, Skipper."

"Let's have a look around, see how the men held up."

Boxer and Clemens got up and used their flashlights to seek out the rest of the crew. Viktor joined them, and they did a head count. Half the men were either unaccounted for, or had died during the whiteout of hypothermia. The mood among the survivors was somber.

Clemens said, "If you don't mind, Skipper, I'd like to just say a little prayer for all the men who didn't make it."

Boxer looked at Viktor, who nodded okay. Boxer put his hand on his exec's shoulder. "Sure, Clem. I'm not a religious man, but if that's the way you feel, go ahead."

Mark Clemens bowed his head, and closed his eyes. Boxer and Viktor stood at ease, heads lowered. Suddenly, a brilliant glare from the direction of the sea lit up the area. The three startled men turned toward the source of the light, hands shielding their eyes.

"Ahoy down there," a voice blared out from a megaphone.

Boxer could barely make out the blackened form of a ship behind the glaring searchlights. He shouted, "Admiral Jack Boxer, Commander of the U.S. submarine *Tiny Tim*."

"Captain Andrew Axelrod here."

Boxer looked at Clemens and Viktor, and broke out in a broad grin. "It's the *Polar King*, men. Let's go home."

CHAPTER 4

"You sure are a sight for sore eyes," Boxer waved toward the ship's bridge. "You didn't arrive a moment too soon."

The ship's captain called back, "How many survivors are with you?"

"I'm not sure. Can you train your lights over there a bit? We got hit by a whiteout. Many of the men are still blanketed by the snow."

"I'll send a landing party to assist you."

"Can you get any closer? Some of the men are in bad shape."

"No problem. The *Polar King* has a reinforced bow. I'll bring her up along the ice shelf. You get your men together."

Boxer made his way back to the largest group of men. Viktor and Clemens followed.

Viktor and Clemens shouted encouragement to the huddled mass of sailors, and helped dig them out of the snow drifts partially covering them. The two execs called out in their respective languages.

As the men began to stir, Boxer sought out Borodine. He approached one small knot of men and brushed snow from them. "Igor? Comrade Borodine?"

The group of Russian sailors shook their heads. One man pointed to a few men twenty yards beyond, and Boxer headed in that direction. The three men sat in an arch, snow piled upon their bent backs. Boxer gently shook one man by the shoulder. The hapless sailor toppled over, a victim of severe frostbite and hypothermia. "My God." Boxer was taken aback. He checked out the other two, who proved to be as dead as their companion. None of them was Borodine.

Boxer began to shout, "Igor. Igor Borodine. Can you hear me? C'mon, you son of a bitch," he muttered under his breath. "Don't die on me now, after all we've been through together. Comrade Admiral Borodine. Can you hear me?"

Several yards away, a parka-clad figure began waving in Boxer's direction. Boxer took off on the double.

A weary American voice called out, "Skipper, Borodine's with me and Mikhail, here."

"Is he alive?"

"Yes, sir. Alive, but not well. He won't make it much longer."

Boxer replied, "He won't have to now. The *Polar King* came to our rescue." He pointed toward the glaring lights of the supply ship.

"Thank God," the sailor exclaimed. "I've never been so glad to see anyone."

Boxer knelt beside Borodine. "Well, Igor. I see that you are still alive. We'll have the MO aboard the *Polar King* fix you up so we can transfer you and your men to a Soviet station."

Borodine managed a weak smile. "Yes, I am alive, thanks to these two." He grasped the American sailor's sleeve with his hand. "Your man Bond, here, and this fuzzy Russian bear Mikhail almost smothered me to death by covering me with their own bodies." Borodine managed a hug of appreciation to the Russian sailor, and placed his hand on Bond's. "They saved my life at great risk to their own. I am very grateful."

"Let's get out of here," Boxer said. "Can you two still manage to help the Admiral to the ship?"

"Aye, aye, Skipper," Bond answered. The Russian didn't understand, and simply smiled and nodded his head, as did his American counterpart.

Boxer led his procession of perhaps threescore men, out of the two hundred that set out from the *Tiny Tim*, and stopped before the dozen American sailors that constituted the landing party from the *Polar King*. Boxer saluted the young lieutenant in charge. "Admiral Jack Boxer requesting permission to board the *Polar King* with my men."

The young officer saluted crisply. "Lieutenant Roy Meade, sir. I regret to inform you, sir, that Captain Axelrod has denied permission for the Russians to come aboard."

Boxer couldn't believe what he'd just heard. "What? These men, Russian and American alike, just went through hell and back to get this far, and your captain is refusing to take them off the ice?"

Lieutenant Meade stiffened at attention. "I'm sorry, Admiral. Captain's orders."

Boxer fumed. "I outrank him and I'm ordering you to take us aboard that ship."

The lieutenant flustered. "Er, sir, Admiral Boxer, this is not my doing, sir. He flatly refuses to aid them in any way."

"But we can't just abandon them. They don't stand a snowball's chance in hell of surviving out here. We lost over half of our force already."

"I'm sorry, Admiral. Captain Axelrod was adamant. No Russians aboard the *Polar King*."

"Perhaps he doesn't understand our situation, son." He reached for the walkie-talkie that one of the seamen carried.

Meade nodded his okay, and the sailor handed over his radio to Boxer. Boxer looked at the instrument, then at Lieutenant Meade. "Patch me through to your captain, will you?"

"Aye, aye, sir." The lieutenant flipped a switch and spun some dials. A red LED light came on and the radio belched a squawk. "This is Admiral Boxer. Patch me in to Captain Axelrod. Over."

No reply.

Boxer repeated, "Admiral Jack Boxer, here. Get me Captain Axelrod. Over."

"Aye, aye, sir," the radioman replied.

A moment passed. Then Boxer heard Axelrod's slightly high-pitched voice come through.

"This is Captain Axelrod speaking."

"Andy, this is Boxer. Let me explain our situation."

"Negative. I am not taking any Russian combatants aboard the *Polar King*. We are a supply ship and my only duty to those men is to notify the nearest Soviet base of their whereabouts. According to Article one zero nine, section zero three four of the…"

"Fuck article one zero nine, or any other bullshit you can come up with, *Captain* Axelrod. These men are survivors of a naval disaster, they have endured the most hellish conditions you could imagine to get here. They actually helped our men to stay alive. And Comrade Viktor Korzenko, here, risked his own life to pull me out of the drink when I was washed overboard. Now for the love of God, get these men out of here."

"Negative. My orders are final."

Boxer was livid with rage. He shouted, "Axelrod, this ice shelf is considered the sea, and the naval code explicitly states that a captain of a ship at sea shall take on survivors of a naval disaster. I order you to…"

Boxer clutched his chest, groaned, and fell to the ice. Clemens was at his side in a moment.

"Skipper, you all right?"

Boxer stared at his exec. He opened his mouth to speak, and a trickle of blood dripped out of the corner of his mouth. Clemens' face went ashen. "My chest. Must have broken some ribs."

Clemens shouted at the young lieutenant from the supply ship. "Meade, tell your captain that the Admiral is in dire need of medical attention. I order you in his name to get him aboard the *Polar King* at once."

Meade relayed the message to Axelrod. He listened, then answered with a smart, "Yes, sir." He turned back to Clemens. "Captain Axelrod says that Boxer can board. I can't take more than two of your men with him, sir. And no Russians."

Clemens returned to the gathering of survivors, and sought out Viktor. He took his fellow exec aside and explained the situation. "I'll try to think of something. Don't give up yet."

Viktor replied. "I fear for the worst. With both your commander and mine incapacitated, I don't think this Captain Axelrod will deal with us fairly, if at all. Why not save yourselves? We will do the best we can."

"Never. Admiral Boxer would not abandon your crew, and I'll be damned if I will, either."

Viktor put a hand on Clemens's shoulder, "On behalf of my men, I sincerely thank you."

Clemens nodded.

"You will make an excellent admiral one day."

"If I live that long. I'm going aboard with the skipper. Maybe I can reason with Axelrod."

"Good luck, then."

Clemens turned away. He spotted his helmsman, and shouted, "Mahony, come with me. We're going aboard the *Polar King* with the skipper."

Mahony came over on the double. "I saw the Skipper go down. Is it anything serious?"

"Looks that way."

Lieutenant Meade walked over to them and announced, "We're ready to take you aboard, sir. They've rigged up a lift for the Admiral."

"Thanks, Meade. Well, let's get moving."

A modified bosun's chair was lowered over the side of the *Polar King*. Boxer was carefully strapped in, and Lieutenant Meade signaled the crew standing by topsides. Very slowly, Boxer was winched up to the deck, and set onto a gurney which was prepared to take him to the ship's infirmary. Clemens and Mahony had to fend for themselves, and they scurried up the rope boarding ladder dropped over the side for them and the landing party.

Boxer tried to prop himself up on his elbows. He coughed, and beckoned a petty officer to his side. "Tell your captain that Admiral Boxer wishes to see him now."

The sailor hesitated a moment.

"Now, please."

The PO saluted, and replied, "Yes, sir, Admiral Boxer." He disappeared, returning in five minutes with Captain Andrew Axelrod.

"Yes, what is it?"

Boxer coughed again. He could barely hold his head up. "Are you forgetting our respective ranks, *Captain*? I am an admiral, and I expect to be treated like one. Your men seem to have no trouble comprehending that, *Captain*."

Axelrod shifted his weight uncomfortably. He was not used to being spoken to like that aboard his own ship.

Boxer forced his voice to come out cold and hard. "Do you understand me, *Captain*?"

"I understand," Axelrod replied, embarrassed.

Boxer growled, "I want to hear, 'Yes, sir.'"

Axelrod glared at Boxer, who seemed much too weak to order him about so commandingly. "Yes, sir," he blurted out.

"I can't hear you, Captain. Louder."

Axelrod's face turned red. Several of his men had stopped to watch the exchange, as did Clemens and Mahony. "Yes, *sir*."

"Much better. Just make sure you remember it."

"And what did you wish to discuss with me, that we haven't already decided."

"We decided nothing. I'm…"

"I'm still captain of this ship. It's my direct responsibility, and even *you* can't remove me of its command. My responsibility is for the safety of my ship, and no Russian combatants are coming aboard. That's my final word on the subject, *sir*."

"I'll have you…" Boxer clutched his chest and gasped in pain. "Take me to your quarters, Captain." He motioned to his men. "Clem, Mahony, give me a hand. We're going to the captain's quarters."

Clemens took his place at the foot of the gurney. "Where's that, Skipper? I've spent my entire tour of duty aboard subs."

Boxer pointed up behind him.

Captain Axelrod nodded to the five-story bridge that towered above deck. "Pilothouse. Up there atop the bridge. My quarters are just aft. We'll use the officer's elevator."

In ten minutes, the procession let out into the spacious personal quarters of Captain Axelrod. The officers' mess was aft, and the officers' sleeping quarters were laid out on either side, separated by a head to starboard, and a stall shower on the portside. Boxer and his men took in the carpeted floor, teak desk and dresser, and the upholstered swivel captains' chairs that made up the furnishings.

"Phew." Clemens was impressed.

Mahony shook his head in disbelief. "This is like a palace compared to the sub."

Axelrod gestured with a sweep around the room with his hand. "Be it ever so humble…"

Boxer cleared his throat. "Captain Axelrod… Andy, look. I'll take full responsibility for the Russian crew. They're exhausted and starving. We've all spent a dozen hours at sea, weathered a severe storm, fought our way across the ice shelf, lost more than half our combined force. The men haven't eaten since before we evacuated the *Tiny Tim*. They're suffering from hypothermia and frostbite. Please… On humanitarian grounds, take them on board." Boxer lay back exhausted. That was quite a long speech for him.

"Sorry. I can't allow that. They're still the enemy."

Boxer lifted his head up slightly, and started to speak. No words came out. He started to croak, and motioned Axelrod and his men closer.

"Skipper, what's the matter?" Clemens's face was pale.

Boxer managed, "I… I can't … closer." He motioned, and Axelrod moved to within a foot of the gurney.

"Well, *sir*, what is it?" Axelrod asked sarcastically.

"Oooh," Boxer groaned and grabbed his chest. He slid his hand inside his parka and clutched his ribcage.

Mahony turned to leave the cabin. "I'd better get the MO."

"No. Not yet." Boxer beckoned Axelrod closer. "Have to tell you…"

Axelrod moved in. "What?"

In one fluid movement, Boxer sat up, swung his feet around and off the side, and placed the barrel of the .45 he'd been carrying against Axelrod's right temple. "I'm sorry it had to come to this, Axelrod. But I'm giving you a direct order to take those men aboard. Now."

"And if I refuse?" Axelrod asked indignantly.

Boxer smiled for the first time. "I'll blow your fucking head off, and feed your worthless carcass to the leopard seals."

"You wouldn't dare. You'll be tried for piracy."

Boxer grabbed a handful of Axelrod's jacket, and pulled him close to his face. He could read the fear in the man's eyes, and knew he had him. "Maybe. And maybe not. I'll take my chances. My guess is that your own men think you're a horse's ass. Now, give the order to take those men aboard."

Axelrod began to shake. Boxer was close enough to smell his fear. The captain squeezed his eyes shut, and blubbered, "I can't do it. If you want to save them so much, you give the order."

Boxer stuck the gun against Axelrod's eye, by now wet with fear. "Shit." Boxer turned to one of the *Polar King*'s enlisted men. "Who's second in command?"

"Lieutenant Meade, Admiral."

"Please summon him. On the double."

"Yes, sir." The sailor found a microphone and pressed the switch. "Lieutenant Meade, Bridge. Please report to the captain's quarters, at once, please."

A moment passed, and the receiver squealed, "Lieutenant Meade, here. Ten four."

They waited several minutes until Meade made his appearance. He stood in the doorway, watching his captain standing there, head hanging in defeat, Boxer sitting nearby, pointing a forty-five automatic at Axelrod's head.

Boxer stared at the young lieutenant, studying the man, trying to decide whether he would turn around and bolt out of the room, or enter and face the consequences. He entered.

Boxer winced, and clutched at the pain in his ribs. In a moment, he addressed the officer. "Lieutenant Meade, I am taking over control of the *Polar King*. Furthermore, I am arresting Captain Axelrod for insubordination, and for refusing to follow the humanitarian rulings of the Universal Naval Code. The code's very specific, Lieutenant. It states…"

"Yes, I know, Admiral Boxer. I'm aware of the duties of a naval officer. To be honest, I'm a little ashamed to have been a part of what happened to you and your men. Please accept my apologies."

Boxer smiled. "No apologies needed, Lieutenant. In fact, I am turning the command of this vessel to you for the duration of this mission. Furthermore, I'll report that you took command under my orders, in front of these witnesses, in the event that Axelrod tries to press charges against you."

Boxer glared at Axelrod. "If he lives that long."

Axelrod cringed. "You heard that," he shouted. "All of you. You heard him threaten to kill me." He looked directly at Boxer. "I'll have you court-martialed for this."

"Better men than you have tried, Andy. And they failed." Boxer turned to Lieutenant Meade. "Lieutenant Meade, please have this man locked up in the brig."

Meade hesitated a moment. He looked at Axelrod, then at Boxer.

Axelrod screamed, "You bastard. I'll have you thrown out of the Navy for this. I'm not through with you yet. I have friends in high places."

Meade nodded to an aide. The sailor picked up the MC mike and called, "NP's to the captain's quarters. On the double."

Within minutes two burly Naval police officers entered the cabin. Lieutenant Meade said, "I've been placed in command by Admiral Boxer. Please escort Captain Axelrod to the brig. He's been placed under arrest by the admiral for insubordination, among other things."

The two NP's looked at each other. It was their asses if they followed the wrong orders. They shrugged their shoulders, and took their captain under each arm. "Won't you please come with us, sir?"

"Right this way, please, Captain Axelrod. Sorry, sir. But orders are orders."

"I give the orders on this ship," Axelrod blasted.

"Not any more, you don't," Boxer said. He looked at the NP's. "Lieutenant Meade is in charge for the duration of this voyage, men. You'll take your orders from him, now."

The two burly NP's saluted. "Yes, sir," they chorused in unison.

Boxer motioned them out with his head, and they half carried Axelrod out to the brig.

"Lieutenant, please order your men to board my entire crew, American and Russian alike. Otherwise I'll have to take the ship by force."

"That won't be necessary, Admiral."

Boxer placed a hand on the young lieutenant's shoulder. "Thanks, son. Thank you very much. You're going to make a fine captain one day."

Meade smiled, then saluted. "Yes, sir. Thank you, Admiral."

"And Meade," Boxer smiled. "If you ever tire of these posh surroundings, and carpeted decks, and you're ready to do a man's job..." There was a twinkle in Boxer's eye. He continued, "I'd be happy to have you aboard any sub I ever command."

Meade snapped to attention and saluted crisply. "Thank you, sir. It would be an honor."

"Thank you, Lieutenant Meade. And now I'd appreciate it if you'd get my men aboard the *Polar King*. They would like to go home."

CHAPTER 5

Under the glare of the *Polar King*'s searchlights, the able-bodied among Boxer's men clambered up the boarding rope cascading down the port side of the ship. Those unable to climb were winched aboard in stretchers lashed to cargo nets. Viktor ushered Admiral Borodine to the head of the group.

"Nyet, Viktor. Let the men go first. Then you and I will bring up the rear."

"But, Comrade Admiral…"

"No buts, Viktor. When we are sure all the survivors are aboard, then we will allow them to hoist us up."

"As you wish, comrade."

Viktor counted heads as the men filed past him to be boarded. There were thirty Russian seamen, and three dozen Americans who lived through the ordeal. And thanks to Boxer, they would all be going home. Quite a guy, Viktor mused in admiration. Quite a guy.

Boxer was on deck to greet Borodine. "Igor, the situation is stabilized now. Our first priority is to check you into sick bay, and have the ship's doc look you over."

"Care for the men first, Jack."

"They will all be given medical attention, comrade. But I'm not about to lose you now."

Borodine motioned Boxer closer. "Jack, you really put yourself at great risk from your government by bringing us aboard. I would suggest you putting us off at the closest Soviet base. I believe Russkaya Station would be the most convenient."

Boxer delved into his memory. "Yes, I believe you're right, Igor. Russkaya Station. Across the Ross Ice Shelf, then west along the coast."

"You amaze me, my friend. Perhaps I could use the ship's radio. I could make contact with Russkaya and see if there are any Russian ships in the area to take us home."

Boxer ushered Borodine toward the elevator to the pilothouse. Lieutenant Meade looked up from his chart table when they entered the spacious cabin. Boxer made the introductions. "Lieutenant Meade, Comrade Admiral Borodine, and his EXO Captain Viktor Korzenko. Admiral Borodine, Viktor, Lieutenant Meade."

Borodine and Viktor saluted the young Lieutenant. "Thank you for extending the courtesy of taking my men aboard the ship."

Meade returned the salute. "I was just following the rules of the International Maritime Code. I consider myself to have answered a Mayday at sea."

Boxer interjected, "It's too bad that your captain didn't see things the same way."

Meade looked a little embarrassed. "I guess it's subject to interpretation. Captain Axelrod is a stickler for the rules, you know."

Boxer smiled. "I'd better not comment on that. It would only get me in deeper than I already am now."

Borodine cleared his throat.

Boxer said, "Oh, yes. Lieutenant Meade, I'd appreciate it if you'd permit Admiral Borodine to use the radio to try to reach the Russian Ice Station."

"Why, certainly. Right this way, Admiral. We will be passing by Russkaya in about thirty hours. Weather permitting, we could put you and your men ashore there."

53

"Thank you. And now if you'll permit me…?"

"Sure. Our radioman will assist you. Mr. Davidson, please try to reach the Russian weather station."

"Aye, aye, sir."

Fifteen futile minutes passed. Finally, Borodine honed in on some Russian-speaking voices, and he smiled triumphantly. Borodine was patched into the base commander. Soon, he was carrying on an animated discussion in Russian. Borodine smiled throughout the conversation. When he finished, and hung the mike onto its cradle, he exclaimed, "Wonderful luck. The last supply plane of the season from New Zealand is at the ice station now. They will wait for my crew and take us back with them."

Boxer beamed. "Now, that is good news. Now, if you don't mind, it's off to the sick bay with you. We've got about thirty hours of nothing to do but get you and some of the other men taken care of. Viktor and I and Clemens will see that everything goes smoothly. Besides, we'll be in the capable hands of Lieutenant Meade."

Borodine stood up and announced, "There's no need for that now. I'm, as you Americans say, fit as a fiddle. What I could really use now is some good Russian vodka." With that, Borodine turned toward the door, took one step, and collapsed.

"Grab him." Boxer was at Borodine's side in a flash. Boxer cradled the Russian's head in his lap, and took his carotid pulse.

Viktor looked worried. "He landed very hard. Is he all right?"

Boxer closed his eyes and shook his head. "Comrade Admiral Borodine is a very sick man. The voyage in the life rafts, and the journey over the ice took their toll on him."

"Will he die?"

Boxer said, "I hope not, Viktor. I really hope not. Help me get him to the sick bay."

"Viktor helped Boxer and Clemens lift Borodine from the deck. In a moment, the ship's medical officer and two assistants burst into the pilothouse bearing a stretcher.

"We'll take it from here, Admiral," the doctor said.

"Thanks. Be careful with him. And make sure you do everything humanly possible to see that he survives."

"Aye, aye, sir." He hesitated a moment. "That goes without saying, Admiral. We'll do the best we can."

At 1100 hours the following afternoon, Boxer poked his head into the sick bay and inquired about Borodine's condition.

"Please come in, Admiral Boxer," the doctor said. "He's still alive, but he's going to need hospitalization for a while, and lots of rest after that."

The acrid smell of disinfectant hit Boxer's nostrils as he followed the doctor into the cubicle where Borodine rested. That and the white shelves and cabinets overflowing with medicines and medical gear reminded him of close calls that he'd had himself in recent years. He felt quite uncomfortable.

The doctor seemed right at home in this environment, and ushered Boxer into the tiny room where Borodine lay on a hospital bed. Boxer was overwhelmed by the array of tubing and IV equipment going in and out of his friend and sometimes enemy. "Is he awake?"

Borodine stirred. "Jack, is that you?"

Boxer moved to his side. "Yes, Igor. I'm here. How are you feeling?"

Borodine smiled weakly. "I'd feel a lot better if this sadist would remove some of this…" He gestured with his head at the IV stand behind him.

The medical officer seemed embarrassed. "Admiral Borodine, I promised Admiral Boxer that I would deliver you to your people alive and in one piece. This is all very necessary."

Borodine continued. "And Jack, I don't even have a pretty nurse to hold my hand and keep me company."

The doctor looked at Boxer as if to say, What am I going to do with this ingrate?

Boxer offered him no help. He just smiled and shrugged his shoulders. "Well, Igor, at least I'm happy to see that you're your old self again. I…"

"Excuse me, Skipper." Clemens and Viktor were standing in the doorway of the cubicle. "Just thought you'd like to know, we're within sight of Russkaya. Viktor has been in contact with the base."

Viktor interjected, "Yes, they are preparing to welcome Comrade Admiral Borodine and our crew with a big homestyle Russian meal and lots of good Russian vodka."

Borodine raised his head and said, "All that is missing is some nice warm Russian women, eh, Viktor?"

Viktor beamed broadly.

Boxer said, "So you see, Viktor, the old sea horse is his old self once again."

"Almost, my friend. Just the thought of getting out of here, and getting rid of all these tubes you've stuck in me, makes my heart feel young again."

The doctor cleared his throat. "Not quite true, Admiral Borodine. Yes, you will be transferred to your base, but the tubes, as you refer to them, go with you."

Borodine groaned.

"Sorry," the doctor continued. "Doctor's orders. It will require one or two of your men to attend to you and this equipment. I'll be happy to train them before you leave. And I have a supply of medication to send along with you 'til you can check into a hospital."

Borodine shook his head, and smiled at the MO. "You're too kind to me."

"I'll send you a bill."

They all broke up at that, Borodine included.

At noon, the sun, still low in the sky, reached the limit of its ascent. Boxer looked at the Russian station from the pilothouse. The view was breathtaking, white as far as the eye could see, dotted by clusters of dome-shaped insulated tents, cylindrical fuel tanks, squat buildings with steaming smokestacks. The hammer-and-sickle flag of the USSR fluttered gently from a pole near the foremost building.

The bellow of the ship's horn brought a dozen orange-clad figures scurrying toward the *Polar King*. They were followed by a giant snow tractor pulling a train of sleds to take the Russian sailors back to camp. Boxer summoned Viktor and Mark Clemens to the pilothouse.

"Please get the men ready for disembarking, gentlemen. I'll see to Comrade Admiral Borodine."

"Aye, aye, Skipper." Clemens turned and went below.

Viktor saluted. "Yes, sir. And thank you, comrade, for tending to Igor. From the bottom of my heart. And from the rest of my men, too."

"You'd have done the same for me, Viktor."

Viktor nodded. "Myself, yes. And Comrade Admiral Borodine, of course. But in my country, this would cause much trouble. Possibly even our arrest or deporture to Siberia."

"I suspect this will cause a flap back home, Viktor. Especially if Captain Axelrod gets his way. We'll just have to deal with that when and if the time comes."

Boxer put his hand on Viktor's shoulder. "For now, though, we must deal with the return of your crew. Please give Clem a hand."

Viktor saluted again, turned and left the cabin. Boxer headed for the sick bay. The MO, along with an assistant and three Russian seamen, were wheeling Borodine out onto the deck in a gurney. Boxer caught up with the group. "Trying to leave without saying goodbye, Igor?"

Borodine pulled himself up on one elbow. "Jack, I want to thank you again for everything you've done. My men and I would never have made it without you."

"I had to make sure someone's still alive who understands what we go through. Sure as hell, most Americans have no idea what it's like doing what we do."

"Likewise, most of my people, Jack. I just want you to know that I'm extremely grateful." Borodine offered Boxer his hand.

"Til we meet again, my friend. Try to take care of yourself."

Boxer shook Borodine's hand, then watched as the gurney was lowered to the waiting Russians on the ice. *Strange*, Boxer thought. *There goes the one man in all the world most capable of destroying me. And yet, we have this unique kinship, this strange bonding that allows each of us to treat the other as a brother. There will never be another like him.*

"That's the last of them, skipper."

Clemens's voice jolted Boxer from his thoughts. "Well, time for one last look at this strange continent. It's as terrible as it is beautiful. It's harsh and violent, and cruel, yet the men who make their lives here share a unique camaraderie. There's no place like it on earth."

Clemens nodded, and the two of them stared off into the distance until the reverberations of the ship's mighty engines told them they were starting off on their way home.

"Well, Clem," Boxer said as they headed for the shelter of the pilothouse, "next stop Norfolk, Virginia."

CHAPTER 6

The *Polar King* reached Norfolk, Virginia, on a clear, bright spring afternoon in early May, with only a few puffs of cumulus clouds overhead. A soft breeze and an ambient temperature of seventy-two degrees swept over the crew of the *Tiny Tim* who had chosen to line the rails of the supply ship heading into port. Boxer was in the pilothouse alongside Lieutenant Meade, helping the young officer guide the hulking ship onto its approach to the channel at the mouth of the Chesapeake Bay.

Boxer pointed out the tugboat steaming out to greet them and pilot them into port when the radioman brought in the message. "Excuse me, Admiral Boxer, sir. Admiral Mason extends his regards and requests you to report as soon as we dock to the base commander's quarters. He has left instructions there for you."

Boxer nodded his acknowledgement, then turned his attention back to the fast-approaching tug.

Meade cast a glance up at Boxer. "Wonder what the old man wants?"

"I'm sure he wants to be there personally at my debriefing. The usual warning about not speaking to anyone until I'm cleared through him."

"VIP treatment."

Boxer said nothing. He was intent on watching the tug take its place at the stern, to starboard. A second tugboat, painted black with the word PILOT emblazoned on both sides of the deckhouse in bold white letters swept across the bow of the *Polar King* in a graceful arch and led the way into port. Finally, he said, "There will probably be an inquiry concerning my commandeering this ship and putting Captain Axelrod under arrest."

He let that statement sink in for a minute. Lieutenant Meade nodded. "Yes, sir. I suppose there will be."

Boxer continued. "There are those who would like to see my ass nailed to the wall, and this will give them an opportunity to try it. I'll have to let the facts of the situation speak for themselves. The second-guessers will try to say that I over-exceeded my authority."

Meade said, "But Admiral, you did the right thing, the only decent thing by taking the Russians aboard the *Polar King*. They would never have made it otherwise. They would have frozen to death on the ice."

Boxer turned his full attention to Lieutenant Meade now that the tugs had taken over some of the task of bringing the ship to port. "Son, do yourself a favor and disassociate yourself from my decision to take over the *Polar King* by force. If memory serves, Axelrod was always well connected, and will stop at nothing to get at me for this. He'll cut you up and have you for breakfast if you take my side."

"But, sir…"

Boxer shook his head. "No buts, son. You'll make a fine captain one of these days, Meade. The Navy needs good men like you. But if you play politics, the Axelrods in the service will try to destroy you. Just tell them you were following my direct orders. That I took the command of the *Polar King*, and you were compelled by my rank to follow my orders."

Lieutenant Meade opened his mouth to protest. Boxer cut him off.

"Clear?"

Meade paused, then shrugged his shoulders and smiled. "Aye, aye, skipper." He'd taken to addressing Boxer as Skipper rather than Sir, as did the men of the *Tiny Tim*.

Boxer clapped him on the shoulder. "Good. Then it's settled. I'll take full responsibility for what happened in Antarctica. It's best that way."

Boxer was met at dockside by two men in civilian clothes in a grey staff car, and sped away to the office of the Commander of the Norfolk Naval Base. Admiral John Mackenzie stood behind his massive dark walnut desk and Boxer was ushered into the spacious room. Behind Mackenzie were the flags of the United States and the U.S. Navy. The walls were decorated with oil paintings of famous sea battles from John Paul Jones' famous battle against the British to the fighting in the Bay of Tonkin. Boxer saluted.

Mackenzie returned the salute, then offered his hand. "Welcome back to Norfolk, Jack. Nice to see you again."

Boxer smiled. "Mac," as the admiral was called by his friends, was a solidly built six footer, with thinning steel-grey hair cut short in military fashion. He had commanded the aircraft carrier *Endeavor* during the Vietnam era. "Thank you, Admiral. Nice to be back."

Mac motioned for Boxer to sit, and slid into the upholstered swivel chair behind his desk. "Hear you had a time of it."

"We had a few close calls, yes. Almost didn't make it back this time."

Mackenzie produced a pack of filter tip cigarettes from a breast pocket, and offered them to Boxer. "I'll stick with my pipe if you don't mind, sir."

"Go right ahead." He lit up while Boxer filled the bowl of his pipe and got it smoldering. Boxer drew deeply and let the smoke waft up toward the ceiling.

Mackenzie tapped off an ash and set the cigarette into a heavy brass ashtray. He folded his hands on the desk. "Admiral Mason is expecting you in D.C. this evening. 1900 hours."

Boxer glanced at his watch. He had less than two hours. "I was hoping to shower and change first."

Mackenzie shook his head. "No time. The old man wants to debrief you himself. And he doesn't like to be kept waiting."

"Mind if I make a phone call first? I'd like to let Admiral Stark know that I'm back, and say hello to a certain lady."

"Sure. Use the phone in the next office. How is Admiral Stark these days? He seems to have dropped out of sight."

Boxer took a deep breath. "He's been better. He's still trying to build up his strength after the stroke he suffered last winter. I've been looking forward to seeing him."

"I've heard you two are very close."

Boxer drew on his pipe and blew another puff of smoke toward the ceiling. "He was a tough boss while he was CNO. After he stepped down because of his ill health, he's treated me like a son. I try to return the favor."

The phone on Mackenzie's desk rang. The admiral grabbed it on the second chime. "Mackenzie."

Boxer watched Mac nodding his head, then glance furtively at him, then back at the phone again. Mackenzie hung up without commenting. He rose from his seat and extended his hand to Boxer. "Well, Jack, your helicopter is waiting to take you to the Pentagon. Good luck with your meeting."

Boxer stood and shook hands with the base commander. "Thanks," he said as he strode to the door. "I'll probably need it."

Boxer was escorted down a long corridor by an attractive young second lieutenant attached to the CNO's office. Boxer followed, enjoying the sway of her full hips under the crisp dark-blue uniform skirt. Boxer sensed that she was well aware of her effect on men, and was putting on a little extra show for his benefit. She stopped at the black door to a corner office suite. She inserted a plastic ID card into a slot in the door, and was buzzed in. She held the door open for Boxer. "Right this way, sir." As she turned toward Boxer, her tailored jacket opened slightly, and he was aware of the heft of her breasts straining at the fabric of her white blouse. "Admiral Mason is expecting you."

Boxer returned her smile. He glanced at the name tag over her breast pocket. "Thank you, Lieutenant Carson." She had tawny blonde hair tucked up into her cap, and blue eyes that complemented her navy uniform.

She smiled at him with full, sensuous lips. "My pleasure, Admiral Boxer. I'll be here to escort you out when you and Admiral Mason are finished." She knocked at an inner office door, then opened it and stuck her head inside. "Admiral Boxer is here, sir."

She stepped aside, and Boxer entered the familiar office. He'd spent many visits here in this room when Admiral Stark was CNO. He saluted Mason when he was across the desk from him. The admiral remained sitting.

"Sit," Mason growled, and Boxer took a wooden captain's chair in front of the desk.

Without preamble, Mason said, "I want to hear from you personally about the Russian Ice Castle. All of the reports so far have been very cryptic. What the hell went on down there?"

Boxer reached into a leather attaché case and withdrew a heavy sheath of papers which he plopped down on Mason's desk. "It's all here in my report, Admiral. I've had plenty of time to prepare this on the trip home aboard the *Polar King*."

Mason pushed the stack of paper aside. "I'll read the damn report later. I want you to tell me what happened in the Antarctic. Our intelligence reports had it that the damn Russians were building a drilling station out of a damn iceberg. True?"

"Too true. They had carved out a massive iceberg using convict labor, and equipped it with a nuclear reactor to power the drilling operation, and to run the engines that would transport the entire station. They almost had the thing operative when we got to it."

"Yes, I understand you've had some success there." Mason opened a humidor and removed two cigars. He offered one to Boxer and clipped off the tip of the other for himself. He got the ash glowing, and sent a smoke ring off to his side.

Boxer was about to fall back on his pipe, but decided he'd enjoy a good cigar for a change. And he had no doubts about Mason's choice of cigars. "Thanks. Don't mind if I do," Boxer said. He cut off the end with a small pocketknife, and lit up. He sat back in the chair. "Yes, Admiral. We destroyed the Ice Castle, but at a terrible cost in lives. The two subs carrying our assault force were lost with everyone aboard. The reactor exploded. They never had a chance."

Mason blew another smoke ring, and shrugged his shoulders. "But it put the damn Russians out of business, didn't it? That's what the mission was all about. That was very important to the President. He'll be very pleased. Besides, you killed a lot of the enemy, didn't you?"

Boxer took a pull on the cigar and let out the smoke. "Too many dead on both sides. A terrible waste of lives. And if we hadn't been rescued by the *Polar King*, we'd all have bought it."

Mason leaned forward in his seat with his beefy forearms on his desk. "Which brings up a rather unpleasant subject, Boxer. Mackenzie called to tell me how you took over the *Polar King* and placed its captain under arrest. In his own brig, no less. You overstepped your authority."

Boxer said, "Axelrod was being an arrogant ass, Admiral. He refused to honor the International Maritime Code. Those Russians and my men were keeping each other alive. In fact, one of them dove into the icy sea to rescue me when I fell overboard. He saved my life."

"Still, they were the enemy. He made a judgment call regarding taking them on his ship. His authority shouldn't have been overruled."

Boxer shook his head. "He made a very bad judgment call, Admiral. He left me no choice. There was no way I was going to let those Russian seamen freeze to death on the ice shelf because of the whim of an officer who should know better. It was my duty to override him."

Mason took another puff on his cigar, and pointed it at Boxer. "You bit off more than you may be able to chew. Axelrod may be a pompous ass... Hell, that's why he's shipping supplies to Antarctica instead of commanding a fighting ship..." A long ash fell from the tip of the cigar onto the desk.

"You know that his father-in-law is Senator Le Roux of Virginia? He'll do his best to have you destroyed."

"That's been tried before."

"Le Roux has a lot of clout on the Senate Armed Services Committee. I wouldn't take him lightly."

Boxer stubbed out his cigar. "Don't worry, I won't. What's done is done. I can only hope that the truth of the situation will prevail."

Mason didn't reply. He looked at his watch and yawned. "It's getting late. Why don't you take the weekend off and report here at 1000 hours Monday morning. That'll give me time to study your report."

"Thank you, Admiral."

Mason stood up. "Monday morning, then. Dismissed."

Mason didn't offer to shake hands, so Boxer got up and saluted. He turned and left the room. Lieutenant Carson appeared promptly in the outer office. Boxer figured that Mason must have buzzed her before standing up.

Carson smiled. "I'll show you out, Admiral. If you'll follow me, please?"

Boxer returned her smile. "Thanks, but it's not really necessary. I've been here before. I'll find my way out."

"It's no trouble, sir. Besides, Admiral Mason's orders."

Boxer enjoyed listening to her voice with its midwestern accent. He said, "Well, we wouldn't want to disappoint the old man, now, would we?"

"No," she smiled demurely. "We wouldn't."

There was no doubt in Boxer's mind that she was flirting with him. What surprised him was how much he missed being in the presence of a woman. It would be good to be with Francine Wheeler again. For the first time in many years, he found himself contemplating marriage again. Yet, as he followed after Lieutenant Carson, swishing her hips for his benefit, he felt the stirrings of desire again. Maybe he just wasn't meant to be married.

Jay Corless Archer and William White were breakfasting with President Spooner in the small dining room of the White House.

Jay was tall, grey-haired, and had a booming laugh, while Billy, as he was called by his friends, was several inches shorter, and dyed his grey hair brown, making him look younger than the other two men, though he was pushing sixty-five. Jay and Billy wore western-cut hand-tailored suits, string ties, and fancy leather boots.

"Well, Mr. President," Jay spoke, spearing a piece of sausage with his fork. "Billy and I are going to Moscow on the twenty-fourth of next month to work out a trade agreement between our company and the Soviets."

"Good," Richard Spooner said. "That'll give you the in you need to find out what the Russians are going to do about that oil field in Antarctica, now that Boxer has destroyed their Ice Castle."

"That, too," Billy replied. "It'll take some doing now, because of that confrontation."

Jay swallowed the sausage and washed it down with coffee. "The Russians will be on their guard, now. We dealt with them in the past, and we always shot straight with them, figuratively, of course. But they'll be wary now of any Americans in their country. Why, the KGB…"

Spooner's face reddened. "Fuck the KGB."

Jay stared hard at the President, then a smile spread across his face. "Not even with your prick, Mr. President." Billy choked on his coffee.

Spooner broke up. "Okay, look, Jay, Billy, this is not going to be without risk. But we've got to be in a position to gain oil exploration rights without going to war with the Soviets about it."

"Understood, Mr. President. Billy and me will do our best to find out what's up in the Kremlin."

Billy said, "And, of course we will expect you to keep up your part of the bargain, too. Your promise to look after Boxer, and keep him out of political deep shit."

Spooner nodded. "That won't be easy, either. Some very heavy hitters in the Senate are already calling for his balls on a silver platter. Did you hear he took over an American ship and locked the captain up in his own brig?"

Jay broke up laughing, and slapped Billy on the back. "That's our boy. You can see, Mr. President, that he's going to need all the help you can give him."

Spooner continued. "Senator Le Roux, the head of the Senate Armed Services Committee, is the father-in-law of the captain that Boxer locked up."

Jay stopped laughing. "Armand Le Roux?"

"Himself."

"Sumbitch," Billy said, reaching for another sweet roll. "Boxer couldn't have picked a worse adversary. Didn't he know that the captain of that ship was related to him?"

President Spooner poured himself another cup of coffee, and sipped it black. "From what Admiral Mason, the CNO, tells me, Boxer couldn't care less. He thought the man was a horse's ass, and took over his ship. And now Le Roux has pressed for a full investigation, an official Naval inquiry. He'll try to have Boxer tarred and feathered."

Jay spoke up. "That's where you come in, Mr. President. Stop him."

"Not that easy. My sources have it that Le Roux's planning to run against me in the next primary. He's got a large following, and almost as much money as you two boys. He'd love to make an issue of me defending the wrong Naval officer. He'll have Boxer charged with treason, then link me to him."

Billy put his sweet roll down, and licked some icing from his fingers. "Just see that Boxer doesn't get hurt, Mr. President, or our deal is off. We're not going to risk our lives and our reputations in Russia only to come home and find we've lost our investment here at home."

"Billy's right, Mr. President. We have to protect each other's interests."

"Then we'll all just have to do just that, boys." Spooner looked at his watch. "Well, gentlemen, thank you for joining me for breakfast, but I have another meeting in a few minutes. No need to get up, boys. Finish up, and just let yourselves out by the back doorway into the rose garden."

As Spooner got up to leave, Jay said, "Oh, by the way, Mr. President, Billy and me are fixin' to throw a big barbeque bash over at my place in Texas before we leave for Russia. You and the missus are sure welcome to join us."

Spooner turned back and smiled as he strode for the door. "Thanks, Jay. I might just take you up on that. I wouldn't want to miss one of your little backyard picnics for the world."

CHAPTER 7

Boxer hailed a cab and was let off in front of Francine Wheeler's brownstone in D.C. at eleven o'clock at night. He'd called ahead, so Francine and Admiral Stark, who'd been recuperating at her place, would be awake when he got there. Francine answered the door.

"Jack, darling, I've missed you so." She threw her arms around his neck and squeezed him to her. She stood on her toes and kissed his lips as he stood there in the doorway.

Boxer returned the kiss, felt her tongue dart between his lips, and hugged her to him. She was wearing the floral perfume that he'd grown to associate with her. "Mmmm. You taste good."

Boxer saw Admiral Stark, dressed in a royal-blue robe over striped broadcloth pajamas and black leather slippers, standing patiently behind Francine.

"Don't try to kiss me like that, young man," Stark smiled. He held out his hand. "How the hell are you, Jack? You look great."

"I'm fine, Admiral. You're looking fit yourself. How's Francine been treating you?"

"She acts like she's my damn boss," Stark said. A smile cracked his lips. "She sees to it that I'm well fed, makes me exercise, cut me down to three cigars a day that she knows about, and keeps hiding my Chivas. It's a good thing she goes off to work sometimes, so I don't go mad from all this good behavior."

"Now, now, Admiral. You know I only do it for your own good."

"Be good to this woman, Jack. Hear me? If you don't marry Francine, and someone else gets her, it'll be your own damn fault." He put a fatherly arm around Francine's shoulders. "Hell, I'd marry her myself if I was five years younger."

Francine laughed. "If you were five years younger, I'll bet I couldn't keep up with you." She turned to Boxer. "Jack, lately when we go out for our morning constitutional, I can hardly keep pace with him. We get back home, I puff all the way up the stairs, out of breath and ready to collapse. The Admiral here starts on his first cigar of the day."

Francine took Boxer by the arm and led him into the room. "Let me take your coat. Here we are going on about ourselves, and you must be bushed. It's almost midnight, and if I know you, Jack Boxer, you were probably up at six."

Boxer slipped out of his coat. "I'd have gotten here earlier this evening, but Mason insisted in debriefing me himself. At least I got the weekend off."

"Wonderful," Francine said. "It'll take me the entire weekend to do all the things I want to do to you." She threw her arms around him again.

Boxer's face got red. Stark just shrugged his shoulders, and sat down on a cream-colored upholstered chair. Boxer followed Francine to the sofa. He said, "I was hoping to spend a day in Staten Island. I'd like to see Chuck."

"Sure. I don't blame you. By the way, the adoption papers will be finalized in about a month. If you'd like, he can move in here with us."

"That's very kind of you, but I'd rather he got the chance to finish out his senior year at New Dorp High, with his friends. Then, he'll be away at college, and it would be nice if he could stay here with us while he's off from school."

Francine said, "Would you like me to go to New York with you? I'd like that very much."

"Of course. I was hoping to see my son John at the same time. The four of us could go somewhere together."

"Wonderful." She kissed him again on the lips.

Stark cleared his throat. "Well, it's getting on to my bedtime. Anyone care to join me in a nightcap?"

"Sounds good to me."

"Me, too," Francine chimed in. "Jack, will you bring me a snifter of cognac? There's Stoli for yourself, and Chivas for the admiral. Oh, and if you can't find the Scotch, the admiral keeps a second bottle in his room that I'm not supposed to know about."

Stark growled, "Damn, girl. Is nothing sacred anymore?"

They all enjoyed a laugh at that. Boxer carried the drinks to a coffee table, and joined the others on the sofa. He watched Francine swirl the brandy in the snifter. She caught his stare, and smiled at him. Boxer hoisted his glass, clinked against the admiral's, and toasted, "Well, here's to good friends."

"To good friends," Stark replied.

Francine snuggled closer to him, and entwined her arm through his. Stark sipped off some of the Scotch, savored it going down, then finished it off in one more swallow. "Well, kids, that's it for me tonight. See you in the morning."

As they watched Stark walk off to his room, Boxer brought her closer to him and kissed her passionately. "I love you, Francine. I really missed you."

She pressed her breasts against his chest. Boxer felt her nipples harden, and smiled. She said, "I love you too, darling. I'm so glad you're home. C'mon, let's go to bed."

Boxer awoke at 0700 to the smell of bacon and coffee. He

quickly showered and dressed, and climbed down one flight of stairs to the spacious kitchen that shared the entire second level of the brownstone with a formal dining room. Francine's business offices occupied the ground level.

"Smells good."

Admiral Stark raised his coffee cup. "Tastes as good as it smells. Francine, may I have a refill, dear?"

Francine brought the coffee carafe to the table. As she poured the coffee she said, "Morning, darling. How would you like your eggs?"

"Over lightly, please. Need any help?"

"Thanks. The admiral already offered, but this is a one-woman job." She placed a steaming mug of black coffee in front of Boxer, along with a basket of freshly made biscuits, preserves, a plate of bacon and sausages, and toast.

Stark forked open a biscuit, stuffed it with four strips of bacon, and chomped away at it. Francine watched him eat, and heaved a sigh of exasperation. "I don't know what I'm going to do about this, Jack. He's supposed to be on a low cholesterol diet."

Stark's eyes twinkled. "I am, dammit. I had to do without my eggs this morning." He speared a sausage link, and bit off half. "Would you please pass the marmalade?"

Boxer chuckled and handed over the preserves. "Francine, Admiral Stark has spent a good many years eating whatever he damned pleased. No one was going to buck the CNO because he ate too much bacon."

"Well, it's going to be salads for lunch, and broiled fish for dinner for a while, Admiral, to make up for this little adventure in gourmet dining."

"Rabbit food. You see what she feeds me?"

Boxer took his plate of eggs, added a rasher of bacon and a biscuit. "It's good for you. We both want you around for a long time."

Stark smiled. "I know that. You've got yourself a wonderful lady here, Jack. Will you pass me the butter?"

Francine rolled up her eyes, shrugged her shoulders, and dug into her grapefruit half and black coffee.

Boxer finished up his breakfast, and brought his plate and cup to the sink. He watched Stark cut off the end of one of his big cigars and light up. "Admiral, Francine and I are going to drive up to Staten Island this morning to see Chuck."

Stark let smoke out and watched it rise to the ceiling where it was dispersed by the slow-moving blades of a ceiling fan. "Good idea. How are the adoption proceedings going?"

"Well, Francine tells me that we'll finalize within a month."

Francine swallowed some coffee and nodded her head. "Yes. We'll speak to Chuck's aunt today. Jack wants to compensate her for having taken over raising Chuck while Rugger was at sea. Which was most of the time."

"Goes with the territory," Stark said.

"I know," Francine replied. She removed the remaining dishes and placed them into the sink. She ran hot water over them and stacked them into a dishwasher. "But in this case, Rugger's absence left Chuck too vulnerable to the peer pressure of the punks in his neighborhood. It took Jack to straighten out the boy's values."

"You give me too much credit. He only needed a little discipline. He had it in him to succeed. He only needed to be shown the way. He's become quite a guy."

Francine nodded. She turned to Stark. "He takes after Jack, now. He's got Rugger's blond hair and Nordic good looks, and Jack's sense of honor and values. He's a match for anyone."

Boxer patted his belly. "Well, we'd better get going. I'll try to get a government limo to take us to the train station."

"Jack, if you don't mind, why don't we drive up in my car? If you don't feel up to the long ride, I'll drive. That way we can have more options open to us."

Boxer thought for a moment. "Fine by me. You drive, and if you get tired, I'll take over."

Boxer and Francine walked out into the street and turned left. Francine stopped at a shiny new black BMW at the curb in one of the scarce parking spaces on the block. "Like it? I bought it while you were gone."

"It's a beauty. Things must be going well at the Wheeler law firm these days."

She smiled broadly, and unlocked the passenger side door. "Hop in, sailor. I'll take you for a spin."

Boxer settled into a deep leather seat, reached over and unlatched the driver door lock from inside. Francine got in and said, "I hope you don't mind the role reversal today. I just love to drive this car."

"I'll just sit back and enjoy."

"There's some classical music tapes in the center console. Just choose whatever you like."

Boxer made a selection and popped the tape into the car stereo. "Just let me know when you want me to spell you."

They got off the New Jersey Turnpike and were over the Outerbridge Crossing into Staten Island in about four and a half hours. Twenty minutes later, they were at the front door of Chuck's aunt Rose Caliendo's modest house on a side street off of Hylan Boulevard.

Mrs. Caliendo became a little flustered standing at the door in front of Boxer and his beautiful woman. She wiped her hands on her apron. "Why Admiral Boxer. What a pleasant surprise. Won't you come in? I was just preparing dinner."

"Thanks. I don't believe you've met Miss Francine Wheeler. She's the lawyer who's helping me adopt Chuck."

"How do you do, Miss Wheeler."

"Please call me Francine. I have some papers for you to look over when you get a chance. Admiral Boxer wants to leave you an annuity fund to help compensate you for all the years of bringing up Chuck while Rugger was away at sea."

"I did the best I could." Mrs. Caliendo sighed. "It was too much for me, what with my brother away most of the time. He needed a man to look up to."

Francine said, "I'm sure Admiral Boxer will provide the guidance he needs."

Mrs. Caliendo took a large wooden spoon from a plate by the sink and stirred a huge pot of tomato sauce that was bubbling on the stove. "Can't let it stick to the bottom, you know, or it'll scorch. I hope you can join us for dinner."

Boxer looked embarrassed. "I'm not sure yet. By the way, where is Chuck?"

"Oh, I'm sorry. Here I go running off at the mouth about my tomato gravy and you came all the way here to see Chuck." She put the spoon back on the plate. "He went to have pizza for lunch with a girl from the high school. He won't be back till supper."

Boxer said, "Francine and I will drive there and meet him. Where is this pizza place?"

"It's called Tony's Pizza Parlor, down Hylan to New Dorp Lane. It's in a small shopping strip at the corner. You can't miss it."

"Thanks. We'd better be going."

As Boxer held the door of the BMW open for Francine, Mrs. Caliendo called after him, "He'd really like to see you."

Chuck Rugger sat in a booth in Tony's Pizza Parlor across a red Formica table from a pretty seventeen-year-old with dark hair and a cute smile. She was munching on a slice of pizza. Chuck sipped from a glass of Coke, then said, "But, Marie, you know I really like you a lot. You're the only girl I've dated in over three months."

Marie washed down her mouthful of pizza with some cola. She looked down at the table, then slowly back up at Chuck. Her face was flushed. "You know I like you a lot, too, Chuckie. But, I'm sorry. I get really embarrassed talking about this. But, you know, well … no condom, no sex. I'm sorry, but with all this talk about AIDS going around, there's no such thing as being too careful."

"But I just know that I don't have AIDS, Marie. Besides, I hate those things."

Marie's face took on an even darker hue of red. "How do you know that I don't, Chuckie?"

"You? But … but… I thought…"

"See? You can't be absolutely sure, now can you?"

"Well, I suppose you're right, Marie. I'm sorry that I've been so boneheaded."

Marie smiled.

Chuck smiled, too, and they both shared a laugh. Suddenly, there was a commotion outside the pizza parlor. They turned to look out the storefront window. "What's going on?" Marie asked.

"I don't know. Looks like it might be a fight. There's some of the hardasses from the neighborhood. They're real brave when it's five of them against one."

"Who's that black kid. It looks like they're ganging up on him."

Chuck craned his neck to get a closer look. "Holy shit. That's Delvon Jackson. I know him from basketball."

"It looks like they're beating him up."

Chuck slid out from his seat. "They can't do that. Delvon wouldn't of started anything with them."

Marie reached after Chuck, but he was on his way outside. "Chuckie, wait. Don't go starting something. Stay out of it."

Chuck strode out to the group of five white youths circled around Delvon Jackson. They were taking turns punching and pushing him from behind. When he'd turn to ward off an attacker, another would sneak in a shot from behind. Chuck turned to the leader of the group, a muscular six-footer with long black hair, whom Chuck had known at school as Vinnie. "Hey, Vinnie, what's up?"

Vinnie shot a jab at the back of Delvon's head. "Nuthin', man. This here punk came strollin' onto our turf and called my girl a slut."

"Hey, that's a lie," Delvon retorted. "I didn't do nothin' to any of you. I was just mindin' my own business."

Someone pushed him from behind. Vinnie pushed him back. "You're the liar, motherfucker."

Someone blindsided Delvon across the face with a backhand. Delvon wheeled and scored a punch to the kid's face that sent blood spurting from his nose. Vinnie moved in. "Okay, you asked for it. Now you're gonna die."

Chuck stepped in front of Vinnie. He was four or five inches shorter than the gang leader, and forty pounds lighter. Vinnie pushed him back. "Why don't you mind your own fuckin' business?"

Boxer had just pulled the BMW into a parking space, and was helping Francine out of the car when he was attracted to the shouting across the street in front of the pizza parlor. He made his way to the outskirts of the crowd. He got there just in time to see the tall, dark-haired boy push Chuck.

Chuck held his ground. "It's five against one. How would you like to go five against two?"

Vinnie sneered at Chuck, and looked at his friends for support. "You fuck with us now, and we'll kick your ass every time we see you at school. How'd you like that?" Vinnie tousled Chuck's hair and pushed his head away.

Chuck continued to roll his head, and slipped a hand under Vinnie's elbow, forcing it upward. He wheeled around, taking Vinnie's hand and forcing it up behind his back, in a hammerlock. Chuck used his leverage to bring a cry of pain from the larger boy. "I said, leave him alone, Vinnie. He wasn't bothering you." With that, Chuck pushed Vinnie off, shoving him into one of his friends.

Vinnie turned on Chuck and roared, "Okay, motherfucker, you asked for it. You're dead meat. C'mon guys, let's get his ass."

The circle tightened around Chuck and Delvon. Boxer changed his vantage point so he could intervene in a moment. Vinnie swung his fist at Chuck in a wide roundhouse punch.

Chuck slipped inside and slammed a fierce jab into Vinnie's face. He felt the nose crunch under his knuckles. Blood oozed from Vinnie's face. Chuck slammed the heel of his left hand up hard under Vinnie's chin, jerking his head backward. Then he wound up and put all his weight behind a drive to the gut. Vinnie went down in a heap.

Someone jumped Chuck from behind, bringing him to his knees. Boxer moved in to help. Just then, Delvon grabbed the

kid on top of Chuck by the neck and lifted him off. "Fuckin'
punk. Can't fight from the front, can you?" Delvon shoved
him out of the way.

Delvon blocked a punch by a third boy, and countered with
two short left jabs and a hard right to the face. The punk went
down.

Chuck yelled, "Look out behind you." Too late. A small
mountain of muscle in a sleeveless black sweatshirt smashed a
filled garbage can down on Delvon's back. Delvon was
knocked to the sidewalk. The hulk advanced toward Chuck.
Vinnie got off the ground and circled warily. The fifth boy
moved in behind the hulk.

Vinnie yelled, "Nice job, Butch. Now let's finish up this
asshole."

"Right, Vinnie." Butch advanced on Chuck, arms
outstretched like a wrestler's. His two-hundred-fifty-pound
bulk loomed over Chuck. He put his head down and charged.

Chuck sidestepped, and lashed a vicious kick into Butch's
groin.

Butch grabbed his balls and groaned.

Chuck moved in and smashed a knee into his face, sending
Butch reeling backward. Chuck finished him off with a karate
chop to the throat. The hulk thudded to the street.

"Motherf—" It was Vinnie charging from behind.

Chuck spun around, catching Vinnie in the face with an
elbow. Vinnie's face looked like hamburger. Chuck swept a leg
hard against the back of Vinnie's knee, and Vinnie went
crashing down. Chuck taunted, "Want any more?"

Vinnie hung his head.

Chuck wheeled around. The hulk lay on the street holding
his throat with one hand and his balls with the other. The fifth
boy looked down at his fallen friends and realized that it was

just him against Chuck now. He put down his fists and backed away. "How about you, punk? Not so tough without your friends, are you?"

Chuck stood there breathing hard, fists down at his side, staring down the crowd that had gathered. Then he helped Delvon Jackson to his feet. "Hey, thanks, man. I owe you," Jackson said.

"Forget it. These punks were asking for it. You okay?"

"Yeah."

A fat man wearing a sleeveless undershirt came lumbering over carrying a baseball bat. He was watching the fight from a window across the street, and recognized his son among the vanquished. "Hey, you. Yeah, you, kid. That's my kid you beat up. I'll kill you for that. You and your friend."

The fat man advanced toward Chuck waving the bat over his head. "Okay, wise guy, now I'm gonna teach youse a lesson."

As Chuck watched astonishedly, Boxer moved out of the crowd next to the fat man. He grabbed the hand with the bat at the wrist, and bent it backward until it snapped. The fat man screamed in pain. The bat crashed to the street, bounced, and rolled off.

The fat man yelled, "I'll kill you. I'll kill you. I'll get the boys down here and they'll kill you."

Boxer slammed a fist into his solar plexus.

The fat man lurched forward, clutching his gut.

Boxer kicked him hard in the ass with the sole of his shoe, sending him sprawling face first into the street.

The fat man groaned, and puked what must have been a recent lunch of spaghetti onto the street.

The crowd was hushed. Boxer looked them over. "Anyone else?"

No takers.

"Good. Then I think everyone should go back home. And someone ought to pull this lump of shit off the street. He's disgusting."

The crowd slowly dispersed. Boxer walked over to Chuck and clapped a hand on his shoulder. "You did well, son. I'm proud of you."

Chuck said, "Aw, it was nothing. Just a little fight."

Delvon piped in. "Nothing, my ass. Oh, sorry, sir. But those five punks would have beat me up if Chuck didn't help me out. And we ain't even hardly friends."

Chuck said, "Oh, Dad, this is Delvon Jackson. We play basketball sometimes. Delvon, this is my dad, Admiral Jack Boxer."

"Admiral? In the Navy? No shit. I never seen an admiral before."

"Are you in Chuck's class, Delvon?"

"Yeah, sort of. But Chuck's goin' on to college. I got nothin' to look forward to."

"You know, Delvon, the Navy's looking for some good men. With your athletic ability, you'd do fine. And I saw you fight. Not bad at all."

"You really think so? Aw, but I hear that the Navy never do no fighting."

Boxer laughed. "Ever hear of the SEALs? They're the toughest little group of fighters anywhere. They're the first ones to get sent in when there's a beachhead to take, or an installation to blow. And then there's the submarines."

"Submarines?"

Chuck piped in, "Yeah. That's what my dad does. He's a submarine captain. Oh, sorry, Dad. I forgot I'm not supposed to spread that around."

"No problem, Chuck. Seriously, Delvon, if you're interested, see the Navy recruiter at the Stapleton base. Tell him that Admiral Jack Boxer sent you and I'll see that you get a tour of one of the subs."

"Oh, wow. Man, that'd be great. Thanks. Hey, and thanks again, Chuck. I'll catch you around school."

Chuck said, "See you."

Boxer turned to Chuck. "You all right, son?"

Chuck smiled. "I'll live. Man, when I saw all those punks beating up on one guy, it made my blood boil. I couldn't stop myself."

"You did fine, son."

Just then, Francine came up. "Oh, Chuck. Are you hurt?"

"No, I'm okay. It's nice to see you again."

Chuck spotted Marie standing by herself on the sidewalk. He walked over to her.

"Oh, Chuckie, you were really great. Like when you first went after those guys, I felt, you know, like why did you have to go help that kid. But when they started picking on you, too, and when you beat them all, like wow, I was so proud of you."

Chuck just stood there taking it all in, a little embarrassed by it all.

Marie asked, "Who's that neat guy that helped you? He looks like a movie actor standing there with that pretty lady."

Chuck smiled. "Oh, that's my dad. C'mon, I'll introduce you."

Marie hesitated. "Chuckie, I won't know what to say."

"Oh, c'mon. They'll be glad to meet you."

"Well…"

They walked over to Boxer and Francine, who were standing on the sidewalk near their car. "I'd like you to meet my friend,

Marie. This is my dad, Jack Boxer, and this is our lawyer Francine Wheeler."

"Pleased to meet ya."

Boxer said, "Well, why don't we drop you young folks off at home. Maybe we can all go out for dinner this evening."

Chuck said, "I don't think so. My aunt Rose is cooking up enough food to feed a small army."

"Yes, we already saw the pot on the stove when we came looking for you."

"Maybe we can all eat at my house, then. How about it, Marie? Dad?"

He shrugged his shoulders. "Okay by me if it's all right with your aunt."

Chuck put his arm around Marie, as Boxer opened the back door for her. "Great," he said. "Let's all go home."

CHAPTER 8

The big tan VL-101 military jet touched down on an isolated runway at Moscow's international airport. A dozen vans and two ambulances approached the plane, sirens wailing, and lined up as the huge cargo door opened from the tail section. The survivors of Borodine's ill-fated mission in the Antarctic were moved into the waiting vehicles. Those that could walk did so. Others were rolled off in wheelchairs, or, as in Borodine's case, were carried off on gurneys.

Viktor Korzenko, Borodine's EXO, walked alongside the admiral as he was transported to one of the ambulances. Borodine grabbed his sleeve. "Wait, Viktor. Have them wait a moment."

Viktor said something to the attendants, and they paused just outside the ambulance doors.

Borodine continued in his weak, frail voice. "I want one last look around."

Viktor put his hand on his mentor's arm, helping him adjust to a better position. It saddened Viktor to see the man who had taught him so much about seamanship and submarines, to say nothing of honor and justice and humanitarianism slipping away from him like this. He had trouble keeping back the tears, and so turned away rather than betray his feelings of impending loss. He turned his collar up against the cold, crisp breeze that swept across the land from Siberia, even in May.

Just then, there was another tug on his sleeve, and he turned to the man on the stretcher. "Viktor, comrade, please come a little closer."

Viktor complied. "Yes, Igor?"

"Promise me you will look after my wife Tanya for me. Our baby is due this month, and her family is back in Vladivostok. It will be very difficult for her."

"I understand, comrade. I will do whatever I can. Now, let's get you to the hospital so you can get well."

Borodine's face suddenly looked sad. "I'm not going to make it, Viktor."

"Nonsense, Igor. The doctors have diagnosed you as having pneumonia. I was assured that the proper European antibiotics have been procured for you, and that as soon as you are well again, you will be testing our newest prototype submarine. Besides, you have to get well. I've been summoned to appear in your place at the investigation of the destruction of the Ice Castle."

Borodine looked at Viktor, too surprised to speak. His eyes asked the question, Why, Viktor?

"Without your help, Comrade Igor, they will cut off my balls and feed them to the wolves."

Borodine smiled for the first time, albeit weakly. "Then I must get better, Viktor, if only to save your ass."

Viktor clapped him on the shoulder. "Thanks, Igor." He was glad to see some of the old spirit return to Borodine. "And I will try to arrange for some pretty nurses to take care of you."

Boxer sat back in his chair and patted his full belly. "Mrs. Caliendo, I can't remember the last time I ate such delicious food." He took a sip from a glass of red wine.

"Ah, it's nothing. I'm so happy that Chuck talked you all into coming back here for supper."

Francine blotted her lips with a napkin, and placed it by her plate. "Chuck kept telling us what a wonderful cook his aunt Rose is that we couldn't resist."

"Well, you should eat some more spaghetti or meatballs. You hardly touched anything except the salad. You're too skinny. Eat. Eat."

Chuck dipped a hunk of Italian bread into the rich tomato sauce. "Aunt Rose, please. Francine's our guest. Be nice." He shoved the bread into his mouth, chomped it down, and followed it with a sip of cola. "Besides," he grinned broadly, "she looks pretty good to me just the way she is."

Francine blushed. Boxer chuckled, and offered his glass up in salute. "I'll drink to that, son." Francine blushed even more.

Marie set her fork down. "Enough for me, too. Thanks, Mrs. Caliendo. Everything was great."

Mrs. Caliendo shook her head in dismay. "You're done eating, too? Eh. You're going to get too skinny, just like Francine."

They all laughed at that.

Chuck speared a chunk of hot sausage and popped it into his mouth. He looked at Francine and then at Mrs. Caliendo. He held his hands in front of him and described an hourglass shape with them. That brought on more good-natured laughter.

Mrs. Caliendo got up and started to collect the dishes. Francine took Boxer's plate and utensils, and her own, and followed suit. Marie caught on, and brought her own plate to the sink. She giggled. "I'd have to wait forever till Chuckie's done eating."

Chuck twirled a forkful of spaghetti around in the pool of sauce on his plate and poised it in front of his mouth. "Hey, I'm a growing boy, remember?" Then he gulped down the food.

Mrs. Caliendo soon had espresso coffee brewing, and took a whipped-cream-covered rum cake out of the refrigerator.

"Thanks again for the cake, Admiral Boxer. And for the wine. I appreciate it."

"Chuck told me how much he likes that cake, so we stopped off at Augie's along the way home to buy it."

Rose Caliendo placed the shiny espresso pot on a trivet and a bottle of clear liqueur in the center of the table. "A little anisette, maybe?"

Boxer smiled. "Great."

Francine poured the steaming black coffee into little demitasse cups, and passed the sugar and a small plate of lemon rind strips.

After coffee, Boxer asked if he could use the phone to call his ex-wife Gwen in the city. He wanted to arrange to pick up his ten-year-old son John on Sunday for all of them to go on an outing. He was told by a servant that Gwen and John were out of town for the weekend. Would there be a message?

Boxer was pissed. He only got to New York once a year or so, and he expected to have John available to visit with. "Just tell her that Admiral Boxer called."

When he returned to the cozy dining room, Francine told him, "We've decided to have a picnic tomorrow. We'll drive out to Montauk Point and walk the beach. And I know of a terrific seafood restaurant."

Boxer said, "John and his mother are away for the weekend."

Francine knew he was disappointed. "Then we'll just have to make an effort to come for a visit again very soon. We don't have to stand on ceremony. We'll just call ahead, and drive up again."

Mrs. Caliendo piped in, "And make sure you stop here to eat. I still want a chance to fatten up the pretty lady."

Francine laughed. "It's hard enough to keep the pounds off without being encouraged to eat so much. I'm stuffed."

Boxer wiped his mouth. "Well, we'd better be going. It's going to be a long day tomorrow. Marie, can we drop you off at home?"

Marie looked at Chuck, blushed slightly, and replied, "Thanks, but Chuck and I have plans for tonight. We have a date."

Chuck beamed. He held Marie's hand under the table. "Yeah. Thanks anyway, but I'll take Marie home by cab. We'll see you tomorrow morning."

Boxer stood up, and held Francine's chair as she got up from the table. "Well then, thanks for a wonderful time. We'll see you tomorrow morning at 0900."

Forty-eight hours later, at 0900 hours, on Monday, Boxer was the key witness before the investigating committee chaired by Admirals Edwards, Newmark, Lewis, and Church. He was being called on the carpet for taking over the *Polar King*, in spite of the fact that he and his crew successfully completed their mission of destroying the Russian Ice Castle. Obviously, someone was trying to get at him for personal reasons.

Boxer was sworn in and seated on a metal folding chair facing the four admirals. Edwards presided. The hearing room was familiar to Boxer; he had been at the center of another inquiry here when his sub at that time, the *Barracuda*, was scuttled by a cruise missile, and Boxer was charged with negligence. Fortunately, he was able to prove that there was no accident, and therefore no negligence on his or any of his crew's part.

The four admirals, none of whom had ever commanded a submarine, were seated at a long wooden table in the front of the room. There was a pitcher of water and five glasses, one for each of them, and a glass for the witness should he become thirsty during the testimony. In front of each of the flag officers was a yellow pad and several sharpened pencils. There was also a microphone set up in front of each of the admirals, recording everything they said into a central tape.

Behind the table, on the left, was a flag of the United States; to the right was the Navy standard. Directly behind them on the wall was a framed eleven by fourteen portrait of the President. The first few rows of seats were occupied by those of Boxer's crew who were not hospitalized or otherwise too incapacitated to appear. There were no television cameras allowed in the room, but the press room outside was filled with news reporters and their camera crews. Linda Johnson, a reporter with whom Boxer had previously clashed, was among them.

Boxer was asked to detail the events leading up to his overthrow of the *Polar King*'s commanding officer and the taking aboard of the Russian seamen along with his own crew. Boxer told the story as it happened, emphasizing the loss of most of the combined Russian and American crewmen in the icy sea and on the ice shelf. Edwards stared at him solemnly and said, "You may stand down."

Boxer's crew were given a chance to add their points of view to the story, but they were constantly cut short by the admirals. Edwards was the most vociferous. He turned to the others and stated, "There's a natural bias on the part of these men toward their commander. I don't believe we can give much credence to their testimony, as they have been obviously all been hand-picked by Boxer for the mission."

Loud groans of disgust rose from the ranks of Boxer's crew in the first few rows. Admiral Edwards rapped his gavel. "Order. This session will come to order or all spectators will be removed." Slowly, the din died off. "I now call Captain

Andrew Axelrod, captain of the U.S.S. *Polar King*. Captain Axelrod, please come forward."

Axelrod strode down the center aisle toward the witness chair. He paused long enough to cast a smug look at Boxer, who had taken a seat with his men in the first row. Axelrod was sworn in, and took his seat. Admiral Edwards sipped some water and cleared his throat. "Now, Captain Axelrod, please tell the committee what happened when you showed up to rescue Boxer and his crew."

"Thank you, Admiral Edwards. My ship, the *Polar King*, was returning to the States after a supply run to the Palmer Ice Station on the peninsula."

Admiral Newmark interrupted. "The Antarctic Peninsula, Captain Axelrod?"

"Yes, Admiral Newmark. We had offloaded enough supplies to last through the Antarctic winter, and we were returning home with some of the scientists who weren't wintering over. That's when we picked up Boxer's Mayday from the submarine *Tiny Tim*."

Admiral Church asked, "And what did you do then?"

Axelrod smiled smugly, and spoke very loudly and succinctly into the microphone in front of him. "I answered the Mayday, Admiral, in spite of a terrible storm that separated my ship from the *Tiny Tim*. I risked my own ship and its crew to rescue Admiral Boxer and his men."

Edwards said, "Please continue, Captain."

"Thank you, Admiral Edwards. Well, at great danger to my ship and my men, I followed the Mayday signal, only to find that the *Tiny Tim* had been abandoned, and the crew set off in inflatable rafts toward the Ross Ice Shelf, about forty miles from the McMurdo Ice Station. I thought that was a very foolhardy thing for Boxer to do, considering the intense storm system they were immersed in, but, nevertheless, I followed their distress signals all the way to the ice shelf itself."

Admiral Lewis cleared his throat. "Tell us what happened next, please."

"We came upon Boxer and his band of survivors along the edge of the ice shelf. In fact, we narrowly averted a disaster when an iceberg calved off as we were about to pull alongside." Axelrod paused for a drink of water. He continued. "At first, I thought they were only members of Boxer's crew. There were about eighty of them, and allowing for some loss of men during the foolish abandoning of the *Tiny Tim* in favor of the ice shelf, I assumed that they were all Americans."

Edwards said, "And were they, Captain Axelrod?"

"No, sir, Admiral. When I heard men shouting and cheering in Russian, I realized what was going on. Boxer had joined forces with the enemy, and had planned to smuggle them aboard a U.S. ship."

The four admirals at the table had a quick, hushed conversation. Edwards said, "And what did you do then, Captain Axelrod?"

"Well, Admiral, I granted Boxer and the Americans permission to come aboard, but not the Russians."

"And…"

"Boxer refused. He said that they would all be coming aboard the *Polar King*. I restated my position. No Russians on an American ship."

Admiral Newmark cleared his throat. "Captain Axelrod, did it occur to you that the Russian seamen might freeze to death on the ice shelf if you did not rescue them?"

"Thank you, sir. I was just coming to that. There is a Russian ice station not far from the rescue area. It was my intention to signal the Russians to come and pick up their people. But because of Boxer's actions, it never came to that."

Newmark chided, "Please refer to Admiral Boxer by his rank, Captain."

"Yes, sir. Well, as I was saying, Admiral Boxer pretended to be having a heart attack or something, and when I had him taken aboard the *Polar King*, he pulled a gun and pointed it at my head."

Edwards asked, "And what did Admiral Boxer say?"

Axelrod looked down at his shoes.

"I asked you a direct question, Captain Axelrod. Please tell this panel what Admiral Boxer said."

Axelrod turned his head around to glare at Boxer, then faced Edwards. "He said he'd blow my fuckin' head off if I didn't take everyone aboard, sir." He blushed. "Those are his words, Admiral. Not mine."

Edwards scribbled some notes on his yellow pad. "Is there anything else?"

"Yes, Admiral. When I protested, Boxer... I mean *Admiral* Boxer had me locked in my own brig. He ordered my men to follow his commands. Naturally, due to his rank..."

"I understand, Captain Axelrod. Is that all?"

"Just that Admiral Boxer took over my ship by force for the benefit of an adversarial foreign power, and justice cries out for his being tried for treason."

Admiral Church leaned forward. "We will make that decision, Captain. Your job is simply to supply us with the facts. Is that understood?"

"Yes, but..."

Edwards rapped his gavel. "That is all, Captain. Please stand down."

Axelrod got up and took his place toward the rear of the room. He was seated next to his father-in-law, Senator Le Roux, and a few lawyer types. Le Roux shook hands with Axelrod, and whispered something into his ear which made Axelrod smile.

Admiral Edwards rapped again. "Is there anyone else present who has something to add to this inquiry? No? Well, then…"

From the rear of the room, in a booming voice, "Excuse me, sir. I would like to say something."

A hush came over the room. All eyes turned to the young naval officer standing at attention. The look of surprise faded from Edwards's face, and he said, "Please come forward, and state your name and rank."

The young man reached the microphone and announced, "Lieutenant Roy Meade, sir. First Officer of the *Polar King*, Admiral."

"All right, Lieutenant, please be seated, and state your case."

"Thank you, sir. I was put in command of the *Polar King* after Captain Axelrod was secured in the brig, Admiral. I would just like to say that I think Admiral Boxer did what he had to do. Those Russian seamen would surely have frozen to death if we'd have left them there."

Boxer's men began to cheer. This was the first voice other than their own in Boxer's favor.

The admirals had a brief, animated discussion. Edwards rapped his gavel for silence. "Go on, please, Lieutenant."

"Admiral Edwards, it took the *Polar King* thirty-six hours to reach the closest Russian ice station. Several of the survivors were near death when we found them. Certainly there would have been many casualties. Admiral Boxer did the only humane thing possible, and under the rules of the International Maritime Code…"

Edwards interjected, "We are well aware of the rules, Lieutenant. Thank you for your testimony. You may stand down, now."

Meade saluted, and took a seat with Boxer's crew. The men made room for him to sit next to the skipper himself. Boxer shook his hand, then whispered that he shouldn't have put his career in jeopardy.

Meade whispered back, "They were trying to crucify you, Skipper. I just couldn't let them do that."

Boxer nodded in Axelrod's direction. "You've just made a powerful enemy, son. I don't envy you."

"I did what I knew in my heart to be right, sir."

Boxer put a hand on Meade's shoulder. "Thank you for what you've done, Lieutenant. You're a very brave man. I'd be proud to have you serve with me."

Admirals Edwards, Newmark, Lewis, and Church conferred for several minutes, comparing notes and opinions. Finally, Admiral Edwards took a drink of water, rapped for order, and spoke into the microphone. "Admiral Boxer, please come forward."

Boxer took his place at the witness seat.

"Please rise."

Boxer did so.

"Admiral Boxer, we find sufficient grounds to recommend that you be tried at court-martial on the grounds of treason."

Boxer's men began shouting. Edwards pounded his gavel until they became silent. "Admiral Boxer, you will stand trial one month from today. Due to your rank, and length of service, you will remain free on your own recognizance. However, you are suspended from active duty, and are to confine yourself to the United States mainland."

Boxer stood there stunned. The interrogation had been a well-orchestrated sham, and they were actually going to court-martial him.

Edwards rapped again. "You may stand down, Admiral Boxer. This session is now adjourned."

Boxer watched the four admirals walk out of the room, with Church trailing the others. He shook his head in disbelief. His crewmen quickly came forward and huddled around him, expressing their astonishment and support.

Next, they had to walk the gauntlet of media people milling around the outer lobby. As Boxer walked through the inner doors, the news people swarmed around him, poking microphones at him, and popping flashbulbs and movie lights into his face. They all began to shout at once. "Admiral Boxer, what do you think of the decision? Admiral, why did you commit treason? Admiral…"

Boxer's men shoved themselves between him and the cameras. Linda Johnson managed to slip through, and sidled next to Boxer. "Well, Admiral Boxer," she sneered, "how does it feel to be on the receiving end for a change?"

Boxer stared hard directly into her face, glaring at her. Then he turned abruptly and strode out into the street.

CHAPTER 9

At precisely 3:30 P.M. Henry Tysin, head of the CIA, switched on the intercom and said, "Ms. Collins, will you please come into my office?"

Lori-Ann Collins was halfway out of her steno chair when Tysin signaled. "Yes, of course, Mr. Tysin."

Tysin switched off his intercom, closed his eyes, and smiled. He enjoyed hearing Lori's soft voice, with just the hint of a southern accent. And now that she had become his lover, he enjoyed many other things with her, most of all, having sex. At that, he mused, she was without equal. He had offered her the opportunity of becoming an agent for the Company, and she not only took him up on that, but repaid him with the most fantastic sex he'd had since his youth. He opened his eyes at the scent of the floral perfume that she favored, and delighted in her presence at the door.

Lori-Ann closed the door. "Yes, Henry? Did you want me to bring you some coffee and a pastry or something for a snack. I was just about to leave for the day."

Tysin patted the slight paunch at his waistband. "Pastry?" He smiled at her. "No. None for me today. I'm starting to put on the pounds. Thanks."

"Well, why did you want to see me at quitting time?"

"Well, first of all, it makes me happy just to see you." She was a tall, svelte, beautiful woman with long, black hair that flowed to her shoulders, with black eyes and a fair, porcelainlike complexion. She was wearing a mid-calf-length blue skirt, slit up one leg to reveal a creamy white flash of thigh, and a sheer white blouse, opened to a V neck. She showed a good deal of cleavage. She was carrying a blue linen jacket that matched the skirt.

"Second," Tysin continued, "I just wanted to let you know that you've been approved to begin classes for becoming an agent."

Lori-Ann turned to lock the door, then wiggled over to Tysin's desk. "Oh, Henry. That's wonderful. You didn't have anything to do with getting approval so quickly, did you?" She held her arms out to him.

Tysin blushed slightly. "Well, I…"

She was at his side, holding out her hand to him. "Henry, I want to kiss you."

Tysin got up from his thickly padded black leather swivel chair and embraced her tightly. He pressed his lips to hers.

Tysin slid his hands down her back and fondled the cheeks of her ass.

"Ooh, I like it when you do that, Henry. Would you like a quickie right here in the office?"

Tysin moved his hands up and cupped each of her breasts. "I'd love to, you know. But I've got some people coming over in a little while. Are you free this evening? Say, about six-thirty?"

She blew a kiss, and turned to unlock the door. "Until later, darling."

Lori-Ann Collins smiled at the armed guards at the several checkpoints throughout the heavily secured buildings that headquartered the head of the CIA. She took the elevator up to ground level into the lobby, and turned on the charm for the two Marine sentries standing guard at the front entrance. She smiled and said, "Goodbye, boys. See you tomorrow."

They each touched the brim of their hats. "Night, ma'am," they chorused.

She rode in one of the olive-green vans that carried nonmilitary personnel to the main entrance of the compound, where she usually caught the bus to her apartment in D.C.

A tall, thin man in his mid-thirties or possibly early forties folded the newspaper he had been reading at the bus stop, and without moving his head in her direction said, "It's such a beautiful day to go for a walk in the park."

Lori-Ann shivered slightly at the recognition of that voice. She glanced at the man, who wore a grey tweed sports jacket and black pants. He was tieless, and needed a shave, whether by neglect or in keeping with the latest fashion trend in sporting a two-day beard. The man sauntered off in the direction of one of the many tiny parks that dotted the otherwise urban sprawl. She waited a few minutes and followed at a discreet distance.

She caught up with him on one of the benches deep within the park, away from prying eyes. He was tossing peanuts to a gaggle of ducks that had waddled up out of the pond to warm themselves on land. "You never answer. I call three times each day as you instructed, but you never answer, and there is never a message. I'm not sure what I'm to do?"

The man tossed a peanut into a group of three of the larger white ducks, and watched them peck at each other to get at the prize. *The man likes being cruel,* she thought, *just for cruelty's sake. Not a man to tangle with. Well, at least we're on the same side.*

"Just do what you always do. I'll contact you when I want you."

"Like this?"

The man called Daniel Frumkin cast her an icy glance. "Like this, or any other way I choose. That is not your concern."

Lori didn't like the way this conversation was turning. She decided a different tack. With a big smile, she asked, "So, what would you like me to do?"

Frumkin glanced in both directions, then, still looking at the ducks rather than Lori, he said, "It is time for you to marry your boyfriend, Ron Baxter. *The third*," he added with contempt. "Gay or not, he will marry you, or you will threaten to expose him."

The smile left Lori-Ann's face.

He continued. "You do not seem very happy to serve your country."

She flustered. "Oh, no. Of course I am. But I've lived with Ron for more than two years, and it will seem like I'm betraying him."

"And he did not betray you by having another man as a lover while pretending to be in love with you? Don't be a fool. You will do as I command, or you will be replaced. Is that clear?"

Lori became scared. She well understood the implications of being replaced. She would never live to meet her replacement.

"I said, is that clear?"

"Yes, sir. Of course. Please forgive me for seeming so concerned for Ron. It just took me so suddenly. Of course he's just a pawn to be used to crush the American imperialist government."

Frumkin smiled for the first time that Lori could remember. "That is better." He took a small hardbound book from his jacket pocket. "This should prove interesting reading."

Lori-Ann eyed the cover. It was titled *The Ancient of Days*. She was not familiar with it. She looked at him with uncertainty.

"A very remarkable book. Quite interesting," he said with just the trace of an accent. "It is not the plot that will be of concern to you, but the photos hidden inside the cover."

Lori made a move to open the book. Frumkin said, "Not here. It can wait till you get back to your apartment."

"Ron and his … his…?"

"His boyfriend?" Frumkin found the words for her. "His lover?"

Lori-Ann blushed.

"Are you shocked that he found a man more attractive than you? Especially since it was your job to find a man to use as suitable cover. Well, perhaps it was tit for tat," he said, turning the screws a bit with his pun.

Lori-Ann puffed out her chest, twisting her torso to give him a good look. "I can assure you that I have ample assets to entice any man that I choose."

"I will be the judge of that."

"My charms have not been lost on my boss, Mr. Tysin," she said, bragging. She would pay the bastard back for his snide remarks. "He can hardly take his eyes off of me." She wasn't quite ready to tell her control about the extent of her sexual relationship with Tysin. She didn't trust him yet; she felt that he would be too willing to sacrifice her if the situation suited him. Better to leave a little unsaid.

Frumkin sneered. "You had better get him under your control soon. So far I've gotten nothing of value from you, and you're the personal secretary of the head of the fucking CIA." He tossed another peanut to the ducks. One large gander moved in close to his leg to snatch a morsel that had fallen. Frumkin kicked it away, setting off a cacophony of squawking ducks scurrying back to the safety of their pond. Frumkin stared hard at Lori-Ann. "Tonight I will see for myself whether or not you have the physical attributes necessary to do your job correctly."

A twinge of fear tied Lori-Ann's innards in a knot. She was not especially afraid of having sex with a man she disliked; she had been trained to do just that very thing. Rather, it was his innate cruelty, his liking to hurt others that she found repugnant. Still, he was her control. To disobey was to die at his hands, and she knew it. She said, "Fine with me. But tonight, I have arranged a date."

"Forget it. Tonight I will find out if you are as good as you think you are. My predecessor gave you high marks. But Leo was an old man, almost seventy, I think. He would have been grateful for anything you did for him sexually."

Lori decided to play out her trump card. "My date tonight is with the head of the CIA, my boss, Mr. Tysin himself."

That caught Frumkin up short. He ran his hand over the two-day-old stubble on his chin. "Interesting. Very interesting." He smiled for the second time that day.

Lori was relieved. She was off the hook, at least temporarily.

"And what time is Mr. Tysin expected?"

"Six-thirty."

"Good. Very good. That will give us plenty of time."

"For what?" Lori couldn't believe that Frumkin would try something with the director coming to visit her at the apartment.

"You will see." He glanced furtively to each side, then behind him. "I will go now. I'll meet you at your apartment at 5:00 P.M."

Lori was almost too shocked to speak. She managed, "I... I live at..."

Frumkin sneered, "I know where you live. I know everything." With that, he turned and walked briskly away.

Francine Wheeler sat in the last row of seats in the hearing room, almost too stunned by the panel's recommendation of Boxer's court-martial to move. She forced her mind to race ahead and realized she had to get Boxer away from the mob of reporters. She slipped through the crowd and outside to the parking lot. In a minute, she had her BMW pulled up at the curb a few feet from where Boxer's crewmen were vainly trying to shield their skipper from the throngs of media people.

Francine honked frantically. She pressed a button on her door, and the passenger window lowered halfway. "Jack… Jack. In here. It's me."

Mark Clemens, Boxer's EXO from the *Tiny Tim*, shoved a video camera out of Boxer's face and shouted above the din, "Skipper, there's a woman in that BMW trying to get your attention."

Boxer caught a glimpse of the familiar car out of the corner of his eye. He said, "Clem, you and the guys block for me. I'm going to slip out of here with the lady. I'll contact you tomorrow."

"Roger that, Skipper." Clemens quickly passed the word along to his fellow crewmen. He shouted, "Now!" and a half dozen sailors held back the crowd of newspeople well enough to have made an American football team's front line smile.

In a flash, Boxer was inside the shiny black BMW. Tires squealed, and they were soon coasting along the freeway, lost in traffic. Boxer placed a hand on Francine's knee. "Thanks for bailing me out. Those newspeople don't know when to stop."

"I noticed that *Live at Five* reporter ordering her cameraman to keep his camera in your face. What a mean little bitch she is."

Boxer turned his head toward Francine. "Linda Johnson? You know that expression they use is true: Hell hath no fury like a woman scorned."

"Honestly, darling. If she can't stand to lose one once in a while, she should turn in her training bra and get out of the game."

Boxer laughed. "You know, there never was anything between the two of us. Some years ago, I was involved in a love-hate relationship with Linda's half-sister, Tracey Kimble." He quickly added, "That was way before I met you."

With a twinkle in her eye, Francine smiled and said, "Yes, darling. Of course."

"Tracey would do anything for a story, to advance her career, even betray our relationship," Boxer continued. "Eventually we drifted apart, and she was subsequently murdered. Got too close to the bad guys."

Francine signaled for a left turn, waited for the traffic to lessen, and turned onto another road. Boxer noticed a sign marked Shore Points.

Boxer asked, "Admiral Stark's place?"

"Uh-hmm. A little peace and quiet for a change. So I guess Linda Johnson wanted to pick up where her sister left off?"

"Half-sister. Well, I guess that was her plan. Seduce Tracey's former lover, see what he was really like in the sack firsthand, and all the while advance her career by exposing my missions to the public."

Francine nodded knowingly. "Nice girl. With friends like that…"

Boxer smiled. "At least with her sister, it was a two-way street. Once she got to know me well, she realized what she could or could not report. But Linda Johnson seems to be on a one-woman vendetta against me."

"I could try to get an injunction against her. Make her keep her distance."

"Thanks, but I don't really want to get involved in a legal battle with her. That might give her more ammunition to use against me."

They drove on for another fifteen minutes. Francine pointed out a roadside tavern done up as a log cabin off to the right. "Hungry yet? It's almost one."

"I hadn't given it much thought, but I could use a bite to eat. And a drink."

"Don't blame you, dear, after what you went through this morning." Francine deftly crossed two lanes of traffic and pulled into the gravel paved parking lot of the Dixie Bar and Grill. Boxer held the door for her and they went inside.

A dark mahogany bar filled most of the interior space, a large oval counter within which two bartenders plied their trade among the several patrons seated on stools on all sides. Glossy wooden tables lined the perimeter of the room. The lightning was subdued. Boxer motioned Francine to one of the tables near a window.

While Boxer and Francine waited, the female bartender ducked under the counter and came up on the other side. "See ya' tomorrow, Earl."

As soon as she was out the door, a husky man at the bar, dressed in jeans and a red-and-black buffalo-plaid shirt growled, "Hey, Earl, now that the boss lady's gone, hows about changin' that crap on the tube?"

Boxer noticed that the twenty-seven-inch TV set over the bar was tuned into a familiar game show. The show's hostess was modeling a long fur coat, which she opened to show off a sleek white mini-dress.

"Yeah, Earl. Put on the fuckin' basketball game or something." The man at the bar's companion, who was even bulkier, and sported a scruffy red beard, slammed his meaty palm on the bar. He lifted off his cap, which boasted *Snappy's Exxon*, slicked back his thinning hair, and put the cap back in place.

Earl, the bartender, said, "Sure, Dave, anything that you and Hooter want." He moved to the TV set and began changing channels.

A news program showed on the screen. A woman on the far side of the bar shouted, "Hey, Earl, that ain't fair. Put back *Fortune Hunters*. Those guys don't own the place."

Earl shrugged, and continued changing channels. A basketball game appeared, and everyone seemed to settle down. Hooter, the first man at the bar, called out, "Hey, Earl. Two more Coors down here."

Meanwhile, a waitress that Boxer judged to be in her midthirties, dressed in brown polyester and heavily made up, produced a pencil from out of her bouffant hairdo. She smiled, wet the pencil tip on her tongue, and said, "Hi, I'm Annie. What can I getcha?"

Francine looked at Boxer and suppressed a giggle. "I'll have a white wine, please."

Boxer said, "I'll have a Stoli on the rocks."

Annie scratched her head. "A what?"

"Stoli… Stolichnaya vodka."

"Oh, vodka. That we have. And what wouldya like to eat?"

Francine glanced at the menu and quickly decided, "I'll have the shrimp salad, please."

Boxer noticed there wasn't much on the menu to choose from. "I'll have the DixieBurger, and fries."

Annie jotted down their orders on her pad, and brought it to the bartender. "Earl, a white wine for the lady, and a vodka for the guy. He asked me for a Stoli-something."

Earl poured jug wine into a stemware glass and placed it on a tray on top of the bar. "We don't have any fancy stuff. If he wants vodka, it's gotta be the house brand."

Dave, the big fellow in the Snappy's Exxon cap said, "Hey, wait a minute. That Stoli crap is Russian vodka." He spun around on his stool to see who had ordered it. "Hey, you," he said, spotting Boxer and Francine seated alone near the front of the room. "This ain't no commie bar, and we don't have no Russian drinks here."

Boxer's face reddened. He started to rise out of his seat. Francine sensed what he was about to do, and placed her hand on his. "Forget it, dear. Please."

Boxer, feeling the tension welled up in him from the events of the morning, sucked in a deep breath and tried to calm himself down. He motioned for the waitress to come over. "Look, forget the vodka. Bring me a Heineken, will you?"

Annie reported to the barkeep. "Forget the vodka, Earl. Make it a Heineken, instead."

This time Hooter piped in, "Hey, what's with all the foreign shit you keep orderin'? You must be a commie." Hooter stared at Boxer. "Wait a minute. I know you. You're the guy we just seen on the tube. Hey, Dave," he said, nudging his partner, "that's the guy who took over that American ship and let the Russians come on board."

"Yeah, you know, I think you're right. We oughta kick his ass real good for him. Show him what we think about traitors around here."

Boxer jumped out of his seat. Francine grabbed his sleeve to hold him back. "Please, Jack. Let's just leave. You've been through enough already today."

Boxer stood there while Francine collected her handbag and got out of her seat.

Dave spat, "Hey, look at the commie hiding behind his mommy." He broke out laughing, poking his partner's ample gut with an elbow.

Hooter joined in, "The commie hiding behind his mommy." The two of them ambled over to Boxer, with Hooter leading the way.

Boxer's jaw clenched so tightly that the muscles of his face stood out. He stood with feet slightly apart, hands balled up in fists at his side. He stared up at the hulk looming over him. "You're in my way," Boxer said.

Hooter said, "What the fuck are you gonna do about it?" He shoved Boxer back with both hands.

Boxer slipped to his right, grabbed Hooter's wrist and elbow, and twisted the arm up behind the man. Boxer shoved him face down onto the table.

Hooter spun around to face Boxer, blood starting to dribble from his nose. "Why, you…"

Boxer lashed out a straight right to Hooter's jaw, powering it with all the pent-up tension and frustration of the morning. He heard a cracking sound, and watched Hooter sink back to the table. Boxer's hand throbbed.

Dave moved closer and bellowed, "Look what you done to Hooter. Now you're gonna pay for this." He grabbed a chair and hoisted it up over Boxer's head. Francine screamed.

Better end this quickly, Boxer thought. He stepped in and unleashed a swift kick to Dave's groin.

Dave dropped the chair behind him and grabbed for his balls.

Boxer closed Dave's eye with a quick left jab. Then he grabbed a handful of hair and slammed Dave's face into a heavy support beam. Dave's face was shattered. "More?" Boxer chided. "You want more?"

Dave shook his head, no.

"Say it."

Dave's nose was clearly broken. He spat out two bloody teeth. "No more, man. Please. No more."

Boxer turned his attention to Hooter. "What about you, lardass? You want any more?"

Hooter just stared blankly in his general direction. Boxer said, "I guess not."

Boxer turned around in a three-sixty. "Anyone else having any problems?"

Earl the barkeep stepped away from the bar, busying himself with wiping the glassware. Annie stood there, holding out the Heineken.

Boxer stared them all down. He linked his arm around Francine's, and walked casually toward the exit. He paused at the door, and turned to the patrons staring at him. He just smiled and said, "Have a nice day."

CHAPTER 10

Borodine lay propped up by several pillows on his hospital bed. He tested his right forearm; an IV shunt had been removed this morning. He glanced around the tiny room, everything gleaming white enamel except for the dull-grey linoleum floor. He felt something missing, then realized that the room seemed emptier without the elaborate intravenous tree that had stood guard at the head of his bed for the past week. Gone were the bottles of serum and dextrose, the tiny plastic bags of antibiotics piggybacked into those, the electric pump that monitored the precise flow of the various fluids into his body.

He noticed, too, the vase of fresh-cut flowers on the shelf of the medicine cabinet to the foot of his bed. Borodine smiled. Either this was a marvelously good stroke of luck, and he was actually going to survive, or he was already dead, hence the flowers and the removal of his intravenous feeding. Then, in walked the rotund, stone-faced doctor, followed by her equally rotund and stone-faced assistant. They looked like female sumo wrestlers in white gowns. He had dubbed them Tweedle-Dum and Tweedle-Dee after the American nursery rhymes, but not within their range of hearing.

"Ah, good morning, Comrade Admiral." It was the doctor, Tweedle-Dum. "And how are we this fine morning?"

Borodine managed a smile. "Good morning, Comrade Doctor Vasilovna. I would feel much better if you would sign me out of here. I'm not used to so much attention."

The doctor removed a clipboard from the foot of the bed and scanned it quickly. "Perhaps sooner than you expect,

111

comrade." She advanced toward him and placed a small digital thermometer into his mouth. "Say ah."

Borodine did so. In about twenty seconds, she removed the device and read the results to Tweedle-Dee. "Thirty-seven point two."

The assistant recorded it on the clipboard.

Borodine watched the doctor walk around to the left side of the bed. She lifted a ruled plastic pouch half-filled with yellow liquid from the chrome side railing, and turned to the other woman. "Two hundred fifty-five milliliters."

That figure was dutifully recorded onto the record as well. "Very good, Comrade Admiral. There is no longer any need for this. Now if you will bear with me for a moment, I will free you from it."

Borodine had almost forgotten about the catheter. He grew embarrassed when the doctor lifted the white sheet exposing his genitalia, and deftly drew out the fluid securing the catheter inside his bladder. He winced as it slid out.

"You will feel more comfortable now." She handed the urine collection apparatus to her assistant, who deposited it into a clear plastic bag and secured it shut. "How do you like the flowers?"

Borodine propped himself up on one elbow, turning to get a better view of the flowers. "Very much, thank you. At first I thought they might be for my grave, but now I like them much better."

"Olga cut them from her garden this morning for you." The doctor nodded toward the assistant, who looked down at the floor and blushed.

"Madam, I truly thank you," Borodine said. "You are very kind."

This made the woman blush even more.

"Oh, I almost forgot," the doctor said. "You have a visitor waiting outside to see you. We will be going now, and so I will send him in."

Tweedle-Dum and Tweedle-Dee left the room, and Viktor stood smiling in the doorway. Borodine was delighted. "Viktor, please come in. You are a sight for these old eyes."

"Not so old. And you look so much better. Your color is back."

"Yes. And I don't feel like a pincushion anymore, with all the needles sticking into me. And I don't have to piss into a bag through a tube. Why shouldn't I look better?"

Viktor moved close to the bed and grasped Borodine's hand. Borodine covered Viktor's hand with his own left hand. Borodine got right to the point. "How is it going with the investigation, Viktor?"

"So far, not so badly, Igor. Admiral Gorshkov has accepted my accounting without comment so far, though I am sure that the KGB is not completely satisfied."

Borodine glanced furtively around the room, trying to spot the hidden microphones that he was certain were in place. "I'm sure they are never satisfied, my friend. That is their purpose, to question everything." He placed the tip of his forefinger to his lips, then he changed the subject. "And how is my wife Tanya doing? Is she ill? Is that why she isn't here with you?"

Viktor smiled. "No, Igor. Her doctors feel that she will give birth any day now, and they didn't want to jeopardize her health, or the baby's. After all, you had a very bad case of pneumonia."

"Yes, I know. The antibiotics probably saved my life."

Viktor glanced at the doorway, then back. "Comrade Admiral Boxer had much to do with saving your life. He risked his career to get you onto that American supply ship. His exec,

Clemens, told me that Boxer actually held a gun to the captain's head and ordered him to take you aboard. You were in very bad shape, then."

"Ah, my friend Jack Boxer. One minute we are trying to blow each other out of the ocean and the next, he risks everything to save my life."

"All of us, Igor. None of us from the *Sea Dragon* would have survived in the Antarctic without his help."

"Well, then, my first wish is that Comrade Boxer is rewarded for his heroics, rather than punished for helping us."

"*Da.* So do I."

Borodine smiled. "And my second wish…"

"Yes, Igor?"

"My second wish is to get out of the hospital and reunite with my wife, and my men."

Viktor looked surprised. "Oh? Didn't they tell you? You're going home today. I'm here to take you home."

The sun shone brightly on Maryland's eastern shore, already burning off the morning haze when Francine first saw the long black limo snake its way along the private drive to their borrowed hideaway. She heard the crunch of tires on gravel as she climbed the wooden porch and let the screen door slam behind her. She called out, "Jack, we've got company."

Boxer had been watching the limo for several minutes from his second-floor vantage point. He had expected to see Admiral Stark. He was surprised when two men stepped out of the back wearing wide-brimmed hats and cowboy boots. Jay and Billy? What the hell were they doing here? Almost no one knew this place existed. He climbed down the stairs two at a time.

Francine snuggled next to him. "Jack, do you know those men?"

Boxer put his arm around her. "I'm afraid so. That's Billy White, the shorter one, and Jay Corless Archer. Texas millionaires. Wheeler dealers. Confidants to presidents. At least the current one."

"Jack? You in there, boy? Hell, come on out and welcome your old friends."

Boxer said to Francine, "It gets pretty thick out there when those two get to talking, but don't let that shit-kicker style of theirs fool you. They're sharp as tacks."

From outside. "Jack Boxer. Rise and shine, boy. It's too beautiful a day to stay indoors."

Boxer shrugged and pushed out through the screen door. Francine followed closely behind.

Billy slapped Jay on the back. "That's why he was holed up inside. Didn't I tell you we should have called first?"

"Hang me if you didn't. Jack, we're sorry if we're intrudin'."

Boxer was sure that they weren't sorry. "Jay, Billy. What brings you two out here so early in the morning?" He felt Francine tap him gently on the shoulder. "Oh, I'm forgetting my manners. Gentlemen, I'd like you to meet Miss Francine Wheeler. Francine, this is Billy White…"

Billy gallantly doffed his Stetson. "Ma'am."

"And Mr. Jay Archer."

Jay tipped his brim. "Howdy, Francine."

Francine smiled broadly. "Hi. Can I offer you gentlemen some breakfast? You must have been up very early?"

Jay said, "No, thank you, ma'am. But we'd sure appreciate some coffee. My throat's drier than a west Texas creek in August." And to Boxer he added, "Mind if we come in and sit a spell with you?"

"Sure. Come on in. By the way, how'd you find out about this place? Very few people know about it, and even fewer know that we're staying here now."

Billy said, "Oh, we asked around some."

Jay added, "Everything and everyone has its price, son. But don't you worry none. Me and Billy are on your side."

Francine put up a fresh pot, and was soon setting a cup of steaming coffee in front of each of the men, and one for herself. "I've got some sticky buns left from the general store up the road." She placed a plate of the goodies on the table. "Help yourselves, men."

Boxer shook his head. Jay patted his belly and said, "None for me, thanks."

Billy reached for a bun. "Don't mind if I do."

Boxer took a sip of his coffee. "Well, guys, what brings you all the way out here so early in the morning, business or pleasure?"

Jay answered, "With Billy and me, business is always a pleasure. But this morning, we're just here on a social call."

Billy took a bite of the sticky bun and washed it down with coffee. "Heard about all that crap you been taking from the press. That investigation was rigged against you, you know."

Jay nodded his head. "Senator Le Roux is trying to fry your ass. That was his son-in-law you put a gun on. Not that he didn't deserve it, though."

Boxer said, "I know all about the connection between Axelrod and the senator. I hadn't imagined that he could buy off an admiral or two."

Billy interjected, "The senator's head of Armed Services. A nod from him is worth another flag to those men if they play along with him. Hell, those admirals are gettin' up there in years, Jack. You know what another flag on their rank will do for their pension?"

"I'm well aware of that. I assumed they had more integrity than that."

Jay shook his head. "Don't assume nothin', boy. I ought to know. Money talks in this town."

"Then things are looking very badly for me."

"Well," Jay began, "part of the reason we made the trip down here is to lend you our own personal support. Anything we can do for you, let us know."

Billy added, "And the other thing, we were discussing your problem with the President last night. He wants you to know, Jack, that he's on your side, too. He'll do whatever he can to help you."

Boxer sipped his coffee. "Very nice of the President. Correct me if I'm wrong, but isn't Senator Le Roux planning to run against Spooner in the primaries next spring? Could that be a factor in his desire to help me?"

Jay shrugged. "Could be, Jack. Remember me just tellin' you, everything has its price. You're a very popular man in this country, Jack. A genuine hero of the people. It wouldn't hurt the President if you come out on top of this thing, and it was known that he was on your side all along."

"All I really want is a fair trial. The facts of the matter will speak for themselves."

Jay gulped down the remainder of his coffee, and turned to his partner. "Well, Billy, time to get movin'. We've got a lot of work before us."

Billy licked the honey from his fingertips and finished his coffee. "Right you are, Jay. Thanks for your hospitality, folks. We'll be on our way. We'll be sure to send the President your regards."

Boxer and Francine accompanied them to the door. As they stepped out onto the porch, their driver got out of the limo and opened both rear doors for them, standing there at attention. Billy started down the steps. Jay suddenly realized something, and turned back. "Oh, almost forgot the most important reason for the visit. Me and Billy are going to the Soviet Union on business in three weeks. We'll be gone for two, three months at least. It'll really sweeten our pockets if we do a good job over there. So we're having a big Texas-style barbeque as a sendin' off party. And you and the pretty lady here are invited."

Billy tipped his hat. "Guests of honor, in fact. It's set for this Sunday back at Jay's ranch. Sure hope you can make it."

Francine leaned next to Boxer as the two men got into the limo and drove off. "Sounds like it might be fun, Jack. And it would take our minds off those Navy problems."

"I'm sure it would be, Francine. But at what cost?"

She looked up at him.

"With those two, it always costs something," Boxer said. "With those two horse traders, it always costs."

Lori-Ann Collins smiled at the driver, aware of his stare as she stepped off the D.C. Transit bus a block from her apartment. He held the exit door open until she was past his field of vision, enjoying the view of her wiggling rear end for as long as possible.

Lori-Ann was fond of innocent flirting and teasing, pleased with the knowledge that she could attract any man she chose to. She needed to feel appreciated, especially by men, and delighted in the warm glow that always seemed to follow a man's appreciative response to the signals she sent out. It had almost always worked for her, since the day when the First

Deputy of the KGB Directorate in Gorky came to the orphanage where she lived, and singled her out of several hundred girls to be pressed into service.

There were certainly more beautiful girls than her in the group. But when the First Deputy stood before her, and cast an appraising eye, she loosed all charms and succeeded at alluring him. She smiled, batted her eyes, and puffed out her sixteen-year-old chest. She needed someone's approval, and she found it that day.

Trained in her craft by the KGB, she became a temptress par excellence, drawing many a traitor out of his clever sinecure and into the hands of her superiors. And, on occasion, she was chosen by this same First Deputy, Valentine Makusky, now the Deputy Director of the KGB's Second Directorate for the entire Soviet Union, for special assignments. If Makusky wished to blackmail a particular political adversary, it was arranged for Lori-Ann to seduce the unwitting man or woman and be videotaped with them in very compromising positions.

That led to her current cushy job in the United States, where she relished the almost unlimited freedom and lifestyles of the capitalists. In exchange, she had to perform occasional low-level spying chores, and attend to the very marginal sexual needs of her former control, Leo. Until she was ordered to seduce the Director of the CIA. She had begun to realize that all her training had been to prime her for this ultimate role. And everything was going fine, everything as it should be until she was passed on to her new control, the man called Daniel Frumkin.

Lori-Ann climbed the short flight of stairs into her apartment building, walking directly to the self-service elevator, and got off at the third floor. She fumbled in her handbag for her key, produced it, and opened her door. Humming a popular song that stayed in her head, she tossed her bag and her jacket into the overstuffed occasional chair near the door, and kicked off her shoes. She locked the door behind her, loosened the button at the top of her skirt, and made herself comfortable. She pulled her blouse out of its confines, and removed the barrette that held her hair in place. One shake of her head and her long black hair spilled over her shoulders.

"Stop." The command was spoken harshly, and in Russian.

Lori-Ann froze long enough to comprehend that the voice was that of her control, Frumkin. "Where? Wha—?"

"Keep your voice down. Stand right where you are. Okay … perfect."

Lori-Ann stood there, shifting her weight from one leg to the other. Frumkin walked into the living room. "It's perfect. Come see for yourself."

She followed him through the foyer into her bedroom. He had her armoire pushed against the wall behind the living room, her clothes strewn on the nearby bed. She looked puzzled. The enigma unfolded as Frumkin guided her to the mini video camera on a shelf facing the wall. Through the monitor she could see her jacket and bag lying on the chair where she had tossed them. "But how…?"

"A hole in the wall. And in the painting over the sofa. You may consider it an improvement to the painting. At least that modern art shit is good for something."

"Mr. Tysin picked it out himself."

"Figures. I have this camera set on a timer. It will go on at 5:45 and run for three hours. Whatever you do, don't let Tysin anywhere near your dresser. If he finds the camera, he will know what is going on, and have you arrested. Or killed."

"He wouldn't."

Frumkin sneered. "I can assure you, he most certainly will. If I were in his position, I would kill you on the spot myself."

Lori involuntarily clutched her arms and shivered. There was no doubt that Frumkin would kill anyone who compromised him. But would Henry? Perhaps…

Frumkin took hold of her arm and escorted her back into the living room. He gave her a gentle shove into the center of the room. "Do your love-making in here. I will move the couch over here, in view of the camera. The chairs will go on this wall."

"In here? But he'll be suspicious."

It happened very suddenly. Frumkin backhanded her face, catching her by surprise and knocking her backward. Lori-Ann's hands went up to her face. Frumkin glared down at her.

"Don't make me damage your face. I don't want him to be suspicious. You will entice him right here, in front of the camera. You will take off your clothes here, and then his clothes, and you will do anything he wants. Only do it right here in front of the camera. Is that perfectly clear?" His voice rose in pitch as he spat out the last words.

Lori-Ann looked down at her stockinged feet. Resignedly, she uttered, "Yes, I guess so."

"Okay, then, I'll leave you now. This is very important. Don't fuck it up." With that he strode to the door, opened it a crack, and looked outside. He turned back into the room, and checked his watch. "It's 6:15. He'll be here any minute. Oh, go put on something sexy and fix yourself up. You look like shit." With that, he quietly closed the door and was gone.

CHAPTER 11

Francine Wheeler circled the block three times before she spotted a red Toyota pulling out of the only parking space in the vicinity of her brownstone. With heavy raindrops pelting the windshield, she darted up the street, nosed the BMW into the tiny area, and swung the wheel sharply to the left. Boxer hung on for dear life.

With a line of traffic honking and blaring their horns at her audacity, she calmly backed into the space until she gently touched bumpers with the car behind. She straightened the wheels and aligned the BMW perfectly. "Not bad," Boxer managed. "Where did you learn that little move? I thought you were going to crash head-on into the car ahead."

"Oh, that? I was a passenger in a long stretch limo once in New York City when the driver pulled that maneuver on Seventh Avenue. He beat out several taxicabs and a Caddy with Jersey plates for that spot." She smiled broadly. "I was so impressed that I paid him twenty bucks to teach me how to do it. It was twenty dollars well spent."

"I'll say. The rain's really coming down heavy. We'll have to make a dash for your house. It's at least a block or so back there." He motioned in the direction with his head.

"I won't melt. And I'm sure you won't. Ready, Admiral?" Her hand was already on the door latch.

"I'm ready if you are. Let's go."

The two of them jumped out and slammed their doors behind them. They jogged through the puddles. Water squished through their shoes, soaked through their clothing, and ran down their faces. They reached the door to Francine's brownstone looking like drowned rats. Francine let them in with her key.

Boxer brushed a wet tangle of hair out of her face and kissed her as they stood there dripping wet in the vestibule. "Jack, I must look a fright. Let's go up and get out of these wet clothes."

Boxer smiled. "Suits me fine."

They climbed a flight of stairs to the living room level, and peeled off their wet clothes. Boxer stood there watching her very carefully undress and gather up her things. She looked up at him and smiled. "I don't know about you, Jack Boxer, but I could use a hot shower."

"So could I. Why don't we shower together?"

"That's the whole idea, silly. Let me have your wet clothing. I'll dump them in the hamper."

Boxer got the shower going just right, and held back the curtain for Francine. She stuck a foot in to test the water, nodded, and climbed in. Boxer quickly followed. She said, "Mmm, this feels good."

Boxer took the soap and lathered her back, gently kneading the muscles of her shoulders and back.

She worked up a rich lather through the mat of hair on his chest, then dropped her hands to his belly and thighs. He ducked his head under the stream of warm water and kissed her lips.

He laughed. "Sure is a far cry from your typical two-minute shower on a submarine. The shower stall's so small that you soap up the walls and spin around to get clean."

That reduced her to giggles. "C'mon, Admiral. Let's get rinsed off and warm up under the covers."

They dried off quickly with thick Turkish towels. Boxer decided, "That's dry enough." He unwrapped the towel from her body and scooped her up in his arms. Then, both of them naked, he carried her to the bed.

As she hung on to his neck, he pulled back the light comforter and placed her gently on the bed. Francine slowly rolled over to make room, and tugged him into the bed after her. She held out her arms, and they embraced, passionately.

Francine clutched him to herself, "Oh, darling, I love you so."

Boxer looked into her eyes. "I love you, too, Francine." He brushed aside a tear from her eye.

"Jack, darling, it's good just to know that we're really good together. You don't have to say that just to please me."

Boxer kissed her lips. "I said I love you because I mean it, Francine. I've felt it all along. You're the first woman in many years to make me feel like this, to give so much of herself and ask for so little in return."

"Oh, Jack. I know I'll never own you. You belong so much to the Navy and your men and your submarines. I'm happy to have you whenever I can."

Boxer propped himself up on the pillows, and took Francine into his arms. He became very serious. "Darling, I… I want more than that for us. I want you to… I mean I'd like you to marry me."

Francine was stunned. She threw her arms around him and kissed him on the lips. "Oh, Jack, are you sure?"

He kissed her back. "Yes, I'm as sure as I've ever been about anything. I'd be very happy if you'd be my wife."

"Oh, yes, darling, yes, yes, yes."

"We'll set the date for as soon as that court-martial business is over with."

Francine primped up her hair. "I can't wait till Admiral Stark gets back here with Chuck to tell them both the wonderful news."

"They'll probably stop off for a bite to eat near the airport before driving back to the house. I guess they'll be here in about another hour or so."

Francine picked up her towel and patted herself dry. "That'll give us just enough time to get dressed and grab something to eat ourselves. And, Jack, I've been giving a lot of thought to the court-martial myself."

Boxer slipped into a fresh pair of skivvies. "Don't concern yourself with it, Francine. The Navy will assign me a counsellor. Being an admiral, I'll automatically get someone of flag rank to defend me."

"I've been thinking of contacting my former law professor at Georgetown. Granville Wilkins is probably one of the best attorneys in the District. I'd like to have him on our side."

Boxer stopped in the middle of buttoning his shirt. "Slick Wilkins? You know him?"

Francine smiled. "Sure. He and I are good friends. I was his star pupil when he guest-lectured on criminal law. Afterward, I clerked for him until I passed the D.C. bar. I'm sure he'd agree to help us."

Boxer rubbed his beard. "Well, if I could get the Navy attorney to agree to some outside help ... why not. I've followed some of Wilkins's cases in the news. They're always sensational."

"And he always wins, Jack. He comes across like a down home country boy from the sticks, but does he know his law. And human nature. I'll call him this afternoon."

Boxer held her in his arms. "Great. Thanks, darling. Now let's get something to eat."

For Igor Borodine, being alive and well again and reunited with his wife Tanya was more than he'd thought possible a few short weeks ago. As they strolled along an unpaved lane in Gorky Park, he linked arms with his pregnant wife and offered her a smile. She responded by pressing his arm to her side and smiling back. Suddenly, she stopped short, a surprised look on her face. "Oh," she exclaimed. She put an assuring hand on Borodine's shoulder. "It was the baby. She's getting impatient."

Borodine placed his broad hand on Tanya's prominent belly. It pleased him to feel the movements of the unborn child within her. "Yes. According to the doctors, you should have given birth a week ago. I hope there's nothing wrong."

"What's wrong is the reckoning of the doctors. I'm just fine, dear. Oh, let's stop awhile here by the bridge."

Borodine escorted his wife to the little footbridge over the river where thousands of Muscovites ice-skated daily during the winter months. Now, at the very end of May, in the middle of the afternoon, they had the area almost to themselves. Lunch hour being over, most people were now at work. "There is a bench, Tanya. Let's sit for a while. Catch your breath."

As Borodine turned to help his wife onto the bench, he caught a glimpse of a figure darting behind a lone conifer. When he sat down beside her, the man emerged and pretended to be interested in something else in the distance. Borodine was pissed. "Bastards. They can't even leave a man alone with his wife without spying on him."

"What?"

"Don't turn your heard. He is standing there with his back toward us next to the tall White Pine over there."

"I see him, dear. Does that mean we are not to go on with our plan to baptize the baby?"

Borodine swallowed. "If that is what you want, then that is what we will do. After the baby is born, we will bring her to visit your relatives in Poland. We will find a way to have the child baptized."

Tanya hugged him to her body.

"And we shall name her for your late mother, Fyodora."

"That is very kind of you, Igor. But what if your mother's instinct is wrong, and she is a he?"

Borodine chuckled, "Her instinct is infallible. At least half of the time. Besides, I watched you pick up her handkerchief from the edge. That means a girl. If you picked it up in the middle, that would assure us that we would have a boy. It's very simple."

Tanya smiled at him. "Does she really believe in that old stuff?"

"To her, it is something that has passed down from mother to daughter, generation after generation. She realizes that is not scientifically feasible, but ... one can never be sure. Besides, she is right at least half the time."

"So, if we have a boy? We shall name him Igor, or, if you like, Aleksandr, after your father."

"If you don't mind, if we have a son, I would like to call him Viktor. As you know, Viktor Korzenko, my second in command on the sub, saved my life, and made it possible for us to be rescued. I would like to honor him as the good friend that he is by naming my son for him."

"Oooh. Help me up, Igor. Viktor ... or Fyodora is telling me it's time."

Borodine helped his wife to her feet, and they walked back down the path toward the street. The man behind the tree left his vantage point and followed after them at a discreet distance.

The door buzzer sounded and Boxer climbed down the two flights of stairs to welcome Admiral Stark and Chuck. "Welcome home, son." Boxer hugged the boy shamelessly. "And thanks, Admiral, for picking up Chuck at the airport."

Stark carried two suitcases in with him. Chuck, dressed in khakis and a faded blue sweater, toted a small knapsack over one shoulder. "Thanks, Dad. Is it all right if I call you that? Seems kind of strange."

"It's official now. Charles Rugger Boxer. Your birth father, Rugger, was a good friend, and I'd have adopted you if only for his sake. But in the past year I've come to see that you're made of the right stuff, and I'm glad to have you as my son on your own right."

Chuck beamed.

Francine said, "Jack and I are so proud of the way you handled yourself with that ugly situation on Staten Island, Chuck. You took charge of the situation just as your father would have."

Chuck blushed. "Now all I need is to have you for my mother. My own mother died when I was so young... I really don't remember much about her."

Boxer put a hand on Chuck's shoulder. "That may come sooner than you think, son. Francine and I are going to get married."

"Wow."

Stark stopped in his tracks. "Wonderful. This calls for a celebration. Chuck, give me a hand at the bar."

Boxer slipped an arm around Francine's waist and they joined the others in the living room. She called in to Stark, "There's some champagne in the fridge. I bought it to celebrate the finalization of Chuck's adoption."

"Fine, fine. A little champagne's good for the spirit." Stark found the bottle and removed the foil wrap and the wire mesh basket covering the cork. He looked over the label. "Hey, this is good stuff."

"Nothing but the best for my men."

Stark held the bottle in one hand and gently twisted the cork. It came out with a pleasant popping sound. "Champagne all around. Here, Chuck, hand these over to Boxer and Francine. I'll pour for us."

Chuck looked at Boxer for approval.

"Sure, son. We've got good reason to celebrate."

Admiral Stark held up his glass. "To Jack and Francine. May they find happiness with each other as long as they live."

The four of them clinked glasses and sipped the champagne.

"Oh, I almost forgot," Stark said in afterthought. "This packet came for you by courier this morning. It's from Texas."

Boxer took the large manila envelope and looked at the return address. "It's from Jay Archer. Wonder what he's up to?"

Francine said, "Well, aren't you going to open it?"

Boxer tore open the envelope and emptied the contents onto a coffee table. There were four airline tickets and a handwritten note inside. Boxer started to read, "'Dear Jack, sorry to be so presumptuous, but I hope you and your friends will be able to attend. We had to move up the date on short notice. I'll have a driver waiting for you tomorrow afternoon at DFW Airport. Jay.'" Boxer looked up. "He goes on to say, "'P.S., Jack I have a big surprise for you. Please be here.'"

Chuck asked, "Who's Jay Archer?"

Admiral Stark answered for Boxer. "Jay Corless Archer is a Texas millionaire, Chuck. His father made a fortune in import-export, in the days when you could keep most of what you made. He invested wisely in real estate and increased his trading empire." He took a sip of the champagne. "And then he did Jay a big favor. He died at an early age, leaving everything to his only son."

Boxer added, "And Jay teamed up with Billy White, another millionaire wheeler-dealer, and the rest is history. They're about to set off for the Soviet Union on a big trading deal."

Chuck asked. "Are we going to go? I've never been on a ranch."

Boxer thought about it a moment. Maybe he should go, for Chuck's sake. The boy had spent his whole life in a small neighborhood on Staten Island. There's another world out there that he'd never been exposed to. Besides, Boxer was curious about Jay's big surprise for him. "Would you like to go?"

Chuck beamed. "You bet I would."

Stark said, "Count me in. I knew Sam Archer when Jay was just a pup."

"Francine?"

She smiled at him. "Whither thou goest…"

"Then it's settled. Tomorrow we go to Texas."

The Texas Air 747 jet taxied to a stop at the Dallas-Fort Worth airport at 11:30 A.M. the next day. Boxer and Stark each took one carry-on bag from under their seats and the foursome made for the moving sidewalk past the luggage area. They were surprised to hear themselves being paged over the intercom. "Jack Boxer party please go to the Texas Air courtesy desk."

They were met at the desk by a tall, lanky man in a western-style chauffeur's uniform topped off by a ten-gallon hat. He held a small cardboard square in front of him that simply spelled BOXER.

Boxer held out his hand. "I'm Jack Boxer. How do you do?"

"Howdy, Admiral. Ah'm Whitey Travers." He shook Boxer's hand and doffed his hat to Francine, revealing a shock of pale blond, almost white hair. "Ma'am."

Boxer said, "This is Miss Francine Wheeler, Admiral Stark, and my son, Chuck."

"Pleased to meet yo'all. The car is raht outside." He took the travel bag from Admiral Stark. Boxer kept his bag at his side. "Yo'all got any more luggage?"

Boxer shook his head. "We're traveling light. There's enough to stay overnight. Then we'll be heading back home to D.C."

"Fine. Raht this way, folks."

They followed Whitey out of the arrivals building. There, parked in a no parking zone, was the biggest white Cadillac stretch limo any of them had ever seen. It had a gaudy, tooled leather brougham roof, gold trim and pinstriping, and a leather-bound pair of steerhorns as a hood ornament. And standing next to it was the biggest policeman they'd ever seen. Whitey said, "Jay's really gone all our for yo'all."

They approached the limo a little embarrassed. Except for Whitey Travers, who approached the policeman and slapped him on the arm. "Thanks, hoss. Ah shore do appreciate your help." Boxer watched him slip the cop a hundred-dollar bill.

The policeman pocketed the money. "Anytime, Whitey. Anytime." He turned to Boxer's party. "Yo'all have a nice visit, folks," and he held the rear door open for Francine.

Boxer saluted and slipped in alongside her, while Admiral Stark joined them in the back seat by the other window. Chuck occupied the jump seat facing them.

Whitey tossed their luggage in the trunk, and climbed in behind the wheel. He turned to face his guests. "Yo'all jist sit back and enjoy the view. We'll be at the ranch in 'bout half an hour."

Whitey Travers drove skillfully, and soon they were driving through a beautiful rolling plain, leaving the hustle of the airport behind. Finally, they came to a barbed-wire fence and turned right, running parallel to it for another several miles. Chuck and Stark watched the steers graze through the fence. Boxer noted the excitement on the boy's face and was pleased that he'd agreed to make the trip.

Soon they came to a gate, where Whitey got out and spoke into an intercom mounted on a post. He unlatched the gate, manipulated a lever on the gatepost, and it opened wide. They drove through on a two-lane dirt road. Boxer noticed the gate close behind them.

They drove on a short distance until they pulled up to a huge white antebellum ranch house. Whitey parked the limo under the porte cochère at the entrance, and helped his passengers out of the car. He rang the front bell, and a white-aproned maid came to the door. "Take good care of these VIP's, Millie. Show them to their guest rooms and let Jay and Billy know they're here."

Then Whitey tipped his hat to the four of them and said, "Been a pleasure, folks. Ah'll be here to bring yo'all back to the airport tomorrow."

Boxer thanked him and followed the maid to their rooms. They were given a three-room suite. Boxer and Francine shared a room with a view facing the backyard, with its small pond and several stands of trees. Servants were setting up tables and chairs, and firing up a large charcoal pit.

Chuck and Stark shared a room with a similar view. The two bedrooms adjoined a common sitting room, complete with a fully stocked bar. "All the comforts of home," Boxer quipped.

Jay Archer personally came up to greet Boxer and the others and offered them a grand tour of his ranch. After they changed to comfortable clothing, they piled into a jeep 4x4 and went for a short ride. Several horsemen rode up and chatted with Jay.

"Ranch hands. All good boys. Ah've been damn lucky."

"I've never been on a horse," Chuck offered.

Jay turned his head toward Chuck. "Well, son. You're welcome to spend some time here as my guest any ol' time you'd like. We'll teach you how to ride, rope, punch cattle. Anything you'd like. Matter of fact, let's make it a standing order. You still in school?"

"Yes, sir. I graduate next month."

Jay said, "Well, son. My graduation present to you is a stay at my place when you finish with school. Anytime. Just pick up the phone, and I'll have plane tickets sent up to you, and yo'all com'on down. How's that sound?"

Chuck looked at Boxer, who smiled and nodded his approval. "Sounds great. Wow."

As they arrived back at the ranch house, Jay said, "Why don't yo'all freshen up some. Dinner'll be around six. Bring your appetites."

As they piled out of the Jeep, Jay took Boxer aside. "Say, Jack, why don't you hang back some. You an' me and Billy can shoot the shit for a while."

Boxer agreed, and sent the others on ahead without him. They walked through the house and out onto the veranda in back. Billy was sitting back on a rocker, his hand caressing the ass of a big, bosomy blonde in a short suede cowgirl dress with lots of fringe. He sat up when Jay and Boxer came into view, but left his hand where it was.

Jay called out, "Howdy, Billy. We got us some company."

133

Billy slapped the girl on the behind and stood up. "Howdy, Jack. Glad you could make it." He motioned with his head toward the young woman. "This here's Lucy Mae. She's one of my protegée's. Ah'm teaching her the ropes."

I'm sure you are, Boxer thought. He smiled at the woman. Lucy Mae returned the smile and waved hello, revealing a flash of milky white cleavage as she did. She whispered something in Billy's ear. He responded with another pat on the ass, and she went off, wiggling as she walked. When she was out of earshot, Billy said to Boxer, "Ol' Lucy Mae thinks you're kinda cute. Them's her words, not mine. I think that ol' gal's got the hots for you."

Boxer was a little embarrassed. "Thanks, Billy. She's not my type."

"Not your type?" Billy couldn't believe it. "Why she's got everything a man could hope for."

Boxer just shook his head.

Jay piped in, "Besides, ah hear she can suck the chrome off a trailer hitch."

Billy slapped his thigh and roared.

Boxer waited till they settled down. "Actually, the lady I brought down with me, Francine Wheeler, and I are getting married soon."

"Married? Yee-haw," Billy roared. "Sumbitch. Well, congratulations."

Jay said, "Couldn't happen to a nicer guy."

"Thanks, boys. But I guess you had some other reason other than offering me a flesh offering to bring me down here."

Jay got serious. "We just wanted to know if we could do anything about that nasty court-martial they rigged up on you."

Billy added, "My understanding is they rigged the investigational hearing against you."

Boxer noticed how fast they dropped the country boy shit-kicker accent when they wanted to get serious. "That's what I figured, too. The captain of the ship I took over has a father-in-law that's a hot-shot senator. Daddy got to someone and they tried to bury me alive." Boxer looked them directly in the eyes. "I'm in the right on this one. I've retained an excellent lawyer, and I'm going to win this thing."

"Who's your mouthpiece?"

"Granville Wilkins."

Jay broke into a widemouth grin. "Slick Wilkins? Why, he and mah daddy done some business back a ways. He's the best all right. Well, me and Billy be happy to kick in for your legal fund."

Boxer shook his head. "Thanks anyway. I've got my own money, and there are no strings attached to it. Besides, he's a friend of a friend."

Billy squared his Stetson hat on his head. "Well, if you need for anything, and ah mean anything, you jist give a holler, and me and Jay will be there with whatever it is you need."

"Thanks, boys. I appreciate it."

Jay finally said, "Ah'm getting mighty thirsty jawin' like this. Let's get something to drink. Dinner ought to be ready in about two hours."

At six o'clock, the backyard filled up with about fifty guests. Stark pointed out to Boxer, Francine, and Chuck several congressmen and senators, some business tycoons, the ambassador to a Caribbean island, and a retired general. All the rest of the men looked well-heeled and influential. There were several wives among them, and a slew of pretty women for those who were down on their own.

Several times, Lucy Mae strolled past Boxer, smiling and shaking her stuff. Boxer ignored her as best he could. He suppressed an urge to giggle. He would never look at a trailer hitch in the same light again.

Jay's wife Louise called them to order with the clanging of the dinner bell, which hung from an old live oak to the side of the eating area. Everyone filed around the table. Waiters made themselves busy serving salad, potato salad, and corn on the cob. Heaped platters of barbequed ribs were placed strategically along the table, along with crispy fried chicken and a small mountain of steaks. Then came the *pièce de résistance*. Several suckling pigs were removed from the charcoal pits and placed on huge trays at either end of the long series of tables.

Jay spoke to Millie, and she quickly returned followed by six waiters carrying two magnums each of Dom Perignon champagne. When all were served, Jay stood up and cleared his throat for attention. "Mah friends, we're all gathered here tonight to celebrate me an' Billy going to Russia on the biggest trade deal we've ever done. And we'll drink to that."

Several people cheered.

"But first, ah have some other great news. Mah good buddy, Admiral Jack Boxer, has just announced his engagement to this fine lady to my right, Miss Francine Wheeler."

Now everyone began to cheer and applaud.

Jay broke in, "So now, I offer up this toast to Jack and Francine, may they forever find happiness together."

Boxer was embarrassed. He raised his glass in acknowledgment. Francine's face turned red.

Billy yelled, "To Jack and Francine," and everyone drank to them.

Suddenly the sound of a large engine was heard, followed by the emergence of two Sikorsky helicopters. Jay looked up at the two whirlybirds. "Our special guest tonight, folks. The President of the United States, Richard Spooner."

A hush came over the gathering as the two choppers set down. Boxer just sat there in awe.

Six stern-faced men in business suits jumped out of the lead aircraft. Two of them were carrying custom-molded aluminum briefcases. Their eyes searched the assembled crowd for anything that looked at all suspicious. Then, their apparent leader whispered something into a lapel mike, and two more similarly clad men emerged from the second helicopter. One of them turned around and offered up a hand to help down the next passenger, the President of the United States.

Bending forward at the waist to keep clear of the chopper's blades, the group headed toward the seated guests. Spooner held both hands overhead in victory signs and everyone at the tables rose to give him a standing ovation. As the secret servicemen fanned out and took positions in and around the yard and ranch house, Richard Spooner shouted over the ebbing din of the helicopters, "Thanks for the warm welcome, everybody. That's why I like coming to Jay's barbeques. I wouldn't miss one for the world."

Jay Archer escorted the President to the place of honor at the head of the table. Boxer and Francine were seated to his right, followed by Admiral Stark and Chuck, who had trouble keeping his emotions under control. He was ready to burst with the excitement of being seated at the same dinner table as the President. Across from Boxer, to the President's left, sat Jay and his wife Louise, a stunning brunette in her late thirties. Billy White was seated next to Louise. He was accompanied by his wife, Holly, also an alluring brunette.

Jay made the introductions. "Mr. President, I believe you know Rear Admiral Jack Boxer."

"Of course. I gave Boxer the Medal of Honor a while back. How are you, Jack?"

"Fine, Mr. President. And may I present my fiancée, Miss Francine Wheeler."

Spooner gave her an appraising glance. "How do you do, Miss Wheeler?"

"Very well, sir. It's a pleasure to meet you."

The President said, "Admiral Stark I already know. How's your health these days, Dick?"

"Almost fit again, Mr. President. If you should need a new CNO one of these days, I might just reapply for my old job."

"We should seriously talk about that. One of the Joint Chiefs is ailing. We might need someone with your experience and outstanding record."

Stark saluted. "Thank you, Mr. President. Oh, I'd like you to meet young Chuck Rugger Boxer. Chuck's dad was killed trying to stop that renegade missile sub several years ago. Jack adopted him."

Chuck stood at his place. "I'm happy to meet you, sir. It's a great honor."

Spooner replied, "It's an honor for me, too, Chuck. You're a lucky lad to have both a natural father and an adopted one who were national heroes."

"Thank you, sir."

The President looked over the group sitting there, hands on their laps. He said, "Food's getting cold, folks. Let's eat. Plenty of time to jabber later."

A secret serviceman stood guard behind Spooner while he filled his plate with ribs and was served a man-sized chunk of the suckling pig by Louise Archer. The President dug in. "Jay, you sure do know how to run a cookout. This food is absolutely delicious."

Jay smiled and put an arm around his wife. "The credit goes to Louise, Mr. President. The sauce is her secret family recipe going all the way back to Sam Houston's time. Between you an' me, that's why I married her."

The President laughed. "Then you missed the best reasons, Jay. Mrs. Archer, not only are you a marvelous cook, but one of the finest looking women I've ever met."

Louise blushed, and continued eating small mouthfuls of food.

After dinner, finger bowls were set out and the guests cleaned up from the messy but delicious food. After coffee, Spooner leaned toward Boxer and said, "Say, Jack, I hear you're having some trouble with your bosses. Why don't you and I go for a little after-dinner walk? Jay, you and Billy care to join us?"

Boxer blotted his lips with a cloth napkin and stood up. The four of them, followed and preceded by two bodyguards, strode off along the path around the small pond. "That's right, Mr. President. I'm up on charges of treason for trying to save the lives of a Russian submarine crew along with my own men. The captain of the rescue vessel took exception, so I commandeered his ship."

Spooner chuckled. "That's the same Jack Boxer that I've grown to know. I'll bet it involved Admiral Igor Borodine."

"Yes, sir. It did. You know, it's strange, but if I ever come up against Borodine in battle, I'd blast him from the sea in a minute. But he's helped me out of desperate situations in the past, and vice versa."

"So I hear. I understand that someone's out to get your ass, son. My sources tell me that there aren't any grounds for your court-martial. But several of the admirals are convinced that they can convict you. I'm not about to let that happen."

Boxer said, "Thanks, Mr. President, but all I want is a fair trial, without prejudice."

Billy piped in, "Mr. President, Jay and I have already offered our financial and political support. And Jack's got ol' Slick Wilkins on his side."

"Jack, boys, that bastard Le Roux is out to get Jack. That much I know. I also know that Le Roux is after my job, and is trying to embarrass me through Jack because I gave him the Medal of Honor. The son of a bitch is my enemy as much as Boxer's, and I'm not about to let him have his way."

Boxer stopped, causing the group to come to a halt. "Mr. President, I appreciate your kind intentions. I'd rather win this case on its merits, rather than being exonerated by Presidential pardon."

"Got your point, Jack. But you can be sure that Le Roux won't get a chance to set up any of his cronies on the bench when you come to trial."

They finished their walk around the pond and stepped back into the clearing where the party was going on. Spooner asked, "Say, Jay, who's that cute number in the suede cowgirl suit? The blonde there with the big…"

Jay smiled. "Big eyes, Mr. President? Don't you recognize her?"

Billy interjected, "That's Lucy Mae, Mr. President. You remember her from your last trip, don't you?"

Spooner gave it some thought. His face lit up. "Lucy Mae? Oh, yes. I sure do."

Boxer watched the dreamy expression on the President's face. Surely he was deep in thought, conjuring up thoughts of trailer hitches. Boxer chuckled to himself.

Spooner shook Boxer's hand. "Well, good luck with your trial, Jack. I don't want to take you away from your lady all day."

"Thank you, sir." Boxer walked back to the party himself. He turned to see the President and his little entourage head for the veranda, where Lucy Mae was standing by to greet them with a big smile.

CHAPTER 12

Lori-Ann Collins stood in the shade of a tree watching the tourists snap pictures of the Smithsonian Institute Buildings across the street. It was a pleasant day, with a gentle noontime breeze, warmed to about fifty-five degrees by the bright sun. Soon the streets filled with hundreds of young men and women headed for lunch.

She waited ten minutes for Ronald Baxter to appear. His tall, lean frame and sharp, handsome features coupled with his impeccable attire made him stand out in the crowd. This was the man she had lived with off and on for the last three years. Her lover. That was a laugh. They had made love about once a month. He was always too busy, or too tired. Same old story. She should have known. She watched him scanning the crowd looking for her, and stepped out from under the shade into the sunshine.

"Ronald, over here," she waved to him.

Baxter spotted her and quickened his pace. He wore a lightweight double-breasted navy-blue suit with a striped Repp tie and burgundy broughams. Mr. Assistant Undersecretary of State for Eastern Europe. How convenient for her.

He came up to her, slicked back his straight blond hair with his palm, and said, "Hello, darling. Is everything all right?"

She smiled back. "Not as right as it could be, Ronald. But we can remedy that. Thanks for meeting me."

"Would you like to go for lunch? I should be able to get away for an hour or so. I know a great French restaurant not far from here. We can walk if you'd like, or take a cab."

"This is more important than lunch, Ronald. It's about us."

"Us? And it can't be discussed over lunch? How uncivilized." He flashed his big white teeth.

Lori-Ann stood with her hands on her hips, feet slightly apart. "Ronald, let's stop bullshitting each other, shall we?"

"Whatever do you…?"

"I want you to stop cheating on me."

The smile left Baxter's face, replaced by a little boy who-me? expression. "Honestly, darling. You're the only woman in my life. I swear it."

"I believe that, Ronald. You know what I mean."

"Really, I…"

Lori-Ann reached into her handbag and extracted a brown envelope. She thrust it at him. "A friend gave these to me the other day. I can't tell you how embarrassed I was."

Baxter stood there, looking puzzled at the envelope in her hand.

"Go ahead, take it. Now, look inside."

Lori-Ann watched the color drain from Baxter's face as he recognized the photos of himself sexually entangled with several other equally good-looking men. He stood there staring at her with his jaw agape. "Where … where did you get these?"

"What does it matter? Someone at your little party showed them off to a friend, who passed them along to someone else, until they trickled down to the person who gave them to me."

Baxter replaced the photos in the envelope and stuffed them in his jacket pocket. "I'll destroy them. They got me stoned at that party, and set up these pictures while I was unconscious."

"Nice try, Ronald, *darling*. I happened to hear from the friend of a friend that you were thoroughly enjoying yourself. In fact, that you were the life of the party."

"I deny it."

"What I can't understand, Ronald, is how you can then come home to me like everything's just hunky-dory."

Baxter ran his hand over his forehead. Tears welled up in his eyes. "Can we … can we go for a walk. People are beginning to stare."

Lori-Ann slipped her arm through his and led him away from the groups of tourists. "Care to tell me the truth, darling?"

Ronald Baxter stopped. He looked down at his spit-shined shoes, not daring to look at her face. He sighed deeply, and placed his hand over his heart. "I'm terribly sorry, Lori-Ann. It's true. I'm gay, and have been since I was fifteen years old. My folks suspected as much, so they sent me to an all-male prep school to make a man out of me. That was a laugh."

Lori-Ann found a handkerchief in her bag and wiped a tear away from his eyes.

Baxter continued. "Well, I got my degree from Yale, my Ph.D. in Poly-Sci at Tufts, and scored a good job at State. At one point, there were some nasty stories being told about me behind my back. You know the kind. It was then that I met you and we became friends. Do you remember the Christmas party we went to that first year? Well, I made it a point of showing you off to all those rotten bastards. The stories stopped right after that."

Lori-Ann shook her head. "So you used me, is that right?"

Baxter backed up a step. "It wasn't like that. Not exactly, that is. I actually found myself liking you."

"Do you like me enough to marry me?"

"What? Are you crazy?"

Lori-Ann gently placed her hand on his chest. "No, I'm not crazy, Ronald. Deeply hurt, yes. Pissed, maybe. But not crazy.

How would it look if my friends found out I was being made a fool of by a gay boyfriend?"

"But I…"

"How do you think the CIA will take it when they find out the secretary of the Director is living with a gay man? They'd throw me out on my ass in a minute."

"But… I'm not so sure that it would work out for us."

"Look, Ronald. It'll be a marriage of convenience for both of us. I'll be able to keep my job, and you'll be able to keep your job at the State Department. But, I'm warning you. You'd better not embarrass me again."

"I won't. I'll be careful. What am I talking about? How did they get those pictures of me in the first place?"

"You have to be more than careful, Ronald. We'll take care of each other's needs for a while. No more boys, Ronald, till this blows over. Neither one of us can afford any trouble. Agreed?"

"Okay, I'll try. No, dammit, I'll do it. There's too much at stake. My career is on the line."

And mine, Ron, she thought. *If you only knew.*

Ronald Baxter put one hand in his pants pocket and stood there a bit more relaxed. "When do you want to get married?"

"This afternoon. We'll find a J.P. and have a civil ceremony today. If you want, we can get married in a church on Sunday."

"This Sunday? Mother will just die."

Lori-Ann smiled at him. "Tell Mother that we eloped, and if she wants to see her baby boy married in a church, it's this Sunday. She can throw a party if she wants. I have no one. My parents are both dead." She was telling the truth.

"Married. I can't believe it. That'll give some nasty-minded people something to think about. Well, let's go find a justice of the peace."

"Oh, and one more thing, Ronald."

Oh, shit, he thought. *What now?* He looked at her quixotically.

"I'm famished," she exclaimed, flashing a row of even white teeth. "Let's go have lunch."

Ronald Baxter breathed a sigh of relief, and they walked hand in hand out of the park.

Boxer's court-martial was set up in the basement grand jury room in the federal courthouse in Washington, D.C. The press and television people were confined to the lobby on the main floor, and spilled out onto the stately marble steps. Inside, the dominant feature of the courtroom was the bench, a highly polished walnut affair, with four highback tufted leather upholstered chairs for the four admirals who presided. For the occasion, the U.S. Navy banner occupied a corner of the room behind the bench, across from the flag of the United States. A 1928 vintage Gordon Grant print of *Old Ironsides* formed a backdrop for the judges.

A court reporter was seated on a chair in front of and to the left of the bench, behind a computerized recorder. The raised witness booth was opposite him, in the same polished walnut as the bench. In front of the bench, Boxer was seated at a table flanked by his official counsel, Rear Admiral Nealy, and Granville "Slick" Wilkins, Georgetown U's finest. Boxer and Nealy were attired in formal Navy dress whites. Wilkins wore a crumpled blue-and-white seersucker suit, with a white shirt and yellow bow tie. Witnesses and spectators, along with a sketch artist, were seated to the rear of a rail that divided the courtroom behind the defense table.

Admiral Pliney, the senior rank on the bench, presided, and called the proceedings to order. Rear Admiral William Bryant opened for the prosecution. "Call Captain Andrew Axelrod."

Axelrod took the stand and was sworn in. Bryant asked him to explain the situation that had taken place in Antarctica.

Axelrod rehashed the story he had told at the inquiry. "I had been steaming home from a supply run to Palmer Station on the Peninsula. The Antarctic Peninsula, that is. Boxer... Admiral Boxer radioed that his submarine, the *Tiny Tim*, was taking on water. Despite having to pass through the eye of a severe storm, I commanded the *Polar King* to answer Boxer's Mayday."

Bryant walked to and leaned against the witness stand. "And what did you find at the sight where the Mayday was issued?"

Axelrod smiled smugly. "The *Tiny Tim* had been abandoned and its crew set off to the continent in a rubber inflatable craft. I understand quite a few of the men perished as a result of that foolhardy move. Had they remained with their ship, I would have rescued them twelve hours sooner, and the ensuing unfortunate incident could have even avoided."

Admiral Nealy stood up. "I object to Captain Axelrod's remarks. They are purely conjecture. He hasn't had the requisite training to determine when a submarine must be abandoned."

Pliney whispered to Admiral Tracey, seated to his right. Then he said, "Captain Axelrod, spare us the embellishments and limit your replies to what you know to be the facts."

Axelrod's face flushed. Something was going wrong. The CNO promised him that the court-martial would go as smoothly for him as the preliminary inquiry had. Mason had told him that the presiding admirals were very understanding of his position.

Bryant turned to the bench, still speaking to Axelrod off to his side. "Captain, please tell the court what happened when you finally caught up with Boxer and his men on the ice shelf."

"Well, putting my ship in even greater jeopardy, I commenced to the Ross Ice Shelf following a signal that Boxer sent from the ice. When I discovered that Admiral Boxer had intended to bring on board a group of thirty or forty of the enemy, I refused to have the damned Russians on my ship."

Bryant turned back to Axelrod. "And Admiral Boxer's reply?"

Axelrod sneered. "He pretended to need medical attention for himself. And when I boarded him out of consideration for his health, he returned my kindness by putting a pistol to my temple and threatening to blow my fucking brains out if I didn't take on the Russians. Excuse the foul language, but that was a direct quote from Boxer."

The four admirals on the bench copied notes on the yellow legal pads before them. Pliney nodded to Bryant.

Admiral Bryant asked, "And then…?"

Axelrod's tone became hostile. "And then Admiral Boxer had me locked up in my own brig, commandeered my ship, and forced my Exec, Lieutenant Meade to take on his entire party, including the Russians. To me, it was an act of treason, to take over an American naval vessel and use it to serve the enemy."

Admiral Pliney leaned forward toward Axelrod. "It is our duty to determine if an act of treason was committed, *Captain.* Not yours."

Axelrod swallowed hard at the rebuff. Pliney said, "Admiral Nealy, you may cross-examine."

Nealy rose and addressed the bench. "Admiral, Mr. Wilkins is assisting the defense and would like to question Captain Axelrod."

The four admirals on the bench huddled for a moment. Pliney pushed his eyeglasses up the bridge of his nose and replied, "Though irregular, it is not without precedent, Admiral Nealy. Mr. Wilkins may cross-examine. We understand his credentials are impeccable."

Wilkins got up from behind the defense table, and strode slowly to the witness stand. He straightened his bow tie, and stared at Axelrod for a long moment. Axelrod squirmed in his seat. "Excuse my ignorance, Captain Axelrod, I spend so much of my time in my ivory tower, insulated from the goings on in the world, that I must have missed something very important. When did we go to war with the Soviet Union?"

Axelrod flustered. "What?"

"You referred to the Russians as our enemy. Your word, Captain. If we're not at war with the Soviets… I'm not saying that I agree with everything they do. Far from it, as a matter of fact. But, as the world today is at peace, relatively speaking, I don't think it is accurate to characterize the Russians as our enemy. Really now."

Axelrod shot back, "You know what I mean. We're in a cold war with the Russians. I consider them my enemy."

Wilkins shrugged his shoulders, "Then I may conclude that they are your personal enemy, Captain. Very well."

That brought titters from the spectators.

Wilkins hitched up his pants, and restraightened his already perfectly aligned bow tie. "Are you aware, Captain Axelrod, that the ice stations are considered sea duty? The military personnel draw sea duty pay, and PX privileges. Correct me if I'm wrong, Captain, but the Ross Ice Shelf covers the McMurdo Sound."

Axelrod didn't reply.

"It's frozen water, Captain. Sea duty. And the International Maritime Code … let's see if I can remember my military law… Article XIV, Section three point … eight, I believe, states that a Mayday at sea must be answered by any vessel in a position to do so. And that all survivors must be taken aboard." Wilkins turned to the bench. "I believe that I have quoted correctly, Admirals."

The four of them whispered among themselves for a moment, Admiral Pliney smiled, and said, "You've done your homework, Mr. Wilkins. You are correct. And, I may add, my colleague, Admiral Oglevie here suggests that you are aptly nicknamed, sir."

Wilkins nodded his appreciation. "I have nothing further for the witness." He turned to Axelrod. "Thank you, Captain Axelrod, for your cooperation. And for the lesson in overstepping one's authority."

Axelrod flustered. He looked to the bench, but help was not forthcoming. He looked over toward his counsel, Bryant jumped to his feet. "I object to Mr. Wilkins ridiculing the witness."

"Sustained. Mr. Wilkins?"

"Sorry, Admiral, I apologize."

Wilkins sat down next to Boxer and gave him an avuncular pat on the back. Boxer smiled broadly.

Admiral Pliney said, "The witness will please stand down."

As Axelrod took a seat in the first row behind the rail, his counsel rose and said, "Call Admiral Jack Boxer."

Boxer started to rise, but Pliney motioned him back to his seat. Pliney then held a huddled discussion with the three other admirals. "That won't be necessary, Admiral Bryant."

A hush went through the courtroom, followed by an outburst of discussion among the spectators. Pliney rapped his gavel twice. He cleared his throat, took a sip from a glass of water, and stated, "What we have here is a difference of opinion as to correct procedures in this incident. Clearly,

Captain Axelrod thought that he was in the right by denying life-saving aid to military personnel of a country with whom we have less than friendly relations." He looked at Axelrod, then trained his attention on Boxer.

"However, there is a higher authority that must be invoked when disasters at sea occur, *even* if we are at war with the parties, Captain Axelrod, which, of course we are not. The world community recognizes this, and makes provisions for the rescue and humane treatment of survivors of naval disasters. This was pointed out very correctly by Mr. Wilkins." He took another sip of water.

"Therefore, we have concluded that there are absolutely no grounds for convicting Admiral Boxer of treason. It is unfortunate that you had cause to disagree with him, and try to usurp his flag rank, *Captain*. And that your actions caused you to be locked in your own brig so that the rescue could be fulfilled." Pliney rapped twice with his gavel. "This court-martial is adjourned. Case dismissed."

As the four admirals rose and left the courtroom via an exit behind the bench, Boxer rose and hugged Granville Wilkins. Wilkins clapped Admiral Nealy on the shoulder. "Thanks for allowing me to help out, Admiral Nealy. I really appreciate your cooperation."

Nealy smiled and said, "Let's just say that your reputation preceded you, sir. It was a pleasure being on your team."

A huge cheer rang out from the rear of the courtroom. Several of Boxer's crewmen pushed forward to congratulate their skipper. "Thanks for your support, men. I thought that bastard had me for a moment there."

Mahony said, "You sure showed up Axelrod for the wimp he really is."

Admiral Nealy said, "You know, Admiral Boxer, you have grounds to press charges of insubordination against Axelrod if you like."

Boxer shook his head. "Just let it rest, if you don't mind. I've got better things to do with my life than seek revenge against a naval officer who made a mistake in judgment. Especially in light of the way things worked out. Let's just leave it alone."

"Fine with me. Just wanted you to be aware of your options." Nealy shook hands with Boxer and with Slick Wilkins. "Well, it's been a pleasure, gentlemen. Good afternoon."

As Nealy left, and Wilkins made his goodbyes, Boxer's men swarmed around him. "Let's go out and celebrate, Skipper."

Boxer put an arm around two of his men. "Love to, guys. Has anyone seen Francine? Or Admiral Stark? I had expected them to be here."

"Negative, Skipper. I was sitting in the last row. I would have spotted them for sure."

"Well, let's have a drink, men. On me. But then I'll leave you. It would be just like Francine to be waiting back home with a surprise for me."

CHAPTER 13

Francine had the dining-room table set for four with her best china, silver, and crystal. There was a floral centerpiece flanked by silver candelabras. The kitchen and dining areas were filled with the good smells of the rack of lamb and roasting potatoes in the oven. There was a medley of vegetables marinating in a pot on the stovetop, needing only a few minutes of cooking time, and mint jelly and a crisp salad waiting in the fridge. A wine cooler stood by to hold the champagne. She was ready to celebrate Boxer's imminent victory.

She smiled at Chuck and Admiral Stark, who were watching her work with the same deftness and efficiency she utilized in her law practice. "Well, men, did I forget anything?"

Stark shook his head. "No. Everything looks ready. You did a fine job. Are you sure you want us to hang the sign before we're sure of the outcome?"

"Hang the sign. Professor Wilkins assured me he had an ace up his sleeve that would clinch a victory for Jack. Put it right over the doorway to the dining room. He'll see it as soon as I walk him in from the living room. It ought to make his day."

Stark shrugged. "Okay. Chuck, give me a hand, will you?"

"Sure." Chuck took the two-by-five-foot banner he had labored over this afternoon to the doorway.

Stark moved a chair close to the doorway and indicated to it with a nod of his head. "Up you go, Chuck. You're much younger than me."

Chuck smiled, climbed up, and taped his sign over the doorway. He jumped down and stood back to admire his handiwork. "Looks pretty neat."

"Very impressive," Stark said.

"I agree." Francine had her thumb up at arm's length, as if she were studying a masterpiece of fine art. "Nice work, Chuck."

It was a drawing of a man in Navy dress whites with a gold star insignia of a rear admiral first level. He had his foot on the neck of a good-sized turkey. It read, CONGRATULATIONS JACK, OUR HERO. DON'T LET THE TURKEYS GET YOU DOWN.

She continued. "Let's see. The roast's in the oven, veggies and potatoes ready, salad in the refrigerator, champagne…"

"Two bottles," Stark added.

"Two bottles of champagne, and something to drink for Chuck." She opened the refrigerator and stuck her head in. "Damn. No soda or milk. How could I be so dumb?"

Chuck said, "That's not dumb. I'm the only one of us who drinks that stuff anyway. I can go out and get some."

"Oh, thanks a million. There's a little grocery store on the corner. Make a right as you leave the building." Francine reached into her handbag and produced a ten-dollar bill. "I really appreciate it, Chuck."

"No sweat. I'll be right back," and Chuck headed for the door.

"Nice kid," Stark said with a smile after Chuck had gone.

"Sure is. You can see some of Jack's influence on him. He was involved in an incident in his neighborhood when Jack and I went to visit there last month. You would have thought that he was a younger version of Jack. I was so proud of him."

Chuck bounded down the short flight of stone steps to the sidewalk, and looked around to get his bearings. It was a nice, residential, tree-lined block with kids and young families and senior citizens all going about their business without the constant fear of intimidation that prevailed where he lived on Staten Island. Two young boys were throwing a big rubber ball to each other, and it got away from the kid closest to him. Chuck kicked the ball back to them. He looked up and noticed two workmen in blue coveralls climb out of a nondescript delivery van looking for the correct address to deliver the roll of carpeting they were carrying.

He turned to the right and went off down the block with Francine's ten-dollar bill crammed into his jeans pocket.

As soon as Chuck was out of sight, the two workmen approached Francine Wheeler's brownstone and checked the bronze numbers above the door against a piece of paper that one of them removed from an inside pocket. The handsome, dark-haired man, whose muscular build suggested that he was used to heavy delivery work spoke to his companion in Italian. "This is it."

"*Bene.*" The second man, slightly shorter than his six-foot-tall companion, but a few years older and with a thick, husky body that was going paunchy with age, nodded his agreement. "Yes. This is the one."

Chuck had gone off without a house key, and so the two men found the door slightly ajar. They entered, and carried their burden up the first flight of stairs without being detected. As they turned the tight corner, the older man, bringing up the rear, bumped against the wall.

Upstairs, Francine looked at Stark, a little surprised. "Chuck's back very quickly."

Admiral Stark stood erect and craned his head toward the living-room door. "Too quick, if you ask me."

Francine smiled. "Maybe it's Jack. He should be due anytime now. I'll set the champagne in to cool."

"Well, I'll go take a look for myself," Stark replied. He opened the door and walked out onto the landing. He heard the men's footsteps at once. Taken aback, he turned to see two men struggling with what seemed to him like a rolled-up carpet or rug. He said, "Can I help you?"

The younger man barely looked up. "*Scusi.* Carpet man," he said in clipped English.

"Carpet? Are you sure you have the right address?"

The carpet man produced the piece of paper from his pocket, studied it while shouldering his heavy load, and nodded his head vigorously. "*Si*, numero one-five-one." He held up the paper for Stark to see, though he was a good ten feet farther up the stairs. "Meester Wheeler, *si*?"

Stark started down the stairs to have a look at the man's paper. He turned his head toward the opened door. "Francine, did you order some carpet to be delivered? There's some men here with a carpet or rug for you. I can't tell which."

He heard some footsteps, and then Francine's voice. "Carpet? No. I didn't order any carpet. Are you sure?"

Stark began to feel uneasy. He turned to the younger man and said in his most commanding voice, "Stay right there. Let me see your papers."

The man began to shake his head, and he dug back into an inside pocket for the paper again. Instead, he removed a heavy, dull-grey Walther 9mm automatic, complete with attached silencer. He pointed it at Admiral Stark's face.

Stark reacted automatically. He turned his head toward the landing and shouted, "Francine, lock the door. Don't let them…"

The man released his grip on the carpet and lunged forward to Stark, bringing the gun down hard as Stark turned to shout his warning. The heavy silencer bounced off the side of his head. Blood splattered against the wall and over the gun.

Stark winced, went down on one knee. He kicked out at the gunman, sending him careening into his partner. The roll of carpet slid down the stairs to the first landing.

Stark tried to get up. The men fought their way back up the stairs. They caught up with him trying to crawl back up to the landing. Francine looked out at the scene in shock. "What the… Who are these…"

"Get back," Stark shouted. "Save yourself."

Francine moved back inside in a daze. She pushed the door closed.

The young gunman ran over Stark, punched his face, and threw himself at the door. The door groaned.

Francine pressed the weight of her body against the door on her side, and tried to twist the lock home.

The man slammed against the door again. On the third attempt, the door crashed open. He pushed Francine back into the living room, and lashed out at her with a vicious backhand across her face. Her hands went up to protect her bloody nose.

The older gunman reached Stark, grabbed him by the throat, and slammed his head against the stairs while choking him. Stark gasped a muffled groan and fell unconscious. His attacker grabbed him by the shirt with both hands and pulled the lifeless form up the remaining few steps and into the room with the others.

The younger man clamped his hand roughly around Francine's mouth to keep her from shouting out. He dug the end of the silencer into her temple. He read the fear in her eyes, and laughed. He squeezed his hand harder against her mouth, and called out something to his accomplice.

The man rolled Admiral Stark over on his back, then looked over at them. He leered at Francine, and sniggered something back. Francine could only make out the word Mario. *So this bastard's name is Mario.* She filed that bit of information away. For when she got free of these creeps.

The heavier man came over to them on the floor and touched her ankle. She instinctively pulled it away. The man chuckled, and grabbed her foot and held it tighter.

The one called Mario said something that made his partner laugh again. She picked out the name Gordon ... or Gordo. She was not sure. What she did know was that they were deliberately hurting her. If only Jack would get here now.

Mario shifted his position, kneeling on her abdomen, bearing down with all his weight, all the while clamping his hand over her mouth and pressing the gun against her head. He said, "Gordo," again, and something she didn't comprehend. *So,* she thought, *his name is Gordo, not Gordon.* She'd remember.

Gordo tossed a handkerchief to Mario. He removed his hand from her mouth and grabbed the square of sweat-stained cloth. Francine opened her mouth to shout at him, and he stuffed the handkerchief inside, almost losing a finger as she bit down at him. He slapped her hard across the face for her troubles. Then, with the weight of his body fully on her, he pressed one hand back over her muffled mouth, and the other hand firmly gripped her by the throat.

What transpired next happened so quickly it caught her completely by surprise. He twisted his body toward her feet, sliding his weight off her as he turned. He grabbed the hem of her wool skirt and pulled it inside out up over her head, effectively locking her arms together above her head. She managed a muffled scream. Someone rolled her over and smacked her hard on the behind. She began to sob. She lay there completely at their mercy. She felt someone bind her arms together tightly.

There was a pause. Then they rolled her over again. She felt a course fiber rug against her bare skin, unlike the plush velour of her own carpeting. In a moment, they had rolled her up in the carpeting they brought with them. She could hardly breathe. Her weak cries remained with her inside the fabric tomb.

A reporter for the *Washington Post* was covering the police blotter at the precinct house when the call came in. He mentioned to the sergeant on duty that he had seen Boxer with several of his men entering Duffy's Tavern downtown on Connecticut Avenue after the trial. A police black-and-white sped him to Francine's house with sirens screaming and red lights flashing. They arrived just in time to see what was left of Admiral Stark being lifted on a gurney into the back of an ambulance.

"Is he...?"

The paramedic slammed the door home, and jerked his head toward a stout man in a tan hat and raincoat who was talking to a small group of uniformed policemen. "You hafta ask the detective. I can't give no comment."

A voice called out, "Dad… Dad… Over here."

Boxer wheeled around to find Chuck surrounded by policemen near the front stairs to Francine's building. Boxer pushed his way through to the boy. "What the hell happened here, son?"

"Hey, you can't go bustin' in here like that," a plain-clothesman shouted at him. "This is a crime scene."

Boxer glared down at the man. "I'm Admiral Jack Boxer. This is my family involved here. You're talking to my son, Chuck. Now what the hell happened? I want some answers now."

The stout man in the tan raincoat bullied his way through the crowd, and stood there facing Boxer. He handed Boxer his card. "Name's Murphy. Francis X., detective sergeant on the case."

Boxer glanced from the card to the man. "I'm Jack Boxer."

"I know who you are, Admiral. We're trying to put the pieces together now. The old man's been beaten up quite a bit."

Boxer turned to watch the ambulance speed off to the hospital. "Will he make it?"

Murphy shook his head. "It's touch and go right now. He's lost some blood, nose looks broken, and his head's all banged up. Fuckin' bastards beat up an old man like that. Oh, sorry, Admiral. Been on the job almost twenty-three years and I still have trouble understanding man's inhumanity to his fellows."

"Don't apologize on my account. Those are my sentiments exactly. How's the woman, Francine Wheeler?"

Murphy didn't answer.

"Chuck?"

Chuck stared at him, fighting back both the tears and his rage. "She's gone."

"Gone?"

"They took her, Dad."

"Who? Let's start from the beginning. What happened?"

Murphy nodded toward the plainclothes policemen milling around them. He said to Boxer, "The boys have been taking a statement from Chuck."

Boxer said, "Okay, let's have it from the top, son."

Chuck thought for a moment, then he said, "It's all my fault. If I didn't go down to the store to get milk and soda for myself, I would have been here to protect them."

Murphy shook his head. "I'm afraid not, son. The people who did this were professionals. Admiral Stark was pistol-whipped near death. They could just have easily shot him. Or you, if you tried to get in their way."

"They took Francine. I saw them, but I didn't realize it till it was too late."

"What?" Murphy asked. "You didn't say anything before about seeing who did this."

Boxer put a hand on Chuck's shoulder. "Who did you see?"

"Well, it was the guys with the carpeting. You see, when I came downstairs to go to the store, there were these two guys carrying a roll of carpet, like they were going to deliver it."

Murphy interjected, "Did you see them get out of a truck?"

"A van," Chuck answered. "A dark-colored van, all beat up: I think it was black or dark blue. Anyway, I didn't notice anything special about it, no name or pictures on it. I really didn't pay it much attention then. Nothing had happened yet."

Murphy was writing in a little notebook. "Then how do you know it was the guys that did this?"

Chuck composed himself. "Well, when I came back to the house, I noticed the same two guys going in the other direction and carrying a bigger roll of carpet. At first, I figured, well, maybe they installed the new carpet and are getting rid of the old one.

"Then, when I went upstairs and saw all the blood all over, and I saw Admiral Stark laying there bleeding from the head, I figured who could have done this? I was only gone for about ten or twelve minutes. I looked all over for Francine, but she wasn't there. Then it hit me."

Murphy turned to Boxer. "If he makes it, your son may have saved the old man's life by his fast action. He called us right away. Got out an ambulance and squad car, and had us looking all over for you."

Boxer put his arm around Chuck. "Good work, son. If I had only been here sooner, this wouldn't have happened."

"Don't go kicking yourself in the ass, yet," Murphy said. "This whole thing seems to have been planned with the knowledge of you being tied up in court all afternoon. Like I said, this was the work of pros."

"But why?"

"To get at me, Chuck. Someone wanted to hurt me, so they tried to destroy the people I hold most dear to me. Thank God you weren't there. They would have killed you for sure if you got in their way."

Detective Murphy cleared his throat. "I'd like to get a make on the two guys that Chuck saw." He turned to Chuck. "You're pretty sure of them, son. Why?"

Chuck said, "Look around you up and down the block. This is a quiet neighborhood, not like back home in New York. The only thing out of place was those two guys."

Murphy nodded. "Okay, I'll accept that. What did they look like?"

"Well, one guy was younger and taller than the fat guy. Not really fat, you know, just sorta heavy."

"Compared to me?" Murphy asked, patting his belly.

Chuck smiled. "About like you, Sergeant Murphy. Only he looked huskier and stronger."

Murphy's face reddened. "Yeah, well I'm a little out of shape, I know. What about the younger guy? How tall? Like your dad? This policeman here?"

Chuck judged the two men. "More like my dad."

Boxer said to Murphy, "I'm six-one."

Chuck added, "He looked like he was about twenty-five or so. Wavy-looking black hair. Italian."

"Italian?" Murphy licked the point of his pencil and wrote in his little book. "How can you be so sure?"

Chuck laughed. "Hell, I go to New Dorp High School on Staten Island. Most of the guys there are Italian. I heard those two carpet guys joking and cursing at each other in Italian."

Murphy looked up at Boxer. "Ring any bells with you?"

Bruno Morell, Boxer fumed to himself. *I almost caught up with that bastard last year in Rome. This time he's coming after me.*

"Admiral?"

"Oh, sorry," Boxer snapped out of his thoughts. "I was trying to think of anyone who could have done this. I've made a few enemies over the years. I'll have to give it more thought."

Murphy had the feeling Boxer was holding back. "Yes. Please do that. Get back to me if anything rings a bell. Meanwhile, I'll be in touch."

"Oh, by the way, where did they take Admiral Stark?"

Murphy replied, "George Washington U. Medical Center. On Twenty-third, Northwest."

"I know where it is. Thanks."

"I'm going back upstairs. I want to make sure they cover the crime scene completely." He paused, and looked directly at Boxer. "I'm going to nail those bastards."

Boxer took Chuck by the arm and led him to where Francine's BMW was parked at the curb. "I want to go to the hospital to check on the Admiral. Then I'm going to drop you off with some of my men. I have one more stop to make."

"Sure. Who are you going to see, Dad?"

"Henry Tysin, son. He's the Director of the CIA. I need to find out some things from him." *And to find Julio Sanchez,* Boxer thought to himself. *If anyone can find Bruno Morell, Julio Sanchez can.* The two of them drove off in silence.

CHAPTER 14

Borodine was granted a two-week holiday to help him recuperate from the debilitating effects the Antarctic had on his health. He was given permission to travel to Krakow, in southern Poland with his wife, Tanya, and his newborn son, Viktor, to visit with Tanya's family. They flew into Warsaw from Moscow, and traveled by rail into Krakow.

They were greeted at the train station by Tanya's family. Borodine was embarrassed by all the fuss they made over him. They treated him like some sort of foreign dignitary. The women hugged and kissed Tanya, and treated her like the long-lost favored relative that she was. And the baby was handled like a precious religious object. Word of the impending baptism had preceded them.

The cortege piled aboard a tram for the short ride to the apartment of Tanya's uncle Tadeusz and aunt Katrina. Their home was in an old grimy tenement building on a street lined with old grimy tenement buildings. No one seemed to mind. And no one noticed the other visitor from Russia who had followed them discreetly from Moscow.

About fifteen or sixteen relatives crammed into the tiny apartment to celebrate the arrival of Tanya's family. Uncle Tadeusz produced a bottle of Polish vodka and showed it proudly to Borodine. Borodine smiled and nodded his approval, though he knew it to be far inferior to the good Russian vodka that he favored. In his mind, Russian vodka was the best in the world, but he would never let on and spoil the festive mood.

Tanya acted as interpreter as Tadeusz filled with vodka every drinking glass that Aunt Katrina could muster up. He raised his glass in salute. After speaking a few words, a cheer went up from the gathering. Tanya said to Borodine, "He says, 'Long life to our dear Tanya, and to her esteemed husband, Comrade Admiral Igor, and to our beloved new baby, Viktor.' They are waiting for you to drink."

Borodine saluted with his glass and downed the vodka in one pull. Everyone cheered and drank from their glasses. Tadeusz refilled any empty glasses. Borodine raised his drink and said, "To my new family in Poland. May your faith always provide for your needs and protect you from your enemies."

Tanya translated and they all drank to that. The old women put the baby to sleep, and the others drank and told stories until the early morning hours. They traded stories with Borodine and Tanya about food and fuel shortages, rising inflation, and the lack of affordable housing. Things were the same in both countries, although both had imagined life to be better in the other's country.

The following day being Saturday, Tadeusz and some of the others only had to work a half day at the steel mills that employed a good part of the city's population. Aunt Katrina took them on a short tour of the neighborhood, and they returned home to prepare for the baptism on Sunday. An old grandmother type presented Tanya with a richly embroidered white baptismal gown for the baby to wear. Tanya had rarely felt happier.

Early Sunday morning, the extended family set out in their best clothing to the Church of St. Stanislas. Though an atheist, Borodine stood reverently during the ceremony, enduring for his wife's sake that which he had been taught to renounce throughout his life. He proudly held his son while the priest stood alongside the basin of holy water and whispered in Tanya's ear. She beamed at her husband, and back at the priest. She said, "My son is to be named Viktor Igorovich Borodine."

Borodine's chest filled with fatherly pride as the priest repeated his son's name and sprinkled holy water on the infant's forehead. He had done it. Christened his son in a Catholic church, for the sake of his wife. It wouldn't sit too well with his superiors in the Kremlin, he was sure. But it was something he had to do. He could only hope that they never found out about this.

No one seemed to notice the stranger in the black overcoat make a quick retreat from the church as soon as the ceremony was performed.

Boxer had called ahead for a meeting with the Director, and Tysin had ordered the security guards at the visitor's entrance to escort Boxer directly to the inner sanctum. The young Marine corporal saluted sharply, and led Boxer, in full dress uniform, to the suite that housed the head of the CIA. The corporal slid his plastic ID card into a slot in the doorjamb and activated a speaker.

A woman with a sweet southern voice asked, "Yes, Corporal Atwater?"

"I have Admiral Jack Boxer with me, ma'am. He has an appointment with the Director."

A buzzer signaled, and the young Marine opened the door for Boxer. They were greeted by a tall, voluptuous raven-haired beauty. "How do you do, Admiral Boxer? I'm Lori-Ann Collins, Mr. Tysin's secretary. He's expecting you inside." She motioned to an inner solid walnut door. Then she turned her sweetest smile on the younger man and said, "Thank you, Harold."

Corporal Atwater blushed visibly, and tipped the spit-polished visor of his cap. He smiled back, somewhat embarrassed. "Ma'am." He snapped to attention, did a rigid about-face, and left the two of them standing there.

Boxer noticed she was wearing a V-necked translucent white blouse over a white, lacy half-bra that left very little to the imagination. *Tysin must be losing it in his old age*, Boxer mused, *to allow the distraction of this bit of fluff. Unless the old boy's slipping it to her himself*, he chuckled to himself. *The secret life of Henry Tysin.* He said, "Thank you." Boxer gestured to the door with outstretched hand. "After you, Miss Collins."

She smiled coyly, turned gracefully with a glance over her shoulder, and swished over to the Director's private office. Three knocks on the door were answered by another buzzer. She opened the door and allowed Boxer to enter.

Tyson rose from his seat, straightened his tie, and said, "Thank you, Miss Collins." And then to Boxer, "Have a seat, please." Tysin remained standing until Lori-Ann left them alone.

So he is having a fling with her, Boxer figured. *Son of a bitch. She's less than half his age. And with a figure like that, she could probably have any man she wanted. Something to keep in mind*, he thought. "Thanks for seeing me on such short notice, sir."

"I've gotten the reports on what happened to Admiral Stark, of course. And your lady friend. Very sorry to hear that. Now, what can I do for you?"

Boxer cleared his throat, and took in the room. It was paneled in dark wood, with wainscoting and elaborately carved molding along the ceiling and baseboard. There were several wooden file cabinets, a two-seater black leather sofa, and another upholstered chair similar to the one in which he now sat. There was a scarlet-edged file folder on the gleaming teak desk, which Tysin promptly removed and locked in a drawer. Boxer said, "I want to find the men who nearly killed Stark and kidnapped Francine."

Tysin picked up a wooden pencil from the desk, and toyed with it, twirling it through his fingers as he spoke. "That's a job for the D.C. police. It's hardly the kind of thing the CIA gets involved with. You know we've no jurisdiction within the country," Tysin said with his best poker face.

"I'm sure she's being taken overseas, if she hasn't been already."

"And what makes you so sure of that?"

"The bastards who did it were professionals."

Tysin shrugged. "So? There are professionals in the U.S. Why couldn't this be domestic?"

"Okay," Boxer said. "Why would anyone have reason to kidnap Francine? She's an attorney, but her work rarely involves her in controversial cases. And Admiral Stark is no longer a threat to anyone. The only reason for harming them is to get at me."

"And you've got enough enemies to make up for the rest of them. Both here and abroad."

"You're right about that. What I'd really like from you is to help me find Julio Sanchez."

The pencil snapped in Tysin's hand. "Sanchez?"

Boxer was puzzled by Tysin's reaction. What was so unusual about bringing up Sanchez's name? They both knew that Sanchez and the CIA often worked hand in hand. "Julio Sanchez, yes. I want him to help me find a mutual enemy. The man I'm sure was responsible for abducting Francine. I'm talking about Bruno Morell."

The color was restored to Tysin's face. He said, "Bruno Morell. I should have known. He'd like nothing better than to hand you back your balls on a platter. And the last we'd seen of him, he was holed up on Sardinia."

"And the two men who made the hit were Italian," Boxer added. "And Sanchez could tread where the Company ought not get involved."

"Agreed. I'll put out the word." Tysin was beginning to relax. He produced a wooden humidor from his desk and removed a long, dark cigar. "Cuban," he said with a chuckle. "I still have my sources there. Care for one?" He pushed the container toward Boxer.

"No thanks," Boxer tapped the humidor. "I'll stick with my pipe, if you don't mind."

"Not at all. Here I am forgetting my manners. Care for a drink? I could use one myself."

"A coffee would be just fine."

"Sure." Tysin pressed a button under his desk. In a moment, Lori-Ann Collins was inside his office.

"Yes, Mr. Tysin?" She was all peaches and cream, Boxer noticed. There was more to this relationship than meets the eyes, Boxer was sure of it.

"Miss Collins, would you please bring the Admiral a coffee? Black, I believe."

"That's right," Boxer said. "You have a good memory."

"It's my business. The usual for me, Miss Collins."

"Yes sir." She smiled broadly. "Yo'all won't have to wait but a minute." She turned and left the room.

When the door closed, Boxer figured he'd stick it to Tysin a little. "Quite a good-looking woman, your Miss Collins. Not the usual fifty-year-old spinster you'd expect at the front desk. In fact, Kinkade's secretary, Gert, must have been at least sixty."

Tysin blushed. "Gertrude Winthrop retired not long after Kinkade died. I guess she didn't want to stick around long enough to break in a new Director. To tell you the truth, I was looking a little ahead to the future when I hired Lori-Ann." The door opened, and Tysin said, "Ah, here's Miss Collins with our coffee."

Lori-Ann set a silver tray on the teak desk, and poured coffee into two fine porcelain cups. She added milk and sugar to one of them and offered it to Tysin, who nodded his thanks. She gave the other to Boxer, as is.

"Thanks very much," Boxer said.

When she had gone, Tysin continued. "When I first saw her, I thought, what a wonderful agent she would make. She's so stunningly beautiful, and with that sweet southern drawl of hers, she could make any man melt. And if we could train her, we could use her to turn certain individuals to our side."

Boxer nodded his agreement. "Yes, I'll bet she could, at that." He swallowed the last of his coffee. "Well, I've got to go now. Please have Sanchez get in touch with me as soon as possible. I'm taking a leave of absence from the service until I settle with Morell."

"What? You can't do that. Mason will shit a brick."

"Mason can go shit in his hat, for all I care. I have to settle this thing with Morell for good. I'll have no peace till I do."

CHAPTER 15

Igor Borodine walked the nine blocks from his apartment in Moscow to the office of Admiral Gorshkov, the Admiral of the Soviet Fleet. The collar of Borodine's coat was turned up against the early-morning chill, even though it was early June. He noticed that the skies were overcast, adding yet another layer of grey to the bleak sameness of the concrete apartment and government buildings in the neighborhood. This was in stark contrast to the blazing colors and bulbous spires of the prerevolutionary churches and palaces that punctuated the skyline in the part of the city that was made the focal point of the official tour groups made up of foreign visitors. Put on a happy face for the world. The citizens of Moscow dare not complain.

Borodine arrived at Gorshkov's office ten minutes early. He was made to wait for almost an hour before the Admiral's secretary, an overweight captain with a sour, jowly face that needed another shave at 0930 hours. Borodine hung his topcoat in the outer office and went inside. Gorshkov rose as he entered, and Borodine snapped a formal salute. Gorshkov extended his hand, which Borodine shook. The Admiral of the Fleet was a heavyset man with a ruddy complexion, a full head of grey hair, and steel-grey eyes.

"Good morning, Admiral Gorshkov."

Gorshkov sat down. "And good morning to you, Igor Alexandrovich. I do not believe you have met Comrade Valentine Makusky."

Borodine turned and noticed for the first time the rosy-cheeked, avuncular-looking man seated comfortably in a leather upholstered chair with his long thin fingers draped over the paunch of his stomach. He had grey hair and wore horn-rimmed glasses that almost sat on the tip of his nose. He looked very soft sitting there next the no-nonsense presence of Admiral Gorshkov. Borodine extended his hand. "Comrade Makusky."

Makusky made no move to rise or to shake Borodine's hand. Borodine let his arm fall to his side after an embarrassingly long period of time.

Gorshkov cleared his throat. "Comrade Makusky is the Deputy Director of the Second Directorate. Please have a seat, comrade." Gorshkov indicated a seat across the desk from both him and Makusky, and midway between them.

Borodine sat, and realized that he'd have to constantly realign his position as he addressed each of them, as if he were watching a tennis match while seated at the net. Bastards.

Gorshkov continued. "Aren't you a little surprised that such a high officer of the KGB is present at our little meeting this morning, Igor?"

Borodine looked directly at his superior. "Nothing that they do would surprise me, Comrade Admiral. They have bugged my apartments in Vladivostok and in Moscow. They have recorded the most intimate discussions between a man and his wife. They have followed me through the streets of the city, through Gorky Park as I strolled with my wife, and —" Borodine glared at the KGB man seated across from him — "they have followed me into Poland where I spent a two-week holiday recuperating from the ill effects of my last campaign down in Antarctica. I suppose he is here to reveal to you that I have committed some fictitious crime against the Motherland."

"My, my, quite a temper we have, now, don't we, comrade?" Makusky smiled with a false sweetness covering the evil that lied within. "I'd better see that we assign more discreet agents in the future to keep you out of mischief."

"Igor."

"Admiral?"

"What I am about to tell you doesn't come easy, even for me. You have been the foremost submarine commander in the Fleet for the past twenty years."

Borodine tried to suppress the shocked look that came over his face. "What are you trying to tell me, Comrade Admiral?"

"You are officially relieved of active duty aboard any submarine. You will be assigned to my office as Assistant Deputy for Submarine Operations. You will be allowed to keep your rank. But you will be assigned to a desk."

Borodine fought down his rage. "But why?"

Admiral Gorshkov shook his head. "Well, for one thing, your health. It would not do for you to take out one of our new prototype submarines and die of pneumonia while aboard. The doctors report that you are not in condition to return to active duty. I have their reports here in front of me." He tapped one of the red file folders on his otherwise uncluttered desk.

Makusky interjected. "Perhaps your kind personal feelings for Comrade Admiral Borodine cause you to delay the most significant reason for his reassignment, Comrade Admiral?"

Gorshkov's face became flush. He growled, "I need no coaxing from anyone to do my duty, comrade. There is no need to hit a man when he is down, especially one who has served the Motherland so faithfully as Comrade Admiral Borodine has for so many years."

Makusky's mask-face never wavered. He acted as if the Admiral's insult rolled right over him.

"Igor," Gorshkov continued, "Comrade Admiral Borodine, there is also the situation of your allowing the baptism of your infant son in Poland."

"Is this a crime against the State?" Borodine let the question out with a controlled softness, fighting down the bile rising within him. "It is a tradition with my wife's family. They are all Roman Catholics, as are most Poles. And they are our close allies, are they not? It is only a custom. It has nothing to do with my ability to command a submarine."

"But can we be absolutely sure of your loyalties now, comrade?" Makusky interrupted. "You were well aware that the Party frowns on such antiquated conventions. An officer can only serve one master, you know."

"The christening of my son has no bearing on my abilities or my loyalties to the Motherland. I object."

Makusky leaned forward, and stroked his beardless chin with his long fingers. "Object all you want. It has already been decided. We are not going to allow you to command any more of our submarines. That is final. And if you continue to argue with me, then perhaps your wife would be interested in some very fine videotapes of you with a certain American woman. A woman, I might add, who was at the same time having an affair with an American Naval officer, your friend Boxer." Makusky almost spit the words out.

Borodine almost rose out of his seat. "That's none of your fucking business. All that happened before I met Tanya. It's past history."

"We would let your wife decide that for herself."

Gorshkov slammed his palms down hard on his desk. "Enough of this. The decision is already made. Comrade Admiral Borodine is reassigned to my office for whatever reasons I deem appropriate. Comrade Deputy Makusky, I believe that our meeting is over. Thank you for joining me here at my office."

Makusky used his middle finger to push his glasses back up on his nose. He leaned forward and rose from his comfortable chair. "Well, then, I bid you good day, Comrade Admiral." He turned to Borodine, a smirk still plastered on his face. He nodded, "Comrade. Good luck in your new assignment. Good day." He stepped gracefully around Borodine and left the room.

When he was gone, Borodine said, "I wish to tender my resignation."

"Denied," Gorshkov barked back.

"But…"

"They wanted to throw you out of the service, and bring you up on treason."

"On what grounds?"

"Grounds? They can always come up with grounds if they so choose. I won't give them the satisfaction of your resignation."

Borodine relaxed in his chair. After a moment, he said, "Thank you for your support, comrade. I thought you had taken their side."

Gorshkov swept the room with his eyes, signaling to Borodine that even in his office, the walls had ears. "There is only one side, comrade. I am only doing what is best for you, and for the Motherland. You will be my assistant. Interesting enough, it comes at a time when we are testing a new prototype to replace the *Sea Dragon*. It will be bigger and faster, with a much larger reactor to fuel it. And more sophisticated electronics. It will be your duty to oversee its completion and testing."

Borodine smiled for the first time that day. "Well, at least my EXO Viktor Korzenko will have the experience of commanding a new prototype class."

"Viktor Korzenko is grounded also for now."

Borodine started to protest.

Gorshkov motioned him to remain silent. "It is already promised to Comrade Captain Anatoli Kilmov, of the North Fleet."

"Kilmov? But surely Viktor is more qualified. I have taught him everything there is to know about submarines, and believe me, he would make an excellent commander of the new sub."

"I believe you, comrade. But a political decision has been made. In light of Viktor's total loyalty to you, and the current problems that you have just been witness to, the Politburo has decided on someone outside your sphere of influence. Anatoli Kilmov will command the new Breshnev class sub."

Borodine sat back resignedly. "As you wish."

"Good. We would like sea trials to commence in one month. Our brothers in Iran would like our assistance in securing a secret mini-sub base in the vicinity of the Straits of Hormuz in the Gulf, They are prepared to launch an all-out attack on the Imperialist oil tanker convoys and the American fleet that guards them. If the Iranians succeed, we would be very pleased. They could accomplish what we could not do without provoking another world war."

Borodine nodded in agreement. "The Americans are already at odds with the Iranians. At very worst, they will try to annihilate the Iranians, leaving the doors open for us to move in."

"Exactly," Gorshkov concurred. "And that will give us the warm water port that we have coveted for so long. Let us hope that our good neighbors to the south succeed."

Boxer had one more loose end to tie up before he could spend full time tracking down Francine and her abductors. He needed some time off from the service. Admiral Stark would surely have understood his plight. Gruff as the old man was while he was CNO, he'd put his career on the line to take care of his men. Not so with Chi-Chi Mason. While Stark paid his dues commanding carriers, then fleets in every military action since Korea, Mason rose to the top using his best move, kissing ass. Boxer was not looking forward to this meeting with Mason.

Boxer was pleasantly surprised to see that his escort to the CNO's quarters was the same pleasant young officer, Lieutenant Kathleen Carson. She saluted him smartly, then smiled and said, "Welcome back, Admiral Boxer. Admiral Mason is expecting you."

Boxer returned the salute and followed her to the elevator down the hall. As soon as they were inside, and riding down to the sub-basement which housed the CNO and several other Chiefs of Staff, she turned to him and said, "I'm very sorry to learn of what happened to your friends, sir."

Boxer's face softened. "They were more than friends, Lieutenant. They were even more than family to me. When the Admiral was CNO, he was a tough taskmaster. Tough, but fair. The kind of CNO that's very hard to replace." He let the obvious implication of that settle in. "Since he'd taken ill, he's been like a father to me. And Miss Wheeler and I were about to be married."

The elevator stopped abruptly at the bottom level. "Well, here we are, Admiral. I just wanted you to know how I felt. I'm sorry for getting so personal."

Boxer allowed her to exit the elevator ahead of him. "No apologies necessary, Lieutenant Carson. It was nice of you to offer your concern." He smiled to show her his appreciation. They walked the rest of the way in silence, Boxer a few paces behind Carson. She had that all-American girl look, pure and wholesome, perhaps a tomboy as a youngster, pleased to be the apple of her father's eye.

They arrived at the CNO's corner suite of offices, and passed through a busy room manned by a dozen officers bent over electronic consoles of various types. A glass planning board occupied an entire side of the room, with its red, blue, and green dots and circles indicating the position of the American fleet and known enemy and allied navies. Many eyes turned as Carson led Boxer to Admiral Mason's inner office. Boxer cut off their leering with a quick glance.

Lieutenant Carson opened the door and stuck her head inside. "Sir, Admiral Jack Boxer is here."

"Send him in." Mason's voice was unduly gruff.

"Admiral Mason will see you now, sir. I'll be waiting here to escort you back out."

Boxer smiled at her, then composed himself and entered Mason's office. He saluted the CNO, and waited for longer than was necessary for Mason to return the salute.

"Have a seat, Boxer," Mason said without preamble. He had been smoking one of his big cigars, which he returned to his mouth. He did not offer one to Boxer. "Well, you were very lucky this time," he said. "You and your big shot lawyer pulled you out of that kettle of fish. There were some members of Congress calling for your head."

"I'm aware of what Senator Le Roux and his friends on the hill tried to do, sir. Just as I'm aware that the senator is also the father-in-law of Captain Axelrod, whom I could have brought up on charges of insubordination. However, I'm not one to get mixed up in politics, Admiral. I'd prefer to leave what has happened at the court-martial in the past."

"Well, I just want to let you know where we stand."

Boxer suppressed a chuckle. "Sorry to have disappointed you, Admiral. I came here to talk to you about the present." Boxer's face turned somber. "I need some time to find my fiancée and her abductors."

Mason snarled, "That's a job for the authorities, not an Admiral of the United States Navy. Let the police do their job."

"It's more complicated than that, sir. I have reason to believe that she's been taken out of the country. This is something I have to do my own way."

"It's always got to be your own damn way. That's what really rankles me, Boxer. You exceed your authority. You always try to take things into your own hands. If you don't agree with an order, you sidestep it. I'll tell you this, I don't like it. Not at all. I want men on my team who'll do as I order."

Boxer could see there was no sense looking for sympathy from Mason. "With respect, Admiral, I didn't come here to argue with you. I'm here to ask you for a leave of absence for a month or so. I have enough sick leave coming to cover it."

"I won't allow it."

"Sir, please be reasonable. This is something I have to settle once and for all. These people have beaten Admiral Stark near death, and have abducted my fiancée right from under my nose. And had the timing been slightly different, they might have killed my son, Chuck. And all to get at me, sir. Time is running out on finding Miss Wheeler. I've got to move on this, and I have to do it now."

Boxer watched Mason set his jaw and cross his arms in front of his chest. Before the CNO could comment, Boxer added,

"Once again, Admiral, I am officially requesting one month sick leave, beginning now."

Mason pulled on his cigar and let the smoke rise to the ceiling. "Let me tell you something, son. And this does not leave this room, understood?"

Boxer nodded in agreement.

"Our intelligence tells us that the Iranians are stepping up their terrorization of the oil tankers plying through the Persian Gulf. Our understanding is that they are building an underwater mini-submarine base in the vicinity of the Straits of Hormuz. Now, we've been able to hold those crazy bastards at bay on the surface, but a small squadron of mini-subs could wipe out our entire convoy protection fleet along with a dozen or more supertankers."

Boxer waited for the CNO to get to the point.

"We've just about completed refitting the *Barracuda*. I want you around in case I need to send you in there to find out what's going on."

Boxer shook his head. "In my opinion, Admiral, the *Barracuda* was too badly damaged. Why don't you pull out the UWIS equipment and the rest of the electronics to use on another super-sub, and salvage what you can from the reactor. I'm afraid the *Barracuda* will crack apart under too much stress."

Mason slammed his fists on his desk. "Dammit. There you go again. I give you an order, and you give me the runaround."

Boxer asked, "Are you denying my leave, Admiral?"

"I need you to drive the *Barracuda*. Didn't you hear me?"

"Captain Clemson is capable of that, Admiral. Especially since this is a reconnaissance run."

Mason's face grew bright red. "No. No, no, no. Am I making myself clear to you. Permission denied."

Boxer straightened his tie, then reached into his dress blue jacket and produced an envelope, which he tossed onto Mason's desk. "You leave me no choice, Admiral. I'm turning in my resignation. As of now."

Mason stared disbelievingly at the envelope. His hand went out to toy with it, to turn it around and flip it over, but not to pick it up. "You can't bluff me, Boxer. I happen to know you have three more years of service before you can collect full pension. You can't resign."

"I just did, sir."

Mason picked up Boxer's envelope and hurled it to the floor. "I'll have your ass for this."

Boxer decided he'd had enough of this. There was nothing else to be gained by remaining with Mason. He rose from his seat and stood at attention. "Is there anything else, Admiral?"

Mason jumped out of his seat and shook a fist as Boxer turned to leave. "Yes. Get the fuck out of here."

CHAPTER 16

As Boxer closed the door to Mason's private office behind him, he was overwhelmed by the hush of silence in the previously humming communications room. It was obvious that the CNO's shouts had carried beyond his door. Boxer spied Lieutenant Carson seated at a desk reserved for her. He nodded and said, "Lieutenant, I am ready to leave, please."

She jumped up and said, "Yes, sir. Ready to escort you out, Admiral."

Boxer gestured with his arm, "After you." He followed her outside, and walked alongside of her down the corridor. As they rode up to ground level in the elevator, Boxer said, "You can drop the Admiral now. I've resigned."

Carson appeared upset. "I'm sorry, sir. I guess you noticed, everyone in the outer office could hear the commotion that took place."

Boxer nodded that he had. As they reached the main entrance, Boxer said, "Thank you for your courtesy, Lieutenant."

Tears began to well up in Carson's eyes. "My pleasure, sir. I'm sorry that things worked out this way. I know the Navy is losing a good officer."

Boxer wiped a tear away with his forefinger. "That's no way for a Naval officer to behave, Lieutenant. Besides, whatever you've heard about me was probably overrated."

She replied, "I was a good friend of Bill Harris, before he died."

Harris was Boxer's Exec aboard the *Sting Ray*, and later on the *Shark*. He couldn't have asked for a better EXO. And he and Bill had been good friends. Boxer said, "Bill Harris was a good man. I'm sure we both miss him."

She smiled back at him. "Well, thanks. I hope to see you again someday, sir."

"I hope so, too, Lieutenant. I hope so, too."

As Boxer returned to Francine's apartment, he noticed a black Mercedes Benz-stretch limo double-parked in front of the building. The driver noticed Boxer staring at the vehicle, rolled down the front window, and slid across the seat. He called out, "Senor Boxer?"

"Who wants to know?"

"Senor Sanchez," the driver replied almost reverently.

Boxer walked to the car warily. As he approached, a rear window partially rolled down. Boxer could make out the face of the man who at one time had been his sworn enemy, and later had become one of his staunchest allies, Julio Sanchez. "Playing games, Julio?"

"Come in, please, Jack. The open window is disturbing the car's climate control."

Boxer laughed and let himself in. It was just like Sanchez to be so concerned with creature comforts. He slid into the soft leather seat next to Sanchez. "Hello, Julio. Thanks for showing up."

Sanchez's big white teeth flashed when he said with a smile, "My pleasure, old friend. We may have our differences from time to time, but when you are in need, I will not let you down."

The two men shook hands, and Boxer got right to the point. "You know why I called, then?"

"*Si*. Bad news travels fast, especially in this town." He pressed a switch on the armrest at his side. He said to the driver, "*Vamonos*," and the car pulled out into traffic.

Boxer said, "I believe that Bruno Morell is responsible."

"I agree. He would be my choice, also, for this type of atrocity. It bears his signature." Sanchez flipped open a small wet bar behind the driver's seat and proudly displayed its contents. "Would you care for a drink?"

"I could sure use one. Got any vodka?"

Sanchez reached in and produced a bottle of 100 proof Stolichnaya. "I hope this meets with your approval. It is the best I could muster at such short notice."

Boxed eyed it admiringly. Best of the best, that's Julio Sanchez. "Thanks."

"Ice?"

"Don't bother. It's been a rough morning. Better make it a double."

"With pleasure." Sanchez doled out a healthy portion of the Stoli for Boxer. Then he poured two fingers of a tawny liquor into a snifter, and brought it to his nose. He savored its essence, and turned to Boxer. "Don Pedro Special Reserve. Twenty-five-year-old Spanish brandy. My personal favorite."

Boxer touched his glass against the other. "To your health, then."

Julio held up his glass in salute. "To friendship. And to success in finding the one who committed this heinous act."

Boxer finished his drink in two swallows. "I've resigned from the Navy this morning."

"In that case, allow me to pour you another," Sanchez said, and refilled Boxer's glass. "I take it that your superior would not allow you time off to search for Francine?"

"Right," Boxer took a sip from the second drink. "I did everything I could to be persuasive, but that Mason's a fucking hardhead. He doesn't like me because of my relationship with Stark, and he goes out of his way to stick it to me. Well, this time he went too far. So I resigned."

Sanchez watched Boxer drain his glass. "Well, you are not alone, my friend. My sources have traced our Mr. Morell to an apartment in Rome. It is said that he is holding Miss Wheeler there. He plans to kill you if you come for her."

"He could have finished me off here, if he'd waited long enough."

"He has more friends in Italy. He could easily slip off back to Sardinia. Or Corsica."

"Then I'm off to Italy. I'll get some things together, and book the first flight out tomorrow morning."

"I will have two of my men meet you at the airport. They know Rome, and they know how to shoot. They will help you find Bruno Morell. And kill him."

Boxer put a hand on Sanchez's shoulder. "Thanks, Julio. They can help me locate Bruno, but I'm planning to kill him myself."

When Francine Wheeler awoke, she found herself lying naked on a small bed, hands trussed over her head, presumably to a headboard or bedframe. There was a wide leather strap around her waist securing her to the bed, though allowing her enough slack to adjust her movements slightly.

She was aware of a sickeningly sweet aftertaste in her mouth, and her lips and cheeks were sore inside and out. With her tongue, she could feel areas inside her mouth where the tissue was split or torn. Her vagina was inflamed, as was her anus, which she was sure was also fissured. Her thighs ached, her arms felt like they were being pulled from her shoulders. A crust of blood and mucus had dried on her upper lip.

She felt sick, like throwing up, and fought hard to suppress the urge to urinate. The last time she had done that, they had beaten her for wetting the bed because they had to change the linens. What was she supposed to have done?

She became aware of the movements of the boat. She remembered that they had taken her aboard the largest pleasure boat she'd ever seen, almost the size of a small cruise ship. Who was responsible for doing this to her? And why?

The TWA 747 touched down at Leonardo Da Vinci Airport in Rome and taxied to a stop. Boxer was up out of his first-class seat before the ground crew had the plane fully positioned for disembarkation. He was the first passenger off the jumbo jet, a black nylon bag slung over one shoulder, a hard look on his face. He wasn't planning to stay in Rome very long. Get in, kill Bruno Morell and bring Francine back with him to the airport, and get out.

Da Vinci was a large, modern international airport, with all the major airlines represented. He bypassed the luggage pickup area and headed for the exit. He was aware of various messages being broadcast over the speaker system in English, Italian, French, and German. It took him a little by surprise when he heard himself being paged in four languages. "Signor Boxer, please report to the TWA courtesy desk."

At the TWA counter, Boxer spotted two men milling about. One of them, in his thirties, wore a brown designer suit, finely tailored to display his well-muscled body. It was cut slightly fuller under the left arm to allow for the gun in its shoulder holster that Boxer noticed. The man had the look of a former football player who had become a bodyguard. Boxer figured he was probably right on that score.

The second man was shorter and thinner, with a pinched, weasel face, heavily pockmarked. He was smoking a cigarette. As Boxer approached, the man dropped his smoke and stomped it out with his heel. He held a small card in front of him with a crudely written BOXER. He looked up hopefully at the well-built bearded man with the black nylon shoulder bag.

Boxer didn't disappoint. He stopped in front of the two men and stated, "I'm Jack Boxer."

The smaller man smiled, "Ah, *si*. We are sent to meet you by Signor Sanchez. My name is Giancarlo. That is Marco."

Boxer nodded an acknowledgment. Giancarlo nodded back. Marco stared, but neither smiled nor otherwise greeted Boxer. *Well, so much for diplomacy*, Boxer mused. *Let's get this over with.* "I believe you have some information for me?"

Giancarlo lit another cigarette with a gold lighter and stuffed it back in the jacket pocket of his expensive-looking tan silk suit. It hung on him shapelessly, appearing too big for his thin frame. Boxer felt sure the jacket concealed a holstered gun also. Giancarlo said, "*Si.* Signor Sanchez has instructed us to take you to meet with a mutual friend." He let the euphemisms sink in. "We are to introduce you to this person and help you get back some property that belongs to you. In any way that is necessary." Giancarlo took a deep drag and flicked ash onto the terrazzo tiled floor. "Come, I have a car waiting."

Boxer followed the thin man to the arrivals exit under the TWA sign. Marco brought up the rear. A policeman was tagging a black Mercedes sedan. Giancarlo spoke to him rapidly in Italian, and slipped him a few banknotes. The policeman stopped writing, looked both ways before tucking the bills in his pocket, and went on about his business.

Giancarlo drove, Marco rode shotgun, and Boxer sat in the backseat. Giancarlo pulled out onto the circular drive and took the highway leading into the heart of the city. He turned his head partway around and asked, "You hungry?"

Boxer shook his head. "I grabbed a bite on the plane. Let's just get on with what I came here for. I have a date with Bruno Morell. Only he doesn't know it yet."

Traffic built up as they approached the city. Giancarlo seemed to delight in darting in and out of lanes, cutting other drivers off, and cursing their mothers when they objected. From time to time, he would roll down his window while trying to force his car into a lane of traffic, make an obscene gesture with his finger, and follow it up with verbal abuse. He usually got his way.

They were soon in the heart of the city, driving up the Via Veneto, swinging past the American Embassy, the Excelsior Hotel with its palm trees in front, and turned right past the Villa Borghese to continue north. They wound their way through several narrow side streets, sometimes scattering pedestrians as the big Mercedes careened around corners at breakneck speed. Mercifully, they came to a stop.

"It is not far," Giancarlo remarked.

Marco opened the glove compartment and removed a small, flat Beretta automatic. He checked the clip, satisfied himself that it was fully loaded, and tossed it to Boxer in the backseat. Boxer slipped the gun into the pocket of his grey windbreaker jacket, and the three men got out of the car.

They walked about a half block, cut through an alley laden with smelly garbage cans, and came out on a narrow street lined with apartment buildings in poor repair. Boxer swallowed hard, and followed Giancarlo to a building in the middle of the block with a brown-painted front door. As usual, Marco followed the others.

They walked gingerly up the porch steps. Giancarlo touched his forefinger to his lips to indicate silence. Boxer nodded and they proceeded into the building. They made their way up two flights of stairs, in single file. Near the third floor landing, a stair creaked. They waited a full minute in silence before proceeding further.

Giancarlo pointed to the door at the end of the corridor to the right. They approached the door, crouched, and Marco and Giancarlo removed their guns from their holsters. Boxer noticed that they were carrying large nickel-plated automatics, probably .44 magnums. Strange that they should provide him with a weapon so impotent compared to theirs. He felt an uncomfortable twinge in his gut.

Giancarlo tapped Boxer on the shoulder, and pointed to Marco. He gestured that Marco was to shoulder the door open, Boxer follow him in, crouching low and moving to the right, and Giancarlo bring up the rear and cover the left. Boxer nodded that he understood.

Marco held his pistol close to his midsection and backed up about five feet from the door to the apartment. The other two men got out of his way. Marco got a running start and smashed into the door with his massive shoulder. The door splintered, and sprang open. Marco charged in, keeping down.

Boxer slipped in and moved to the right, gun drawn. They were in a kitchen. He looked around the room, then closed in on a series of rooms with closed doors.

Giancarlo flew past him to the left, contented himself that the kitchen was empty except for themselves, and took the lead past Boxer and Marco. Suddenly, Boxer watched in disbelief as Giancarlo's head seemed to burst apart like a smashed melon.

Giancarlo's body lurched forward. A red splotch appeared on the back of Giancarlo's tan suit, and the man crumbled to the floor.

Marco wheeled and leveled his gun at a gunman behind Boxer. Too late. Boxer heard a muffled thunk, thunk, thunk. Three bloody rosettes punctuated Marco's chest. His face stared back in disbelief. A fourth bullet wiped that expression away.

Boxer dove for the floor, somersaulting over his forearm and coming up facing the direction the shots came from. He tried to bring up his Beretta. He found himself staring down the silenced barrel of an automatic pistol equal in size to the guns of the two dead men. Boxer dropped his arm to his side and stared into the face of Bruno Morell. He shook his head. "Bruno. You were expecting us."

Morell pointed his weapon directly at Boxer's head.

"Well, well. If it isn't Jack Boxer himself. How nice of you to come."

CHAPTER 17

Igor Borodine toiled over a small stack of paperwork in his tiny sub-basement office one level below Admiral of the Fleet Gorshkov. He leaned over a computer-generated spreadsheet, going over column after fine print column until his back ached and his eyes burned. He called to his assistant. "Well, Viktor, at least the old man allowed us to stay together in this hole. I am grateful for that, but I'd rather they had made you the commander of this new *Breshnev*."

Viktor Korzenko was flipping through some spec charts. "You are kind, comrade. I appreciate you looking after me."

"What else can I do? You are my only child's godfather." He squinted at a particular column of figures. "Hey, come here a moment. Something's not right here."

"What?"

"Bring the sheets for the reactors. I don't like the looks of this."

Viktor found the requested specs and laid them on top of the spreadsheet. He checked the figures of both documents against each other. "I see what you mean, comrade."

"The *Breshnev* is one hundred and ninety meters long with a twenty-five meter beam. It displaces twenty-five thousand tons, dived, and they are trying to power it with these remarkably small reactors."

"They are trying to save money," Viktor responded. "Already, this sub cost enough to feed the city of Kiev for a year." Viktor's family was from the Ukraine, a fact that he didn't publicize because of the traditional ill feelings between the Great Russians, who formed the Soviet Union's leadership, and his ancestors.

"Maybe so, but this is no place to scrimp. According to what I am seeing here, the reactors are only capable of providing 40,000 shp. A ship this size requires at least twice as much shaft horsepower. I'd better have a talk with Comrade Admiral Gorshkov before the *Breshnev* goes on her sea trials."

"Are you sure that is wise, Igor? After all, you are only on this new job for a week, and you are going to report a major flaw in the design of our new class of sub?"

"I am sure."

Viktor paced nervously back and forth across the twelve-foot confines of the little office. True, it was larger than his quarters on the sub, but it was too tight a fit for two men and all this computer equipment and filing cabinets for his liking. He crossed the room in four paces, wheeled, and blurted out, "Please reconsider, comrade. I fear for your safety if you disclose this error. Many high-level heads will surely roll. And be sure, those involved in the error will try to take yours along, too."

Borodine rubbed his beard while listening to his exec. He sighed, shook his head, and said, "Viktor, Viktor. I can do nothing else. It is my duty to stop this mistake from happening. I'm going up to see the chief."

"Well, if I can't stop you, at least let me go with you."

"No, comrade. I must do this myself. Let me have the specs. I'll be right back."

Viktor watched Borodine leave their tiny hole in the wall office, and thought to himself, *I hope so, old friend. I sure hope so.*

Borodine approached the heavyset captain in Gorshkov's outer office and asked for an immediate audience with the Admiral. "It's urgent that I speak to him now."

The jowly officer made a dour face and said, "And what is the nature of your business, comrade?"

Borodine knew better than to trust something of this importance to a subordinate. "It is personal and confidential. Now kindly tell Comrade Admiral Gorshkov that I have a message for him, and let *him* decide if he will see me."

"Very well. But you are wasting your time. Comrade Admiral Gorshkov is a very busy man."

Implying that I'm not worthy of his time, you bastard, Borodine fumed to himself. He waited without uttering a word. Several minutes passed, and Gorshkov's aide returned. "The Admiral will see you. Please do not waste his time."

Borodine walked past him into Gorshkov's office, and closed the door behind him. He saluted the Admiral, and sat when Gorshkov nodded to a chair across the desk from himself. "Captain Yoshkar tries to protect me from my enemies, both real and imagined." He smiled at Borodine. "And from my friends, too, I'm afraid. What is on your mind, Igor Alexandrovich?"

"I have the duty to inform you that I have discovered a serious design flaw in the new *Breshnev.*"

"Oh come now, Igor. Do you really believe that you could find fault with such a magnificent submarine that has taken many years and countless millions, billions, probably, to perfect? Are you sure that it is not just jealousy that prompts you stop the testing?"

"Jealousy? What do I care about jealousy? If the nuclear reactors aboard the *Breshnev* are as inadequate as they appear from the specs, they are likely to overheat the system and, Lenin's ghost forbid, cause a meltdown. I am trying to save the lives of a hundred and twenty good men. And, of course, the billions that it cost to build the sub."

"Show me your proof," Gorshkov demanded, no longer the good-natured old friend he professed to be only moments ago.

Borodine laid out his spreadsheets on Gorshkov's desk. On this he placed the charts and specs that he'd gotten from Viktor and pointed out the discrepancies to his superior.

Gorshkov studied the material and came to the same conclusion. "What are we to do now, scrap the whole design?"

Borodine shook his head. "I don't think so, Comrade Admiral. I think we can retrofit the reactor systems from a *Typhoon* class sub. The two are roughly equal in size. It will take several months, but in exchange, you will have a truly magnificent submarine capable of carrying a landing force of one hundred men in addition to the crew, a missile compartment equal to the best in the world, and the fighting capabilities of any SSN hunter-killer, except maybe our own *Alfas*."

"You really think so?"

Borodine knew his job was on the line. "Yes. Make the modifications. It will be worth the delay. If everything else is as good as it looks, we will have the best in the world."

"Yes. That is good, Comrade. It seems that I made a wise move, making you my deputy for Submarine Operations. But the Iranians are screaming for aid. What shall I send them, now that the *Breshnev* is going to be refitted? They can't wait for another four to six months."

"Why not send Kilmov in an *Alfa*? He is currently commanding the *Y.K. Narodnay*, I believe."

"You've got quite a memory, Igor. Or have you been checking up on the competition?"

"Just a good memory, Comrade Admiral. Actually, Admiral Narodnay, whom the sub was named after, was my instructor at submarine school a lifetime ago. Good man, too."

"Yes, I remember him, also. Khrushchev purged him. Breshnev brought him back from retirement to teach at the academy. Good man. And yes, I do believe you are correct. We shall send Comrade Anatoli Kilmov to the Persian Gulf aboard his *Alfa*. Then we will put an end to the American presence in those troubled waters for good."

"You set us up?" It was more of a statement than a question. Boxer already knew the answer. They'd been had.

Bruno Morell nodded his head. "You were too easy. You telegraphed your every move." He motioned to the two corpses on the floor. "And those two bozos couldn't find their asses with both hands if I didn't lead them to this place." He spat at them.

"Why, Bruno? Why did you have to involve my family and friends in this? If you wanted to kill me, there were lots of opportunities back in the States. Why this charade?"

"So you really think I kidnapped your fiancée? I'd have nothing to gain by doing that. Why should I go to so much trouble, and expense, to kill you? As you seem to know so well, I could have had you killed anytime I chose. Could have even done it myself. No. Think again."

Boxer slowly rose from the floor. At least he'd die with some semblance of dignity. Bruno didn't seem too anxious to shoot him, anyway. At least, not yet. "No, I think I've got you pegged right, Bruno."

"What do you think I'd do with her if I took her? Keep her here? Do you really think so? No. The man who had your Francine Wheeler kidnapped had an ulterior motive."

Boxer was on his feet now. "Just what are you talking about, Bruno? Stop playing games with me." He moved a step closer to Morell.

Bruno aimed the automatic at Boxer's chest. "Don't try anything funny with me, Boxer. You're still alive right now because it suits me. Don't press your luck. Now move over to that table and sit your ass down. Do it now."

Boxer backed over to the table, never taking his eyes off Bruno Morell. Or the gun. He pulled a chair out with his foot and sat himself down in it.

"That's better. The man who kidnapped Francine Wheeler sells women." He let that sink in, watching Boxer's face fall. "The fact that he could make twenty, thirty grand didn't hurt any. And all the while, he was sticking it to you, Boxer. Sorta paying you back for getting in his way once before with this sort of thing."

Boxer was sorting through the details of what Bruno was telling him. It was possible. Was he telling the truth? Or was Bruno trying to use him for his own needs? "Are you implying…"

"I'm not implying anything. I'm telling you the truth. Julio Sanchez had your woman snatched."

"But… Admiral Stark was almost killed. They almost beat him to death. Sanchez knew the Admiral. You don't think he…"

Morell laughed. "Don't be so fucking naive. Stark got in the way. Nothing more, nothing less. Believe me, I've been keeping tabs on Julio Sanchez. He framed me several years ago on that Libya fiasco. Sanchez set you up, and made me take the fall for it."

"Bullshit."

"I don't think he realized what the barbarians were going to do to your men."

Boxer's face bore the rage that had been pent up inside him since that day when he'd seen a hundred of his men impaled on stakes on the beach in Libya. From that day, he'd sworn to kill Bruno Morell. He shot up out of his seat and started toward Morell.

Bruno fired a shot into the floor at Boxer's feet. "Next shot won't miss, I promise you. Sit back down. I could have taken out your knee. Or killed you, for that matter."

"I've had nightmares since that scene on the Libyan beachhead. I lost almost all my men on that mission. Sanchez said you set us up. And he's the one who brought you aboard the *Turtle*. I figured he should know."

"Like I said, Sanchez sold you out, and put the blame on me. I barely escaped with my own life. True, I sold my influence to the Russians on occasion. True, I work as a double, at times. Part of my job at the CIA." He laughed. "Used to be, anyway. That was before Sanchez and Tysin teamed up to do me in."

Boxer perked up. He'd been trying to find an opportunity to jump Bruno. And now this? "Tysin? What about him?"

"I still keep my hand in Company business, Boxer. Well, not a hand anymore. Let's say a finger or two. I still have friends at headquarters. People who know me better than to think I'd sell you out on that botched mission. They look out for me. Protect me. So what I'm going to tell you is the truth."

Boxer glared at Morell.

"Just sit and hear me out. If you get up again to jump me, I'm going to shoot you. That's a promise. *Capisce?*"

"I hear you."

Morell was still standing over Boxer with his gun. Now he put his gun hand down at his side. "Henry Tysin paid Julio Sanchez ten thousand dollars, in addition to the twenty grand or so Julio's made on the sale, to kidnap Francine. Take her out of the country. Sell her to some Arab sheik somewhere in the Middle East."

Boxer stared incredulously. "But why?"

"To get at you, Boxer. Tysin hates your guts. Tried to have you killed when you returned to Norfolk from a mission. You know. When the *Barracuda* was hit by those missiles. That was Tysin's doing. I know. He tried to get me to do it."

"And you didn't?"

"I already told you. I could kill you anytime. Why go to all that trouble?"

Boxer rested his palms on the table. "Go on."

"Tysin knew about all the trouble his predecessor Kinkade had had with you through the years. He wanted you out of the way from the start. Get his own people in."

Boxer shook his head. "Kinkade and I were adversaries. But in the end, he left his entire estate to me. Did you know that?"

Bruno shook his head no.

"No? I'll bet Tysin didn't know, either. Kinkade and I had respect for each other. And that's how it ended. Tysin's another story."

"He wanted you out from the start."

"Well," Boxer said, looking directly at Morell, "I started off by wanting to kill one man. And now I have to kill two others instead. If what you've said is true."

"It's true. Trust me."

"Hah. Trust me. Famous last words. Give me one good reason to trust you, Bruno."

Morell thought it over for a moment. He raised the automatic, pointing it directly at Boxer, and walked over to the table. He said, "I can see that everything I've said so far isn't going to convince you."

Boxer didn't take his eyes off the automatic weapon. It loomed ominous as Bruno stood over him, pointing the weapon at his head.

What happened next turned Boxer into a believer. Bruno grasped the silencer end of the gun in his left hand and placed it on the table in front of Boxer. Boxer sat there staring at it.

"Go ahead, take it."

Boxer hoisted the pistol in his hand. He removed the clip. It was still loaded. He slammed it back into the handle and pointed the gun at Bruno's midsection. He registered a round into the chamber, and wrapped his finger around the trigger. "Shoe's on the other foot now."

"So it is. Now it's up to you."

Boxer let a long moment go by. He placed the heavy pistol on the table between them. "Okay," he said. "Let's get Julio Sanchez."

Captain Mark Clemens stood alone at the foot of Pier 24A, his raincoat collar turned up against the grey, early-morning fog that enshrouded Norfolk Naval Base. At the far end of the pier lay the refurbished super submarine, the *Barracuda*. The black silhouette of the control tower loomed over the pier. Clemens was anxious to start this tour of duty as Exec of the *Barracuda*, sorry that Boxer would not be the commander, and hopeful that the new captain, Roger Waldron, would be half as good as his former mentor.

Through the mist, Clemens could make out the forms of three official Navy cars, followed by several troop carrying trucks. His new captain and crew. Waldron climbed out of the first vehicle, and was followed to the pier by a dozen other officers in full uniform.

As they approached, Clemens dropped his duffel bag at his side and saluted. As they returned his salute, he said, "Captain Waldron, I'm Captain Mark Clemens, your new EXO." Clemens handed him an envelope bearing his orders.

Waldron was tall and trim, with a muscular, square jaw which sported a cleft chin. Clemens thought he looked more like a daytime soap opera star playing the part of a naval officer. Waldron said, "My new exec? Must be some kind of mistake. Clark here is my EXO. Let's go below and have a look at these orders."

No hello, no handshake, no greeting of any kind. Not like Jack Boxer, Clemens thought.

The two of them walked the length of the pier in silence, followed by the other officers. The crew piled out of the trucks and followed suit. Waldron entered first, followed by the officers, the chiefs, then the other enlisted men. "Come into my quarters," Waldron told Clemens. "Clark, you, too."

Clemens didn't like the way Waldron addressed him. They both had the same rank. It was a political decision that gave command of the *Barracuda* to Waldron. Sort of a slap on the wrist for anyone associated with Boxer.

"Now, let's have a look at your orders again. My understanding is that you sailed under Jack Boxer. Isn't that right?"

Clemens beamed. "Sure was. I was exec on our last mission to Antarctic. We destroyed a Russian oil drilling platform carved out of an iceberg. Nuclear reactor and all."

Waldron read over Clemens's orders. "Says nothing about being my exec, here. BUPERS cut these orders. I told the CNO that I didn't want any of Boxer's boys on my ship."

"What?"

"That's right, Clemens. Boxer was court-martialed for being a traitor, and I don't want any of that stigma aboard my sub."

Clemens turned livid with rage. "Are you fucking crazy? Admiral Boxer was completely exonerated of those charges, and you know it."

Waldron slammed a fist on the table. "Don't you talk to me like that. I'm captain of this ship, and I demand your respect."

"Respect isn't something you demand, Waldron. You earn it. And Admiral Boxer earned the respect of all his men many times over. And furthermore, my rank qualifies me as captain or EXO of this sub."

Waldron was furious. He hoisted his leather briefcase onto the chart table and withdrew a handful of envelopes. He tossed two of them on the table. He ripped open one labeled Commander Clement Clark, and scanned it quickly. "Here. Clark is my exec. Signed by the CNO himself."

Clemens found it hard to believe that this was happening to him, but Mason's signature was at the bottom of the page, and the CNO superseded everyone else. Then he read the contents of the second envelope that Waldron handed him. His orders were to orient Waldron and his officers with the UWIS and other sophisticated electronics, and then to remain ashore at the base pending reassignment. Son of a bitch. Well, at least he wouldn't have to sail under this asshole.

"Let's get started with the briefing," Waldron said. "We sail at 1800 hours tomorrow, and I want the men to be ready. We've been through this gear at the training grounds in San Diego for the last two months. All the men are experienced, and itching for some action. We've been Boxer's backup for too long. Now it's our turn."

Well, at least that explained some of the hostility, Clemens figured. "What's the assignment?"

"Can't discuss it. Off the record, though, we'll be ferrying a squad of Marines to the Persian Gulf. The Ayatollah and his goons are threatening to shut down the shipping lanes again. This time they're talking like the cat that got the cream. We're going to have a look-see for ourselves, and take care of business if we have to. And speaking of business, let's get started ourselves. We're wasting time here. We sail tomorrow."

CHAPTER 18

As the noontime sun rose over the Cammarata Mountains of Sicily, a three-seater Bell helicopter swept over the coast and headed toward a two-hundred-foot motor yacht slowly cruising the waters offshore. The boat gleamed white against the brilliant blue waters of the Mediterranean Sea and left a foamy white trail in its wake. The pilot pointed her out to his only passenger. "There she is, signor, the *Sea Breeze*. Magnificent."

"Yes, she is a beauty. Take us down."

The chopper bore down on the yacht, circled once to alert the captain of its arrival and finally homed in on the red landing pad on the *Sea Breeze*'s massive foredeck. Julio Sanchez hopped out onto the deck, crouching low to avoid the whirling rotors as several crewmen approached the chopper to secure it to the deck. Sanchez headed back toward the pilothouse.

The yacht's captain, a massive three-hundred-pounder with a full dark beard touched the gold-braided peak of his cap as Sanchez approached. "Senor Sanchez, a pleasure to have you aboard."

Sanchez smiled, "Ernesto, *cómo está?*"

Ernesto Hidalgo was the *Sea Breeze*'s permanent captain, and like Sanchez himself, of mysterious Latino origin. "I'm well, sir. It's a beautiful day for a sail."

Sanchez nodded. "And the woman?"

The smile left Hidalgo's face. "She's still below ... with those two pigs." He motioned belowdecks with his head.

"Well, then, if you'll excuse me, I'll go have a look for myself." Sanchez made his way down a flight of steps to the next level and turned toward the guest sleeping quarters at the stern. He heard voices coming from a room on the port side and let himself in unannounced. Both Mario and Gordo were forcing themselves on the woman at the same time. The two men were laughing and joking all the while.

Sanchez flew into a rage. "Imbeciles," he shouted. "Pigs. What are you doing to her?" He pushed the one called Gordo away from the head of the bed. "Look what you've done."

Gordo stood there, staring dumbly at Francine's face.

"Get off," Sanchez yelled at Mario. "Get the fuck off of her."

Mario got up slowly and glared at Sanchez, upset for being chastised, but not fool enough to take on his new boss with all of Sanchez's own people on board.

Sanchez walked to the bed and took a good look at this woman with whom he'd had a brief affair some years back. She'd come to hate him, and they'd kept their distance ever since. And now, thanks to a deal he'd made with CIA Director Tysin to get at Boxer, she was once more his. He leaned close to her and lifted her swollen, battered face in his hands. As her eyes opened, he said, "Do you know who I am?"

Shock registered as Francine recognized him. She nodded her head, and managed, "Julio? Julio Sanchez?"

"Yes. It is me." His eyes took in her body. It was covered with bruises and red welts. Her once beautiful figure was now a sorry sight. He stared at her face, into her pleading eyes. He placed her head back down onto the mattress, got up and turned on the two men.

"Look what you've done to my property. How do you expect me to sell her to anyone now? She looks like shit. Who is going to buy someone who looks like this."

Francine couldn't believe what she was hearing. His property? So it was Julio who had this done to her.

"I ought to have you both killed and thrown overboard," Sanchez continued.

Mario and Gordo looked at each other, trying to size up their chances of overpowering the entire crew, or of making good an escape. They didn't look hopeful.

Sanchez continued his tirade. "Just look at this room. It looks like a pigsty. It smells like a toilet. And look at the two of you. You make me sick."

Sanchez glared at the two men, one at a time. When he got no response, he threw up his arms in disgust. "Bah, worthless. Both of you. And now the woman. I'll have to dispose of her now. Sell her to some farmer or fisherman on Sicily. She would have brought thousands in the Emirates, or Qatar."

Finally, Mario summoned up some courage. "Signor Sanchez, all is not lost. She is young enough to recover from this. She is strong, I can tell you that."

Gordo chuckled at his partner's glib remarks. "*Si*, she is strong. She gave us quite a fight in the beginning."

"Yes," Mario interjected. "Come see for yourself."

Francine began to whimper as Sanchez walked back to the bed followed by the others.

Mario continued, "Now she will do anything you want. She no longer puts up a struggle. We have destroyed her will to resist."

Sanchez ran his hand over her body, roughly fondling her here and there. She merely cringed slightly at his touch, and sobbed. He said to the others, "Okay, I shall see for myself. Turn her over. Then get the fuck out of here."

As the *Barracuda* steamed into the Gulf of Oman, Captain Roger Waldron was signaled by his radioman. "Conn, message for the captain from Admiral Rodgers."

Waldron hurried to the radio room and made his way to a man wearing a headset, hunching over a writing table. His left hand was fiddling with a switch on his radio console. "What do you have for me, Bloom?"

"Your orders, sir. From the Admiral of the Fleet himself."

"Hmm." Admiral Rodgers was the commander of the Seventh Fleet, patroling the Indian Ocean, with responsibility for the Persian Gulf. He took the coded message into his quarters a dozen feet from the inside bridge and fed the data into his decoder. He was to proceed through the Strait of Hormuz into the Persian Gulf. His mission was to check for submarine activity in that narrow waterway in the vicinity of the various small islands off the coast of Iran. He was to seek out a suspected mini-submarine base among the Islands of Qeshm, Hormuz, Qeys, Larak, and the Isle of Lusi, and destroy the base.

So, he was going to see some action after all. This was the moment he'd long been waiting for. He walked to the command center on the bridge and gave the orders to proceed into the gulf. "DO… Bring us down to one five zero feet. One zero degrees on the diving planes."

"Aye, aye, Captain. One five zero feet."

As the *Barracuda* dropped from periscope depth down to one five zero, the helmsman brought the helm to the midline to reduce drag, and the EO revved up the turbine to make three-quarter full ahead.

The diving officer signaled, "Conn, DO… Passing through one zero zero feet." Then one minute later, "Passing through one two five feet."

The helmsman pulled back on the yoke that housed the wheel, signaling the EO to reduce speed. At the same time, the

DO eased the diving planes back to null. "Conn, DO... We're at one five zero feet, Captain."

Waldron checked his DDRO against the manual diving bubble. Both were at null. "Good work. Helmsman, make for course three two zero degrees."

"Roger that, Captain. Making course three two zero degrees."

"EO, Conn. Make full speed ahead. We have a date with the Ayatollah. At four zero knots, we should be through the strait in about an hour. Meanwhile, I want all hands at battle stations."

The EXO nodded, and gave the command over the intercom. "All hands to battle stations. All hands to battle stations."

The crew moved about the sub quickly and precisely to their stations, considering that there was barely enough room in the passageways for two men to pass shoulder to shoulder.

Forty-five minutes later, the sonar officer reported, "Conn, SO. Target bearing zero seven five degrees... Range twenty-four thousand five-hundred yards... Speed one five knots... Depth zero eight five feet. It's a diesel, Captain."

Waldron's adrenaline began to pump, though he kept a relatively calm demeanor. He had his target. Now to go for the kill. He punched the raw data into the COMCOMP. He asked, ID?

SOVIET WHISKY CLASS SSK TYPE V
ELECTRIC DIESEL ENGINE
1350 TONS DISPLACED DIVED
EST. SPEED ONE EIGHT KNOTS SURFACE
EST. SPEED ONE FOUR KNOTS SUBMERGED

Waldron turned to his exec. "Clark, the Russians haven't used one of these babies outside their area in ten years. Chances are it's an export picked up by the Iranians." He flipped a switch on another console, and the image of the sub could be seen on the UWIS heading for Qeshm Island, off the Iranian coast, just past the bend of the strait. "Let's take it out. The mini-sub base must be on the lee side of the island, facing the mainland."

Clark gave the thumbs-up sign and stood by the Fire Control console. This would be his first kill. He was looking forward to it.

Over the intercom came the SO's clipped, dispassionate voice. "Conn. SO. Target bearing zero six zero degrees... Range twenty thousand yards... Speed still one five knots... Depth zero seven five feet. She's heading for the eastern end of the island, sir."

Waldron clicked on his MC mike. "Helmsman, change course to three five zero degrees. EO, maintain flank speed."

"Changing course to three five zero degrees, Captain."

"Engine full speed ahead," said the EO.

Waldron spoke to his EXO, "This is going to be easy, Clark. Almost a practice run."

"Conn, SO. Target just ran behind Qeshm Island, sir. She's beyond the reach of the scope."

"We go in after her, then. What's our range to the island?"

"Range twelve thousand yards, sir."

"Okay. Helmsman, change course to zero one zero degrees."

"Aye, aye, Captain. Changing course to zero one zero." He pushed the rudder over to starboard, and the ship responded.

Waldron checked the depth gauge against the DDRO. "We're heading into shallow water," he told Clark. "DO,

Conn. Diving planes up zero five degrees. Bring us up to one zero zero feet."

"Roger that, Captain."

Waldron felt the sub tilt upward at the bow, and he was pleased. The crew was performing well. His exec, Clark, pointed out their position on his screen. They were at the eastern tip of the island. He keyed his MC mike. "Helmsman, hard left rudder. We're following the target behind the island. Given his speed relative to ours, we should be buggering the bastard in minutes."

That brought laughs from Clark and a few of the junior officers on the bridge.

"Conn, SO. Target bearing three three seven degrees… Range six thousand yards… speed one four knots… depth six zero feet."

"Good work. Now we've got the bastard where we want it." He keyed the forward torpedo room. "TO… Load and arm tubes two and four."

"Aye, aye, sir. Loading two and four."

The FO reported, "Arming two and four, Captain. We're at zero minus thirty seconds, sir."

"Conn, SO. Target dead ahead, Captain. Range four thousand yards … speed one four knots … depth zero five zero feet."

Waldron nodded at Clark. "Fire two and four."

"Firing two and four," Clark repeated. He pressed the red firing button and two fish thrust forward from the *Barracuda* at seven zero knots.

"Multiple targets dead ahead, Captain." There was noticeable anxiety in the SO's voice. "Looks like a cluster of twenty of more, sir."

"Must be mines," Waldron remarked to his EXO. He keyed in the engineering officer. "EO … come to full stop. Repeat. Come to full stop."

"Conn, SO. Target bearing one eight zero degrees … range four thousand yards … speed four five knots and closing fast, Captain. Depth zero five zero feet. We've got a visitor on our tail. Another sub."

"Damn, we've been sucked into a trap." He keyed his aft torpedo room. "TO … load and arm tubes ten and twelve. Repeat… Load and arm ten and twelve."

"Multiple targets bearing one eight zero degrees, Captain. Range two thousand yards … speed zero seven zero knots and closing fast."

"Torpedoes," Waldron said to his exec. For the first time, Clark was witness to profuse sweat running down his captain's face. Clark tried to swallow down his own sudden panic.

"Mines dead ahead, Captain. We're not slowing fast enough."

Waldron began to shout into the MC. "I know damn well we're not slowing fast enough, dammit. EO … one-half reverse."

"Aye, aye, Captain. One-half reverse."

"Fire torpedoes ten and twelve."

"Aye, aye, sir."

But it was too late. The first two contact mines blew out the *Barracuda*'s bows at the same time three torpedoes slammed into her from behind. Waldron was thrown into a bulkhead where he struck his head. He was dead before his body hit the deck. Clark watched seawater enter the inner hull as the *Barracuda* broke apart. The cooling system for the reactor cracked under the impact of the explosions. This was followed by the reactor overheating to a meltdown of the radioactive core. The *Barracuda* was finished.

Captain Anatoli Kilmov watched and listened in his *Alfa*-class sub, the *Sea Ghost*, and was very pleased with the trap he'd devised. For good measure, he ordered two more torpedoes fired into the tangled mass of titanium, steel, and electronics gear, just to discourage any survivors. There were none.

CHAPTER 19

Boxer braced himself in his seat while Bruno Morell's open speedboat raced across the Tyrrhenian Sea, pounding against the chop on the short trip to Sicily. Julio Sanchez's yacht had been sighted by someone who owed Morell a favor.

Boxer and Bruno were dressed in civilian clothes: fishermen's pants, caps, and shoes, cotton kit tops, and windbreaker jackets to ward off the sea spray. Two of Morell's men sat in the rear of the boat, dressed similarly, and sporting UZI automatic machine guns. A third UZI was on the seat next to Bruno. Boxer still carried the small Beretta automatic in his jacket pocket.

One of the gunmen, a young, dark-skinned, bushy-haired man named Aldo Fagiole was the first to sight the *Sea Breeze* on the horizon. "Over there, Bruno. Off the starboard bow." Aldo pointed with his UZI.

The other young gunman, Nicky Capoletti, joined his partner along the gunwales, shielding his eyes with his hand. "Son of a bitch, there she is. What a beautiful boat."

Bruno nodded, and began a sweeping approach toward his prey. When they were less than a mile away, Boxer pointed out a small green helicopter taking off from the *Sea Breeze*'s foredeck. The chopper circled the yacht once, swung around closer to the speedboat for a better look, and took off toward the Sicilian coast. It soon disappeared inland.

As Bruno closed in on the *Sea Breeze*, the larger boat increased its speed to about fifteen knots and headed directly at the speedboat. Boxer was about to shout orders to evade the attempted ramming, but Bruno knew his business. He veered out of the way at the last moment in a display of bravado, and used his superior speed to pull alongside the *Sea Breeze*, staying roughly amidships. Aldo and Nicky strafed the pilothouse with their UZI's.

Captain Hidalgo steered hard left, causing a wake which almost flipped the speedboat. Bruno Morell cursed and fell behind the yacht. He came up on the *Sea Breeze*'s starboard side, and again Aldo and Nicky fired at the pilothouse. This time, they were answered by a half dozen armed men shooting at them from the main deck with everything from revolvers to shotguns. Hidalgo swerved at them again, once more trying to ram the smaller boat.

Bruno hollered to Boxer, "Pass me that blue gym bag near your feet."

Boxer bent down, picked up the bag, and handed it over.

With one hand on the steering wheel, Bruno unzipped the bag, and felt inside it. "Good. Now we will teach those fuckers a lesson. Aldo. Nicky. Take these."

Each man helped himself to two of the hand grenades they found in the gym bag. Bruno smiled when Boxer looked surprised. "Go ahead if you like. I'm going to pull close alongside. Then you and the boys let them have it."

"How can we be sure exactly where Francine is being kept. What if we get too close and kill her?"

Bruno nodded. "Good point. What do you want to do?"

"Do you have a megaphone? Or a speaker?"

"Under the seat behind you. All the safety gear's in there."

Boxer said, "Let's try a little diplomacy first."

Bruno Morell shrugged. "It's your party."

Boxer put the loudspeaker to his mouth. "Ahoy, captain of the *Sea Breeze*. You have someone aboard that we want. Let us board and retrieve her, and we'll allow the rest of you to go unharmed."

His request was answered by a volley of shots from the yacht.

Bruno laughed. "So much for diplomacy."

"If one of your boys has a good arm, let him try to loft one up near the pilothouse. They wouldn't keep Francine in there; she'd just get in their way."

Morell turned his head. "Nicky, see if you can hit the captain with one of those."

"Right, boss." Nicky pulled the pin and popped the lever off a grenade. As Bruno pulled as close as he could to the yacht, Nicky heaved the heavy projectile with all he had.

Bruno roared away from the *Sea Breeze* just in time to see the grenade explode. It fell short of the pilothouse, but the concussion blew out all the starboard windows. They heard someone scream.

Several men rushed to the rail and fired at the speedboat. Aldo returned their fire with his UZI. Several men fell back. Shattered glass went flying in all directions.

Boxer picked up the speaker. "Ahoy, *Sea Breeze*. This is my final offer. Come dead in the water and drop a boarding ladder, or we will destroy all of you."

Minutes passed with no reply or visible slowing of the yacht. "That's it, Bruno. I'm going to try to board her. Nicky, you've got a good arm. See if you can get a grappling line over the starboard rail. I'm going up."

Aldo said, "I'll go, too."

"Good. Hand me the bag of grenades."

Morell pulled the speedboat as close as he could. Boxer yelled, "Now, Nicky."

Nicky whirled the line over his head and heaved. The metal claws found their mark on the starboard rail, and wrapped tightly around it.

And then the *Sea Breeze* slowed until it came to rest dead in the water. Someone yelled over the side, "Okay, don't shoot anymore. We're putting over a boarding ladder. Stand by."

Boxer replied, "We're standing by. Don't try anything foolish."

Moments later, a folding aluminum ladder was rolled over the side of the yacht. Boxer said to Morell, "Once I get Francine safely out of there, I want Sanchez, and anyone else who had anything to do with this."

Bruno nodded. "Then I'm going up with you, too. You'll need all the help you can get. Nicky can stay with this boat."

"Thanks. We'd better get going."

Bruno said, "Aldo, you go up first. Shoot anyone who gets in your way."

"Right, Bruno. My pleasure." He reached over the side of the speedboat and got a handhold on the ladder.

Boxer watched him climb aboard, then he slung the bag of grenades over his shoulder and followed Aldo. Bruno brought up the rear, UZI in hand. The three of them moved swiftly to the pilothouse. Boxer put his Baretta to Ernesto Hidalgo's head and commanded, "Get all your men in here, now. And I want to see all the weapons tossed over the side."

Hidalgo shouted orders in Spanish and Italian. Several men entered the cabin. "Guns overboard, men," he said.

The crewmen reluctantly complied, while Bruno and Aldo glared at them from behind their UZI's. Boxer said to the yacht's captain. "Where's Julio Sanchez? And where's the woman you've taken aboard?"

Hidalgo shrugged. "Senor Sanchez isn't here. And the woman is probably below somewhere."

Boxer's face turned scarlet. Bruno interceded. "Allow me, my friend."

Bruno pulled a switchblade from his pocket and clicked open the six-inch blade. He dug the point into the captain's thick neck. A rivulet of blood trickled down Hidalgo's clean white shirt. "Don't fuck with me, fat one. I will cut your head off and feed it to the fish in a second if you don't tell me where Sanchez is."

Hidalgo sensed that Bruno meant every word. "Senor Sanchez flew off in the helicopter just before you got here."

Bruno drew the sharp blade about an inch across the captain's neck. This time the blood flowed freely. "And the woman?"

Sweat trickled down Ernesto Hidalgo's forehead and rolled off his cheeks. He knew that this was to be his moment of truth. "She is one level below in an aft cabin."

"Alone?"

Hidalgo started to lie that she was alone. The tip of the knife sticking him in the neck dissuaded him. "There were the two who were with her all along. They might still be there." Then he added, "They are not my men, senor. I don't care about them. But please spare the others. They were only trying to defend themselves."

Bruno said, "We shall see. It depends on how well you all behave. Believe me, Captain, if you or any of your men give us trouble, you will all die. *Capisce?*"

Hidalgo nodded. He certainly did.

Boxer reached into his pocket and took out a handkerchief, which he tossed to Hidalgo. "That should stop your bleeding. Now have all your men lie facedown on the deck. Now."

Hidalgo put the cloth to his neck, and barked the order. The men did as he said.

Boxer said, "I'm going down there." Gun in hand, he headed for the steps.

"Aldo, stay here and keep an eye on them. If anyone moves, kill them all."

Aldo's smile was not missed by Ernesto Hidalgo. "No problem at all, boss. No problem at all."

Bruno charged down the stairs after Boxer, catching up to him on the landing below. Guns at the ready, they headed to the stern cabins and kicked in the farthest door on the left. The slamming door left a hollow sound. The room was empty.

"No sense being polite now," Boxer said. "They know we're here."

Bruno nodded, and kicked in the door of the center cabin. That was also empty. Bruno whispered in Boxer's ear, "Remember the lesson I taught those two assholes that Sanchez sent to get me in Rome. Don't make the same mistake twice."

Boxer gave the thumbs-up sign, and they each stood to one side of the remaining cabin door. Bruno kicked the door open and stood back. A fusillade of fire struck and splintered the bulkhead opposite the doorway.

Boxer dove in on his belly and fired off two rounds at the man who stood there in the center of the room. Gordo wheeled toward Boxer and leveled his automatic at him.

Before Gordo could fire, Bruno jumped in and sprayed the gunman's thick body with the UZI. Gordo seemed to disintegrate in front of them in a splattering of blood and gore.

A voice called out, "Don't shoot. Don't shoot. I'll kill the woman right now if you don't put down your guns."

Bruno looked over at Boxer and shook his head no.

"I mean it. I'll kill her." It was Mario, with a chokehold around Francine's neck, her naked body held in front of him as a shield. "I mean it. She don't mean nothing to me. Either I get out of here alive or she dies with me."

Neither Boxer nor Bruno moved.

Mario placed the tip of his gun barrel into Francine's ear. "I mean it. Put your guns down right there and back out of here. I'm taking a lifeboat out of here, with the woman. If you follow me, I'll kill her."

Boxer shrugged, and tossed his Beretta onto the bed. Bruno followed suit and placed the UZI on the ground at his side.

"Now back up."

Boxer eased himself back out of the cabin, trying to figure his chances of jumping the guy without getting Francine killed. Not good, he thought. But not impossible. Especially with Bruno at his side. He could not bear to look at Francine. She was battered unmercifully, and could do no more than whimper. He wouldn't be able to depend on her to help them. Bastards. They would pay dearly for doing that to the woman he loved.

Mario backed up the stairs to the upper deck, keeping Boxer and Bruno at bay with his threats. Bruno, like Boxer, was looking for an opportunity to strike. He wasn't as concerned with what happened to Francine as was Boxer. Still, he'd like to spare her if possible. There was no way he'd let this jackal get away.

Mario half dragged Francine along with him to the stern rail, where three lifeboats were held on davits, in position for escaping should the crew have to abandon ship. He was concentrating on his escape plan so intently that he failed to notice Aldo following his movements with the barrel of his loaded UZI.

Both Boxer and Bruno must have sensed this at the same time. They followed Mario and Francine to the stern, keeping about ten feet away from them, watching for that moment of distraction when they could make their move.

Now Mario was faced with the task of climbing into the lifeboat while still holding Francine in front of him as a shield. Then he would have to lift or drag her in with him and work the winch that would lower him to safety. He thought for a moment, then transferred his pistol to the hand holding Francine around the neck.

Boxer and Bruno rushed him from opposite sides. Mario's first shot whizzed past Bruno's head. Bruno pulled up short. Boxer flung himself at the gunman, knocking him backward. A shot roared from Mario's automatic and struck Boxer in the shoulder. Blood gushed from the shoulder wound, but Boxer managed to throw his body over Francine's. He crashed down to the deck on top of her.

Bruno looked toward Aldo and shouted, "Now, Aldo. Now. Shoot."

Aldo stepped into the clear and emptied his clip into Mario. The blood-splattered body was lifted up and back out of the lifeboat and over the stern rail. Then, it looked as if he'd been thrown upward. Nicky was firing at the falling figure from the speedboat below. The remains of the gunman Mario settled onto the sea. In moments, the bravest of the Mediterranean fishes were nibbling on their windfall meal.

Boxer scooped Francine up in his arms. He yelled, "Someone get me a blanket."

In a minute, a deckhand came forth with a woolen blanket. Boxer took it from him, and as gently as he could, wrapped it around the naked body. Francine was shaking uncontrollably, alternately sobbing and blabbering nothings. Boxer carried her downstairs and placed her on her bed.

As soon as she realized she was back in the room where she'd been held prisoner and violated so brutally, Francine screamed and huddled in the corner. Any attempts by Boxer to comfort her were futile. She was carrying on completely out of control. Boxer felt the bile rise in his throat. He hoped she was not beyond help.

On the drive back to Da Vinci Airport, Boxer sat in the back of the rented sedan next to Bruno Morell while Aldo Fagiole plied the auto through traffic. *Strange bedfellows*, Boxer thought. *I came to Italy to kill this man for past crimes against my men and treason against my country. And for what I thought he'd done to Admiral Stark and to Francine Wheeler. And now he is giving me a lift to the airport.*

Boxer stared out the window at the nightmarish traffic snarls, and laughed as Aldo rolled down his window to curse at the driver of an offending yellow cab, and to give him the finger. Some things never change in Rome. At least in the few short weeks since Boxer had arrived. He turned to Bruno Morell. "I want to thank you for arranging the sanitorium for Francine. The administrator promised me that she would receive the best treatment possible."

"Yes. If one has the means, they will provide state-of-the-art psychiatric care with around-the-clock nurses and aides. And the villas are really beautiful. The Piedmont is where the rich and famous come to dry out or to recover in a splendid setting with the best care, and out of the limelight. And when they go home, it is as if they had been on a vacation." Morell knew that this was a gross exaggeration, but he wanted to spare Boxer's feelings.

Boxer knew it was a lie, also. He also knew the reason for it, and accepted it as such.

"Here we are, boss. The TWA terminal," Aldo announced.

Bruno offered Boxer his hand. "Well, good luck to you. And good hunting."

"Thanks. I'm going home to look after Admiral Stark, and check on my son Chuck. But then I'm going after Julio Sanchez, and kill him."

Bruno nodded his head. "I don't blame you a bit."

Boxer's expression became solemn. "You know, Bruno, I really don't know what happened that day on the beach in Libya. You and Sanchez each blame the other. I do know what you did for me here in Italy, though, and I'm grateful for it."

Bruno acknowledged that with a nod.

Boxer continued. "I'll tell you this, though, so there's no mistake. If I ever get proof that you betrayed us to the Libyans, I'll come back here to kill you."

As Aldo came around to open Boxer's door and hand him his travel bag, Bruno Morell leaned back in his seat. "I'll be here, my friend. I'll be right here."

Boxer slung his bag over his right shoulder. The left had been heavily bandaged, and his left arm was in a sling. Boxer knew he was very lucky that the bullet fired in the shootout went clear through the muscle tissue, sparing him a permanent disability. He waved off the redcap baggage handler and strode briskly to the TWA departure desk. His reservations had already been confirmed.

He smiled back at the beautiful brunette customer service rep and said, "I'm Jack Boxer. You're holding my ticket for me."

"Thank you, sir. Are you checking that bag?"

"No, I'll carry it on with me."

"Very well, sir. Here's your ticket and boarding pass. You'll need to pass the bag through the security detector over there."

As Boxer turned to head toward the security devices, he thought he caught a glimpse of her signaling to the two policemen standing nearby. All of a sudden, they approached him. "Signor Boxer. Please come with us."

Boxer looked puzzled. "What's this all about?"

"Right this way, please."

Boxer turned to find himself facing an American civilian in a grey dress suit and tie, and a U.S. Marine Corps sergeant. The man in civvies said to him, "Admiral Boxer, I'm Captain Morrison, naval attaché here. I have a personal message for you from the CNO, Admiral Mason."

CHAPTER 20

Boxer was escorted to a small, windowless room deep within the Immigration Department complex of the airport. The walls of the room were painted a drab grey, and except for a table and half a dozen chairs, the room was devoid of furnishings. Boxer felt sure that very few outsiders even knew this place existed.

Captain Morrison motioned Boxer to have a seat near one of several telephones on the table. Then he turned to the two Italian policemen. "Thank you, officers. We truly appreciate your assistance. And now, if you'll please excuse us...?" He indicated the open doorway with a sweep of his hand.

The two policeman nodded and marched stiffly out of the room. Morrison said, "Sergeant Reynolds?"

The Marine snapped to attention and marched to the door, closed and locked it, and stood at attention just inside the room. He was in full dress uniform, with a .45 automatic holstered at his hip, and he looked as if he meant business. Was he there to keep him in, or to keep anyone else out, Boxer wondered?

Morrison produced an envelope from an inside jacket pocket and handed it to Boxer. "Admiral Mason has instructed me to give you this, sir."

Boxer hefted the envelope in his hand, unopened. "What is it?"

"Your new orders, Admiral Boxer. As you'll soon find out, there's been a disaster off the coast of Iran."

Boxer looked up.

Morrison continued. "Captain Roger Waldron had taken the *Barracuda* into the Persian Gulf last week in a search and destroy mission."

"Oh, yes," Boxer said. "The supposed mini-sub base."

"Exactly. Admiral Rodgers of the Seventh Fleet was in contact with Waldron in the Gulf of Oman, prior to the *Barracuda* entering the Straits of Hormuz. That was a week ago. There's been no contact since."

Boxer shook his head. "It would be normal for the *Barracuda* to maintain silence in the search and destroy. But a week? I fear for the worst."

Morrison slumped into a seat across from Boxer. "So does the CNO. Why don't you open your orders, Admiral?"

Boxer tossed the envelope onto the table. "I'm retired. I turned in my resignation to Mason last month. Now I'm involved in a personal problem, and I no longer take orders from Mason."

"I was informed about Admiral Stark, sir. As CNOs go, he's the best I've served under. I understand that he's doing quite well. The doctors at Walter Reed have given him an excellent prognosis."

Boxer smiled. "He always was hardheaded."

"Thank God for that," Morrison replied. "And I'm sorry to learn that your lady was kidnapped."

"That's the unfinished business that I have to take care of, Captain. So, considering that Admiral Mason wouldn't allow me to take a leave to settle this thing, I turned in my resignation. And now that I am no longer in the Navy, I am free to pursue those ends. So if you'll excuse me…?"

"I can sympathize with you, sir. And frankly, that's the response that was expected. If you'll please bear with me for a moment, there is someone who wants to speak with you."

Morrison took a black leather case from the Marine sergeant, and opened it on the table. He disconnected the telephone line from the phone, and inserted it into a device in the black case. Then he ran another line into the telephone.

Boxer smiled. "Scrambler?"

Morrison looked over the room, sweeping the four walls and the door with his eyes. "Can't be too careful." Then he dialed a number. In a moment, "I have Admiral Jack Boxer on the line. Yes, I will."

Boxer took the phone that was offered to him. He had a puzzled expression on his face.

Morrison said, "Stand by for the President of the United States, sir."

Boxer watched the Marine sergeant snap to rigid attention at the very words. He held the phone to his ear for almost a minute. At last he heard, "Jack, is that you? This is President Spooner."

"Mr. President."

"Good to hear you again, Jack. I'm calling to ask you a personal favor. In fact, to do your country a favor. I hope I can count on you."

"You know I resigned from the service under duress, sir."

"Bullshit, Jack. I told Mason that no way was I going to accept your resignation. I had him put you in for a month of leave to take care of personal matters. And I told him he damn well better cooperate with you on this mission or I'll have his ass." Spooner dropped his voice. "That's privileged info, Jack. Just between the three of us. Well, five of us, actually. Jay Archer and Billy White helped me track you down."

"Well, Mr. President, I appreciate your going to bat for me, but I found out who was responsible for what happened to Admiral Stark and Francine Wheeler, my fiancée."

"A very fine woman, Jack."

Boxer suppressed the tears welling up in his eyes. In a broken voice, he said, "She's in very bad shape, now, sir. Her abductors broke her spirit as well as her body. I've got her in the Piedmont Clinic here in northern Italy, the best around. But the doctors are not very hopeful."

"Very sorry to hear that, Jack. If there's anything I can do, just ask. We've got the best medical care available for Admiral Stark. He's coming along fine. The docs tell me he's cranky and barking orders at everyone."

"Sounds normal for him," Boxer said. At least that was news to be grateful for. He said, "Mr. President, I've got to find the man responsible for this."

"I understand, Jack. Take care of this mess in the Persian Gulf for me, and I'll see to it that you get time off to do just that. Oh, and Jay and Billy wanted me to tell you that anything that you need, money, someone to press the right buttons, whatever, they'll take care of it for you. Anything at all."

"I have money, sir. And some connections. But I'll keep it in mind. You do realize, Mr. President, that it would take at least a month to assemble a new crew and strike force, and get them and a capable sub into the Persian Gulf. I could be finished with what I have to do by then."

"You'd be surprised what the Navy can do if the President prioritizes something. There's a *Los Angeles* class submarine waiting for you out in the Gulf of Oman, with your man Clemens in charge till you get out there."

"I'm not even going to ask how you managed that, sir. What about a strike force?"

"Not to worry. We found an old friend of yours to help us out. General Fitzpatrick, my NSC adviser loaned me Colonel Will Pickens. Jay and Billy say he's a good ol' boy."

Boxer chuckled. "Will Pickens was my right hand during the Discovery Day celebration, back in '92."

"Yes, I'm aware of that. You boys did a fine job that time," Spooner added. "Colonel Pickens grabbed us some Marines and a squad of SEALs, so I think you'll have the manpower you need."

"That should do the trick, Mr. President."

Spooner was elated. "Then you'll do it for me?"

Boxer paused. "There's just one more thing, sir. Admiral Mason forced me to resign. I'd like to hear him ask me back aboard, and assure me of his cooperation." The long silence that followed caused Boxer to believe that he'd just gone too far.

Then the President burst out laughing. "Glad you're on *my* side, Jack. Stay put there. I'll have Mason get back to you in a minute."

"Thank you, Mr. President." But the line had already gone dead.

A minute turned into ten. Then, the scrambled phone rang again. "Mason here."

"Boxer here," he mimicked.

Mason noisily cleared his throat. "Well, I suppose the President gave you your next mission."

Boxer smiled. "Well, actually, I haven't read the orders yet. President Spooner said he'd have you fill me in, and then if I was satisfied, I'd accept."

"Don't toy with me, Boxer. I don't like this one bit. Now read those damn orders, and report to Admiral Rodgers at once."

Boxer gently placed the receiver on its cradle. He looked up at Morrison. "Well, I'm out. I don't have to take that crap, and I won't."

The phone rang again. "Mason here."

"Yes?"

"You get me pissed off, Boxer. I'm sorry I lost my temper."

Boxer pictured the CNO squirming uncomfortably in his leather seat, knowing he'd have to report to the President that he'd blown the one chance that Spooner had bought for him. Mason knew his career was at stake. And so did Boxer. "No problem."

"Look, Boxer, we think that Waldron lost the *Barracuda* with all hands. At least there's been no sign of the sub, or any survivors. And no word of the *Barracuda*."

Boxer shook his head. "That's a lot of good men lost."

"That was a billion-and-a-half-dollar sub."

That's one of the things Boxer hated about Mason. Besides being a pompous ass who put political decisions ahead of military ones, he valued his toys much more than the lives of the men who sailed them. Nonetheless, Boxer ripped open the envelope on the table before him. "Let's see what the orders say."

While Boxer perused the paperwork, Mason ran over the details with him. "You'll command the *Halsey*, a conventional nuclear SSN of the *Los Angeles* class. Her crew is twelve officers and one hundred and fifteen enlisted men."

"I'm aware of that, Admiral. I trained on those hunter-killers. They fire Mark 48 wire-guided torpedoes and Tomahawk missiles. And there's some very good sonar. But I'd like to replace some of the enlisted men with officers. On the *Shark* and *Barracuda*, we ran with about twenty percent."

"No time to get them together. Besides, the electronics are not nearly as sophisticated as you're used to having. The BQQ-5 long-range sonar is good, and she tows the BQS-15 for shorter range. Fire control is fully computerized. But there's no

UWIS or COMCOMP. The chiefs can handle all there is aboard. And Mahony and most of your surviving crew are aboard, along with Captain Clemens. You should be all right."

"I hope so, Admiral." Boxer hung up the phone. "I really hope so."

Within hours, Boxer was speeding towards the Seventh Fleet at Mach 2 speed aboard an F-14 Tomcat interceptor feeling mighty glad that he was a submariner and not an aviator. When the fighter touched down on the *Rickover*, Admiral Rodgers's flagship carrier, Boxer climbed out the moment the cockpit opened, and headed up the several flights of steps to the Admiral's bridge. Rodgers greeted him, read over his orders, and asked Boxer if he was hungry.

Boxer eyed the posh quarters, and the two waiters in starched white uniforms standing by to take their orders, and was tempted by the offer. "Thank you, Admiral, but I'm anxious to get aboard the *Halsey* and meet my men."

"I know just how you feel, Jack," said the white-haired Rodgers. "If I were in your position I'd be chaffing at the bit to get started, too. Have some coffee with me while we get my personal tender ready to take you to your sub."

Boxer relaxed a little, and nodded to the waiters. "Black, please."

They looked at Rodgers, who beckoned them out. In a few minutes they returned bearing a silver tray with porcelain cups and a silver coffee service and a large plate of miniature pastries. Rodgers smiled his gratitude.

"Help yourself, Jack. The bakers do a wonderful job on those pastries." Rodgers patted the slightest hint of a paunch on his otherwise trim sixty-year-old body.

Boxer hadn't eaten in almost twenty-four hours. Just as well, he thought, because the flight on the Tomcat jet would have cost him at least his last meal. He poured himself a cup. "Admiral?"

"Thanks, black for me, too." He reached for an almond Danish, and polished it off in two bites. "By the way, Jack, how's Admiral Stark doing?"

"I understand from the President that he's recovering nicely, thanks."

"He was a good man. A good CNO."

"That seems to be the consensus," Boxer nodded. "I'm quite fond of him."

"And he was very proud of you, Jack. He told me that on several occasions."

A young ensign with a blond crewcut stood in the doorway. "Admiral Boxer, the tender is ready, sir."

"In a moment," Rodgers said. "Tell them to stand by."

As the officer left, Boxer washed down one of the little pastries with his remaining coffee. "Well, I'd better get started. Thanks for your hospitality."

Rodgers shook hands and said, "Well, good hunting."

"Thank you, Admiral. I'm dedicating this kill to Admiral Stark." Then he followed the ensign down to the flight deck. Once in place in the small boat, they were lowered over the side along with two enlisted men. One of the sailors cast off the davit lines when they reached the surface, and the ensign took them to where the *Halsey* had hove to.

Boxer saluted his new deck crew who quickly summoned Captain Clemens, who was joined on the outside bridge by Chief Mahony, Boxer's longtime navigator. As the tender returned to the *Rickover*, Boxer shook hands all around, and quickly caught up on the news of his men. "The CNO really got you men out here quickly," he remarked.

"Quick isn't the word for it," Mahony quipped. "Believe me, we left many a broken heart ashore, this time. They had SP's track us down and drag us back to base kicking and screaming."

"He tends to exaggerate," Clemens added. "The *Halsey* was here waiting for us. I don't know how, and didn't ask. I was just happy to learn that you'd be our skipper again."

"The President made me an offer I couldn't refuse. How about we go below and meet everyone?"

"Sure thing. There's about forty of us left from the Antarctic. Most of the new guys have a lot of experience."

Mahony held open the hatch and followed Boxer and Clemens below to the command room. They were met by a fortyish sailor dressed in sparkling clean denims and black rubber-soled shoes that were spit-shined to a brilliance. Clemens made the introduction. "Admiral Boxer, I have the pleasure of introducing Master C.P.O. Amos White, the chief of the boat. Whitey, meet Admiral Boxer."

"Pleasure to serve under you, Admiral. I've heard only great things about you from your men."

Boxer offered his hand to White. Like himself, the chief had salt-and-pepper hair, though Whitey had his trimmed almost to his scalp. He had a square face with bushy eyebrows that matched his hair, and was a little thick around the middle, though very muscular. He had a firm handshake that Boxer liked. "Pleasure's mine. What shall I call you?"

"Well, sir, the men call me Whitey, or just the Cob. There's a few other names, too, but never to my face."

"Very well, Whitey it is. By the way, you can drop the Sir, and Admiral stuff. My men just call me Skipper."

"Thank you, sir. I'll try to remember."

Clemens added, "Whitey serves as DO when we're involved in any action. He has the most years of service, and knows this ship better than anyone. With the possible exception of yourself, Skipper."

Boxer asked, "Has the strike force gotten here yet?"

"Just yesterday," Clemens answered. "Let's go forward and meet Major Roland Jones and his merry men, Rolly's Rangers."

"You kidding?"

"No, Skipper. Jones is the meanest, toughest-looking son of a bitch that I've ever seen. Marine Corps has been training men for an elite force similar to the SEALs, except they work on land as well as on and under the sea. Also, we've got a half dozen SEALs on board, too. They're cross-training with Major Jones."

Boxer, Clemens, and Whitey passed through the galley and mess hall to the cramped quarters of the strike force. As soon as Major Jones spotted Boxer's uniform, he jumped to his feet and shouted, "Admiral present."

Eleven other men rose in unison and stood at rigid attention.

"At ease, men." Boxer looked them over. They were as rugged-looking a group as he'd ever fought with. And their leader, Roland Jones, was the biggest, meanest man he'd seen. Jones's shaved head glistened with sweat. A droplet rolled down his cheek and was sopped up by a short cropped mustache. Eleven sets of eyes watched him, not daring to stand at ease until Rolly did.

Finally, Roland Jones relaxed his stance slightly, and separated his feet just a bit. Boxer figured that served as "at ease" for him. The remaining Rangers followed suit. Boxer saluted Jones. The major saluted back, very crisply.

Boxer said, "Major Jones, I'd like to commend you and your men on your *esprit de corps*. I'm very impressed. However, that was your last salute while you serve with me. And also the last time you stand at attention aboard my submarine. You're likely to split your heads open on the bulkheads. Okay?"

Jones snapped to attention and saluted. "Yes, sir."

"And your last 'sir'. The men call me Skipper, which suits me fine."

"Yes, sir."

"Yes, Skipper."

"Yes, Skipper."

Boxer managed a slight smile. "Good. I want to spend tonight going over this ship, and meeting the rest of the men. I'll be having a meeting at 0600 with Captain Clemens, my exec, Chief White, and yourself."

"Yes, Skipper." Jones smiled for the first time, though just barely.

"Relax, men. You'll be seeing plenty of action by this time tomorrow. Meanwhile, get some rest."

Boxer spent the next several hours reacquainting himself with the *Los Angeles* class sub. He toured the fore and aft torpedo rooms, met the sonar officers and techs, checked out the missile control consoles and the navigation and diving controls. He was pleased that some of his former men were at each position, and well integrated with the new people. Everything seemed to be running well.

"Aren't you going to get any sleep, Skipper?"

Boxer turned to find Clemens standing there watching him. "It's been so long since I've slept that I hadn't given it much thought."

"It's 0200 hours. I'll stand watch. Why don't you catch forty?"

"Well, maybe a short nap is in order. Maintain present course and speed until I wake up. That should put us at the mouth of the Persian Gulf. At the Strait of Hormuz."

"Roger that, Skipper. See you at 0600."

Boxer stifled a yawn. He'd been awake for almost twenty-four hours. "Okay, then. See you at 0600."

CHAPTER 21

At 0530 hours, Boxer arose from a fretful sleep filled with the images and sounds of the *Barracuda* being attacked and sunk in the Persian Gulf, with the sailors screaming in agony as they were being blown or crushed to death, or drowned trying to escape. He tried to shake the morbid thoughts from his mind, and made a trip to the head to splash cold water on his face. He carried a steaming cup of black coffee back to his quarters, and reflected on the day ahead of them. At precisely 0600, he switched on the MC mike above his bunk and summoned his key players to his tiny cabin. "This is Admiral Boxer... Captain Clemens, Major Jones and Mr. White please report to my quarters."

Whitey had been standing outside Boxer's door, waiting to be summoned. To him, five minutes early was on time. In less than thirty seconds, he was joined by Clemens and Rolly and they stuffed themselves inside Boxer's cramped quarters.

"Please be seated, men. Rolly, you and Clem take my bunk. Whitey, you can sit there," he said, pointing to his chair. Boxer stood with his back to the door. "We'll be entering the Strait of Hormuz at approximately 0700. That means we'll take her down from present periscope depth to one zero zero feet and keep as far from the Iranian coast as possible. My plan is to monitor the gulf as far west as possible and return along the Iranian side. My best guess is that the Ayatollah's boys have their mini-sub base near one of the small islands that dot their coast."

Clemens asked, "What if we encounter the enemy sooner?"

"I think that's what happened to the *Barracuda*. I feel that the Iranians, with possibly the Russians supporting them, tried to draw off the *Barracuda* and destroy it before Waldron could locate their base."

"So we attack?"

"I'd rather try an end run first. If we can avoid contact until we find their base, the mission will be the better for it."

Roland Jones cleared his throat. "If we spot an enemy sub, why don't we just blow the motherfucker out of the water? Then we can do what we came for."

Clemens blushed. Whitey suppressed a smile. Boxer said, "Well put, Major. But our assignment is to locate and destroy the suspected mini-submarine base. We've already lost one of our subs trying to do that, and chances are that they'll expect us to try again."

"So they'll be waiting for us," Clemens finished.

"Right," Boxer continued. "And once we skirmish with one of them, we'll attract the others like sharks drawn to blood. And we'll have to leave without achieving our objective." He turned to Rolly Jones. "Got that, now?"

"Got it. Sorry I spoke out of turn."

"Don't be sorry. I'd rather have you say what's on your mind than stifle a possible good idea. Now, Rolly, get your men ready in scuba gear. If and when we locate their base, it will be your job to destroy it. I'm sure I don't have to tell you how to go about it."

Rolly Jones smiled broadly. "No, sir, Skipper. You sure don't. We're just itching for some action."

Boxer smiled back. "I'll try my best to see that you get some. Whitey, I'll want your crew on full alert as of 0700. The gulf is shallow and I don't want to run aground. Keep an eye on your depth gauge."

Whitey said, "Right, Skipper. I've done this before a few times."

"I'm sure you have, Whitey. Clem, who do we have on sonar?"

"SO is Howard Freedman, Skipper. The guys call him Hi Fi. He looks like a be-bopper, but he's got one of the best ears in the business."

"Okay. Tell him we're going in under full silence. No active sonar. We'll use only the passive sonar in the bow and the towed array. I don't want to give our position away."

"Roger that, Skipper."

"We'll go in at five knots and drift. Notify the EO. If we encounter something, well try to avoid it for now."

"Right, Skipper."

"Whitey, I want everyone in their bunks except Major Jones's squad and the men on duty."

"Aye, aye, Skipper. I'll see to that. No flushing, no garbage disposal, no dispensing machines, nothing. If anybody farts, I'll have him scrubbing the decks with a toothbrush."

The others laughed at that. Boxer said, "Okay, men, you all know your assignments. Let's go do it."

Just past the northernmost tip of Oman, where it juts into the Gulf after leapfrogging a section of the United Arab Emirates, SO reported an enemy sub. Boxer said to his EXO, "Mark, you take the conn. I'm going to see what Hi Fi's up to."

"Roger that, Skipper."

Boxer found Freedman at his sonar console, listening intently to his earphones, while keeping an eye on the multi-color Spectogram reproduction of the sounds. The color patterns help to distinguish between submarines and other ocean-going behemoths, such as whales. "What do you have for me, Hi Fi?"

SO removed one earphone, still listening with the other ear. He had short dark hair, cut shorter on one side, with two parallel stripes carved into the other. "Got you a sub, Skipper. Actually, I think I've got two. Have a listen."

Freedman tossed a spare headset to Boxer and plugged it into his console. Boxer slipped it over his ears.

Hi Fi asked, "Hear that faint chug-a-chug-a-chug-a sound? That's a diesel. We don't use them at all anymore, but the Russians still do."

Boxer acknowledged SO's briefing with a nod. He already knew that, but let the young sonarman go on.

"The Russians mainly use them close to home, off of Scandinavia, in the Baltic and the Barents seas."

"They teach you that in sonar school?"

"No, sir," Hi Fi said, pointing to his dolphins. "I try to learn as much about the ship as I can. I'd like to make a career of the Navy."

"Well, you're doing just fine. You said there were two subs out there."

"Yes, Skipper. The other signal is fainter, but the Soviet *Alfas* have a distinct sound signature. I'd know it anywhere. Look here on the scope."

Boxer watched the SO point out the area around Qeshm Island, a mere ten kilometers away. "Good work, son. We'll maintain silence and try to give them the slip."

Hi Fi smiled and gave the thumbs-up sign.

Boxer walked to the control center and told Mahony, "Come to course two two five degrees."

"Aye, aye, Skipper. Coming the two two five degrees."

Boxer watched Clemens plot their position. He said, "We're trying to slip past the guardians of the gate."

Clemens chuckled, and pointed to a screen on his console that detailed their immediate area. "We're here, now. In five hours we'll be beyond Qatar and Bahrain. Then we should be able to cross the gulf and look for that sub base."

"Roger that, Clem. Meanwhile, we'll just keep her steady as she goes."

At 0230 hours, Boxer gave the order to change course for the Iranian coast. "Mahony, come to course three five zero."

"Aye, aye, Skipper. Coming to three five zero."

Whitey had just come on watch as diving officer, and was not happy with what he read on his gauges. He motioned for Boxer to come to his station. "Skipper, there's only five zero feet under the keel. The water's too shallow here."

"We'll keep to the main shipping channels for a while. Good work."

Whitey nodded and went back to studying his console.

Boxer keyed the helmsman. "Mahony, bring us around to zero seven five degrees."

"Roger that," Mahony replied, and put the helm across to reverse their earlier route through the gulf.

At 0300, the one of the men in the communications division handed Boxer a message. Boxer looked at the sheet written in code and walked it back to his quarters. He told Clemens, "ELF message from Admiral Rodgers." The ELF was an Extra Low Frequency radio message beamed off a satellite and able to penetrate the sea to be picked up by a submarine. The message came through one letter at a time, and was excruciatingly slow. Boxer put the message through his decoder and ran it at high speed. He reread the message twice and keyed Major Roland Jones.

"Rolly, to my quarters, please."

In a few moments, Jones was at the doorway to Boxer's cabin. "Come in, please."

Jones stood next to Boxer, who was seated at the table, with the decoded message and a chart of the area around the Strait. "What's up, Skipper?"

Boxer pointed to the chart. "Right here. That's our target. The Admiral just sent us word that our satellite got some good infrared close-ups of the mouth of the gulf on its last pass. It looks like the mini-sub base is on the mainland across this narrow channel from Qeshm Island. That's where we spotted to two enemy subs on the way in. It's their job to keep outsiders out."

"And our job to get in there and blow it up."

"Right, Rolly. Have your men slip out in the two Subskimmers and head for the target. Meanwhile, I'll try to draw those two subs out here. Pull them off your backs, if I can. If any of us survive, we'll rendezvous here, at the tip of Oman."

Jones rubbed his shaved head with his fingertips. "What do we do if this sub gets sunk?"

Boxer smiled. "Then I'd suggest that you and your men learn how to speak Farsi."

Rolly Jones laughed. "In that case, we better wish each other good luck."

Boxer accompanied Rolly as far as the control room. The major continued forward past the galley to his quarters in a converted missile compartment. "Suit up, men. We got work to do."

The commandos donned deep-blue wetsuits, and began strapping various weapons and explosives to their bodies. They would wait until Boxer brought them closer to their target. Then, they would board the two transporters that looked and acted like rigid-hull inflatables on the surface, but could be maneuvered and even parked underwater. No one knew just what kind of opposition they would meet, if any. They did know that their only hope of escape lay in these two vessels. And failure to escape meant certain death.

Boxer keyed his engineering officer. "EO... Come to full ahead."

"Aye, aye, Skipper. Full ahead."

The *Halsey* raced toward the mouth of the Persian Gulf at almost forty knots, flank speed for this *Los Angeles* class sub. As they approached the Strait, they drifted in at three knots, virtually silent. SO sent a message to Boxer. "Target bearing zero eight five degrees... Range six thousand yards... Depth zero five zero feet... Speed zero one five knots, Skipper. It's our friend, the diesel, sitting right off Qeshm Island."

"Thanks, Hi Fi." Boxer keyed Rolly Jones. "It's time, Rolly. The Subskimmers are clipped onto the deck. You'll find the fittings already attached. You inflate them from the sub's own pressure system."

"Roger that, Skipper. We're on our way."

"Good luck."

One by one, Rolly's Rangers slipped out through the forward escape hatch, and headed for the Subskimmers. Finally, there was a radio signal from Rolly indicating that they were off.

Boxer nodded to Clemens, and said, "Now to take some of the heat off of Rolly's men." He keyed the engine room. "EO... Full ahead. Let's make some noise to let them know we're out here."

"Roger that, Skipper. Full speed ahead."

"Mahony, head off a bit. Course one zero five degrees. We'll drive right past them."

In a few minutes, the pinging of the diesel sub's sonar registered in the *Halsey*. "Good," Boxer said. "They found us. Mahony, change course to one one five degrees. We'll try to draw them away from the island, and buy Rolly some time."

"Target bearing zero four five degrees... Range four thousand yards ... depth zero four five feet ... speed one five knots. Skipper, he's making a dash for the lee side of the island."

"Seems as if our friend wants us to follow him. Let's send him a present, instead?' He keyed the forward torpedo room. "TO ... load and arm tube one."

"Loading one, Skipper."

Boxer walked over to the Fire Control Console. "FCO ... slave fish one in on the target with your sonar."

"Aye, aye, Skipper."

"Fire one."

"Firing one."

Boxer and Clemens watched the wire-guided torpedo snake its way toward the target on the FCO screen.

"Target out of range, Skipper." SO reported. "She's ducked behind the island."

"FCO, blow the torpedo. Let them think we're going to follow them in. I'm beginning to smell something here and I don't like it."

Clemens nodded. "They're making it look too easy."

"That's what I'm thinking," Boxer concurred. "Let's pull back and see what happens. "Mahony, change course to two two zero degrees. DO ... bring us down to one zero zero feet."

"Coming to course two two five, Skipper," Mahony replied.

Whitey said, "Diving to one zero zero feet."

"Second target bearing zero eight five degrees, Skipper. It's our *Alfa*. Range three thousand five hundred yards... Depth zero seven zero feet... Speed four five knots and closing fast."

Clemens pointed to the blip closing in on them on his screen. "Do we go in for the kill?"

"Not yet. We have to buy Rolly's guys more time. We head off. "Helmsman, change course to one nine four degrees."

"Roger that," Mahony answered.

As they reached the shipping channel, Boxer ordered, "DO ... bring us down to one five zero. Diving planes at one zero degrees."

"Aye, aye, Skipper."

Boxer touched the klaxon button, and braced against a bulkhead as the *Halsey* blew some forward ballast and nosed downward. He watched the bubble indicator overhead reach the null reading as they leveled off.

"Coming to one five zero," Whitey announced in his dry monotone.

"Target bearing one eight zero degrees... Range seven thousand yards... Depth one zero zero feet... Speed four eight knots, Skipper. That *Alfa* is gaining on us."

"What about the diesel?"

"Negative. Skipper, multiple targets closing fast on our tail... Range five thousand yards... Depth one two five feet... Speed seven zero knots. Four fish, Skipper."

Boxer pressed the klaxon button twice. "Dive... Dive... Whitey, go to two five zero feet. Mahony, hard right rudder."

Almost immediately, the ballast tanks blew, and the *Halsey* went down hard and to the right. A tremendous explosion rolled over the hull. The *Halsey* jerked up and down, hit the bottom hard, and rolled onto her port side. Boxer shouted, "DCO ... report the damages."

The damage control officer responded with, "Aye, aye, Skipper."

A second explosion rocked the *Halsey*. Boxer was thrown to the deck. He reached for his EXO, to pull himself up. Blood from his shoulder wound soaked through Boxer's white shirt, and he dropped back to the deck. The *Halsey* rolled back on her side, and the lights went out.

CHAPTER 22

The blast sent a huge geyser of water heavenward from the site of the former mini-sub base. Chunks of concrete and twisted steel broke the surface and came back down to rest on the bottom. Rolly's Rangers watched from the relative safety of the beach. "Okay, men. Let's get the fuck out of here."

"You don't have to tell me twice. Let's hit it." Lieutenant Sam Fleury, Rolly's second in command hopped off the flat black rock he was sitting on and ran toward the breaking surf. He was followed closely by Rolly and the ten other Rangers.

Twelve men crashed through the breakers as one. Then, shots rang out. "Over there." Rolly pointed to a dune above the beach.

Fleury slipped a waterproof pouch off his back and removed a small automatic machine pistol. He ran a hand over his blond crewcut, and waved Rolly away. "I'll hold them off. Get moving."

Rolly Jones shouted back, "Give us a minute or two and head straight out. We'll come by to pick you up."

Fleury fired a burst at the dune and headed away from the rest of the men. Rolly dove under a breaking wave and followed his men out to the buoy that marked the parking area of the two Subskimmers. He was a world-class swimmer, and reached the two vessels a few strokes ahead of the others.

Rolly signaled the sergeant in charge of the other craft, motioning him to head for the Arabian Peninsula. He headed his own vessel due east. He hoped he could get to Fleury in time.

Sam Fleury fired one last long burst at the figures running toward him on the beach. At least three men went down. Fleury threw away the gun and swam out into the gulf. Shots whizzed past his head from behind. He just about had it made. They could never catch him now.

He swam for all he was worth, straight out into the gulf, using a nice, steady crawl stroke that was well suited to his long muscular arms. Then he heard the drone of a motor. Rolly had come for him, after all. He headed toward the noise.

The sharp retort of shots being fired brought his head up out of the water. A row of tiny plumes rose from the water heading toward him. Just missed. Damn. Sam Fleury drove himself down and farther out to sea. More shots were fired. The sounds of the motorboat came closer. Then it was upon him.

Fleury felt something hit his thigh. It took a long moment for him to realize that he'd stopped making forward progress. He couldn't move his leg. He looked down to see a deep gouge torn out of his hamstring muscle by the propeller. The more he tried to kick away, the worse it hurt. Still he pressed on.

He felt a sharp slap in the back, then another. Fleury bobbed to the surface to see the speedboat circling him, coming in for the kill. Men were shouting at him in a strange language. And then he saw Rolly and four other Rangers rise from the sea behind him. Rolly still had his machine pistol.

"Save yourselves," Fleury shouted. "I'm too far gone."

Rolly fired a burst at the advancing speedboat. One gunman took a hit in the chest and fell over backward. "No way, man. We're all in this together. I'm coming to get you."

"Kill me, man. Don't let them take me alive."

Rolly fired another round at the motorboat. "Hang on just a little longer. I'm almost there." He turned to the man handling the eighty horse merc outboard. "Can't you go any faster?"

Another spray of fire caught Sam Fleury in the head with Rolly only five feet away. The water turned red. Sam Fleury's body began to fill with water and started to sink. Rolly fired at the speedboat. "Bastards. Fuckin' bastards. You killed him."

A man in the bow stood up and aimed at Rolly. Jones emptied his clip into him. "Die, motherfuckers, die."

Two Rangers pulled out grenades and lobbed them at the speedboat as it bore down on them. Rolly yelled, "Jump! Dive!" Five Rangers hit the water as twin explosions burst over them, tearing away the bow of the enemy speedboat.

Eight or nine Iranian frogmen wearing only swim trunks or shorty black wetsuits and air tanks dropped silently into the gulf. Their leader caught sight of the Rangers and followed in hot pursuit.

Cletus Sawyer, a lanky, twenty-year-old Ranger caught up to Rolly and tapped his leg. Rolly looked back at the men following them, and turned to take them on. Cletus fired two shots from an air rifle, hitting one of the enemy frogmen. Rolly gave him a thumbs-up, and hurried to signal the others. Cletus fired again, and swam after him.

Rolly tagged his men and turned their attention to the frogmen following them. They watched them overrun Cletus Sawyer, who was still firing at them when the stainless-steel spear pierced his chest. Now it was four Rangers against eight of the enemy. The Iranians formed a wedge and swam into their midst. Rolly dove deep and came up under the point man, driving the twelve-inch blade of his scuba knife up into his bare solar plexus. *That's for Cletus, you bastard.*

He dodged a spear and headed for another enemy frogman. Two other Rangers spread out along the flanks of the wedge. The fourth Ranger dove deep and made his way to the rear. In close ranks, the air rifles could do more harm than good, so the Rangers moved in with only their knives. It was going to be man to man.

Rolly made fast work of two men by severing first their air hoses, and then their throats as they surfaced for air. *That's for Sam Fleury.* Five left.

The Ranger on the left flank was locked in a death grip with his man. Rolly ducked away from an attacker and cut the Iranian's air hose. The flank man finished him off. The odds were now even. Four Rangers and four Iranians. The enemy didn't like the odds, and tried to escape.

They found themselves surrounded front and back and both sides. The Rangers moved in for the kill. In a flurry of flashing steel and writhing muscle, all four Iranians and one more Ranger died. The sea turned red from all the blood. Rolly Jones glanced at the blood flowing from a long cut on his arm, and motioned for his men to surface.

They pulled off their masks and air hoses, breathing the fresh air, drawing in deeply. Rolly got his bearings, and headed toward the Subskimmer. It was now reduced to a blazing wreck, along with the Iranian speedboat. Talk about being up the creek without a paddle. But at least the three of them were still alive.

Rolly Jones tried to make up his mind. To swim back to shore was the shortest distance. But that would be almost certain suicide, perhaps a slow death by torture at the hands of the crazies on land. On the other hand, the Arabian coast was eight or ten miles away. He'd swum that far before. But now he had a mean-looking gash on his arm. And it was starting to throb.

And then he heard the sound of a motor, faint at first, then growing louder and louder. The three Rangers turned in unison to see another boat bearing down on them. *Friend or foe*, Rolly asked himself. He looked at his two men, then at the blood oozing from his wound. "We shall just have to see," he said aloud. "We shall see."

"Clem ... help me up."

"Skipper, you okay?"

Just then, the emergency lights came on, bathing the interior control room in a dull yellow glow. "I'll live," Boxer grunted. "I opened up this shoulder wound."

"I didn't know you were wounded. Let's get you fixed up."

"First things first, Clem. Let's assess the damages." Boxer keyed the damage control officer. "DCO... Report to the bridge, please."

Clemens took the mike. "Medic to the control room."

"There may be others who need him more than me, Clem. He may be busy with them."

"Can't run a ship without a captain. And this captain can use a doc right now."

"Maybe you're right." Boxer felt a stickiness on his left side.

"The whole left side of your shirt is bloody, Skipper. Let's have a look." Clemens helped Boxer remove his shirt. The gauze bandage covering the shoulder was blood-soaked. Clemens got a pocketknife from his pants and began cutting away the bandage.

"You called, Mr. Clemens?" It was C.P.O. Pulasky, the ship's quartermaster, who doubled as the MO. "Oh, Admiral Boxer. Let me take a look at that." He plopped his black medical kit on a console table and found a compression bandage. "This ought to stop the bleeding, sir."

"I'll be all right. The other men may need you more than me."

"I'm afraid some of the men didn't make it, sir. I've got two DOAs and a lot of broken bones. Did we take a hit?"

"A near miss, I think. The concussion slammed us against the bottom."

"Freedman picked up an explosion just as we took the blast, Skipper."

Boxer managed a smile. "The mini-sub base, I hope. We're not that far away. That may explain why we're still alive. The same concussion may have stopped that Soviet *Alfa*."

"Let's hope so."

Then, over the intercom, "Conn, DCO."

Boxer took the mike. "Go ahead, DCO."

"We've got trouble with the forward ballast tanks, Skipper. I'm afraid that once we surface, that's it. We won't be able to resubmerge. We can maneuver within a fifty-to seventy-foot depth range by using only the aft tanks."

"Hmmm," Boxer replied. "Is that it?"

"Sorry, Skipper, but the air scrubber isn't working properly. We can buy some time if we kill the AC now."

"It'll get hotter than hell in here," Boxer said, rubbing his beard. "Go ahead, do it. I'll order the men to dress down."

"Conn, SO." It was Hi Fi Freedman. "Target bearing one six zero degrees ... range four thousand yards ... depth two zero zero feet ... speed twenty knots, Skipper. She's pulling away."

"Thanks, Hi Fi." He turned to Clemens. "She's running from us. Must have sustained some damage of her own."

"Can we still take her?"

"We can damn sure try, Clem." Boxer keyed the MC mike. "Aft TO, arm seven and eight. Forward TO, arm tubes two and four."

"Aye, aye, Skipper," both men replied.

"Okay, Mr. Clemens. Let's get ourselves an *Alfa*." Boxer keyed the engine room. "EO, conn. Give me flank speed. Engines full ahead."

"Roger that, Skipper."

As the massive turbines roared back to life, the full lights came back on in the control room. SO called in, "Conn, SO. Target dead ahead ... range three thousand yards ... depth two zero zero feet ... speed two zero knots on course zero three six degrees."

Clemens plotted the relative positions of the two subs. Boxer could see that they were gaining on the *Alfa*. "DO ... take us up slowly to one five zero feet."

"Aye, aye, Skipper. Diving planes at zero five degrees."

"Good man, that Whitey," Boxer said to Clemens. "Really knows his stuff."

"Too bad he's not an officer. He'd make a great DO on our next prototype."

Boxer put his hand on Clemens's shoulder. "As far as I'm concerned, Whitey can be the DO on any sub I ever command." He pointed to the screen in front of Clemens. "I'm going to try to keep that *Alfa* between us and the coast. Then we'll keep cutting the distance."

"Catch them between a rock and a hard place, eh?"

"That's a nice way to put it."

"Conn, EO," the engineering officer's voice interrupted. "The turbines took a beating. I've got a bearing out of alignment. Sucker's banging away inside. I've got to cut the speed."

"Roger that," Boxer said. "What can you give me?"

"Thirty knots, maybe. Twenty would be within the safety zone."

"Okay, EO. Give me thirty knots. We won't get a second chance at this baby. We have to go for it."

"Aye, aye, Skipper. You've got thirty."

Boxer plotted a course running parallel to the coast, about a mile offshore. "Got to keep boxing them in," he showed Clemens.

"Multiple targets bearing zero nine zero degrees, Skipper," SO reported. "Range fifteen hundred yards ... speed seven zero knots and closing fast."

Boxer shook his head. "Can't dive," he told Clemens. "Got to shoot them out of the water." He keyed sonar. "How many torpedoes, SO?"

"Two, Skipper. Range now one thousand yards."

Boxer keyed the aft torpedo room. "Arm seven and eight."

"Seven and eight armed, Skipper."

"FO, fire seven and eight. Slave them onto the targets."

"Roger that."

Two blasts ripped over the *Halsey*. The lights dimmed, and then returned to normal. They had won that round. A draw would be more accurate. Boxer said to Clemens, "Now to drive that *Alfa* into shore. Forward TO, arm two and four."

"Tubes two and four armed, Skipper."

"Mahony, change course to zero three zero degrees."

"Aye, aye, Skipper. Zero three zero degrees."

"FCO ... home your sonar onto the target."

"Roger, Skipper."

"Fire two."

"Firing two," FCO replied.

The guidance wire played out behind the Mark 48 torpedo as it sped toward the target at seventy knots. Aboard the *Alfa*, Kilmov tried desperately to outrun the fish. And failing that, he tried to outmaneuver it. He headed ever closer to the Emirate coast.

The FCO followed the target on the type 2020 sonar slave display. He followed every turn of the target, signaling the data through the guidance wire to the Mark 48. The torpedo slowed, turned, speeded up, all in response to the fire control system. Finally, "The fish has the target on its internal sonar, Skipper."

"Great. Let her loose, FCO."

"Aye, aye, Skipper. With pleasure."

Kilmov tried one last desperate maneuver. Too late. The *Alfa* hit the beach at the very moment the Mark 48 torpedo found its target. The explosion tore out the bows of the enemy sub.

"Bingo," FCO reported. "It's a hit."

SO keyed the bridge. "Conn, SO. I believe the target is aground."

Boxer smiled and nodded to Clemens. "Good work." He keyed the forward torpedo room. "TO … arm four."

"Aye, aye, Skipper. Tube four armed."

"FCO … fire when you have the coordinates."

FCO did a quick calculation on his computer. "Four away, Skipper."

A blast sent the *Halsey* rocking. The bow began to head downward.

"Whitey…"

"Under control, Skipper." He compensated with the diving planes and blowing forward ballast.

"Direct hit, Skipper," FCO reported.

Boxer managed a smile. "Whitey, let's take her up. Nice and easy as she goes."

"Roger that, Skipper. Five degrees on the planes. Blow forward ballast, nice and easy. You realize that we can't resubmerge, sir?"

"I understand, Whitey. I want to take a look for myself. Take us up to periscope depth."

"Aye, aye, Skipper."

When they reached the proper depth, Boxer twisted a dial and the periscope rose out of the water. He pressed his face to the foam cushioning around the viewfinder. "One of the torpedoes scored a direct hit on the bridge. She's aground and ablaze. Come take a look, Clem."

Clemens took his place at the periscope. "Sure is a beautiful sight, Skipper. Are we going to finish her off?"

"No need for that, Clem. That *Alfa* is out of action. I'll radio her position to Admiral Rodgers. He can deal with the survivors and the salvage. We've got to rendezvous with Rolly Jones and his Rangers."

Major Roland Jones tread water, his knife at his side, his airtanks almost empty. This might be his last stand, he realized. He watched the motorcraft close in on him and the two other survivors. Then a smile creased his face. "Hey, it's the sarge, and the guys. What a sight for sore eyes."

Sergeant First Class Carlos Rivera waved from the bow as his Subskimmer approached the three heads bobbing in the water. "Hey, you guys need a lift?"

Rolly reached for the outstretched hands and pulled himself onto the overcrowded vessel. "Our spirits could sure use a lift. Fleury, Sawyer, and Marino didn't make it."

Rivera crossed himself. "Sorry about that, Rolly. They were good men."

A second Ranger was hauled aboard. "Mean Gene" Greene was a six-footer with dark close-cropped hair, almost black eyes, and a permanent tough, hard look about his face brought about more by his sharp angular features than his disposition. Nevertheless, the nickname Mean Gene stuck with him. He said, "It was two to one against us, and we kicked their asses."

As the third survivor was pulled aboard the boat, Rolly said, "Sarge, we're never going to make it to the other side before dark if we don't move it."

"You got it, Rolly. We're on our way."

"Hey, man, what the hell is that sticking out of the water?"

One of the men shielded his eyes and stared at the surface of the gulf toward the Iranian side. "Must be some kind of vent pipe."

Rivera squinted against the glare of the late-afternoon sun on the water. "Vent, my ass. That's a fuckin' periscope. Must be Boxer come to rescue us."

Rolly stared at the pipe protruding from the surface. "I don't know. Boxer said he'd meet up with us on the Arabian side of the gulf. We're right in the middle."

The submarine rose out of the sea with decks awash. The conning tower loomed over the tiny inflatable. The chug-a-chug-a-chug-a of the diesel engine could be heard over the din of the Subskimmer's outboard. In a minute, the tower was filled with sailors and officers crowding the bulwark, peering at them with binoculars, pointing machine guns at them.

Rivera shrugged. "Why do I get this sinking feeling we're in deep shit here?"

Rolly quipped, "You know what they say, man. If it looks like shit, and smells like it … just keep smiling and ease that M-16 over near me. Anybody got any grenades left?"

"I got two," Mean Gene replied.

"See if you can get one to Shorty," Rolly said quietly. Shorty was six foot six.

The deck hatch on the sub opened, and several crewmen climbed out. Someone reached behind and lent a hand to the man who was apparently the ship's captain, judging from all the gold braid on his uniform and scrambled eggs on the brim of his cap. He stood at attention on the deck and shouted at them in a strange language. He was followed by a junior officer, who translated. "Our honorable Captain Aran Kashan serves you with notice that you are under arrest for crimes against the people of Iran. You will return as our prisoners and stand trial in our courts. When you are found guilty, you will be punished in accordance with our laws."

Rolly told his men, "Okay, now, everybody smile and nod your heads. Let these jackasses think we'll go with them. When I say, 'Motherfucker,' fire everything you got and dive over the side. We'll take as many of them with us as we can. Agree?"

Rivera smiled and nodded his head. "See. How'm I doin'? Just make sure you don't say motherfucker when you don't mean it."

Roland Jones turned to the captain and his interpreter. He smiled and nodded his head. He could make out his men doing the same thing out of the corner of his eye. He shouted across the closing gap, "Tell honorable Captain that we are his prisoners. But tell me why you said we will be punished *when* we are found guilty instead of *if* we are found guilty?"

The interpreter translated for the captain, and then more loudly for the crew. The captain thought that was very funny, and began to chuckle. The crew picked up on this and they all began to laugh at Rolly.

Jones said to his men under his breath. "Well, I guess this is it, guys. Been nice teaching you everything you know. Ready?"

"Yeah, man. Do it already. We're ready."

Rolly shouted to the submarine, "Honorable Captain, I have one more thing to say."

The interpreter whispered in the captain's ear. The captain looked at Rolly and shrugged.

Rolly shouted, "Die, motherfuckers." He scooped up the M-16 and fired a short burst at the captain and his flunkies. Other Rangers swept the deck clean, killing or wounding everyone on board.

The Iranians returned fire from the bridge. One ranger took a hit, and collapsed over the side. "Now," Rolly shouted to Mean Gene.

Mean Gene lobbed his grenade in a high arch. It came down in the conning tower. The explosion took them all by surprise, and they were all blown apart.

Shorty said, "Hey, wait a minute for me, guys. I gotta deliver a present to the Ayatollah." He dove over the side, and scrambled onto the deck of the submarine. The hatch was still open. A sailor stuck his head out to see what was going on. Shorty kicked his face, and the sailor slipped below. Then, Shorty pulled the pin, flipped the lever, and dropped his grenade into the opening. He said, "Been nice meetin' you," and he leaped off the deck, swimming with all he had.

Rolly shouted to his men, "Abandon ship," just as reinforcements made their way to the bridge and opened fire on them.

Rolly surfaced about twenty yards to the lee of their vessel, which was being shot to pieces by the submariners. "Well, guys. Looks like we're out of options."

Rivera pointed toward the west. "Maybe not, Rolly. I think we've got some company."

Shorty, a full-blooded Cherokee, grinned. "This is the first time that I've ever been glad to see the cavalry coming."

The U.S.S. *Halsey* rode on the surface a few hundred yards away. Clemens was in the control room; Boxer had the conn from the outside bridge. He spoke through a loudspeaker. "Ahoy there aboard the *Hezbullah*." The name was painted on the side of the bridge. "This is Admiral Boxer of the U.S. Navy, and those are my men that you're firing on. Put down your arms at once or we will sink you."

Rolly Jones shouted, "Give 'em hell, Skipper."

The Iranian sailors on the bridge went wild, started shouting and cursing at Boxer. Several machine-gun bursts were fired at Boxer, mostly deflecting off the bridge's armor plate, some coming very close to hitting him. Boxer said, "Well, we asked you nice." He keyed the control room. "Mr. Clemens, fire tube one."

"Yes, *sir*. One fired."

The torpedo streamed along just below the surface, speeding toward its target. Boxer yelled, "Rolly, keep your men clear."

The next instant there was a loud thunk, followed by a huge explosion. The Iranian sailors were thrown from the bridge. The *Hezbullah* split in two. Fire broke out, followed by a secondary explosion. A cheer broke out among Rolly's Rangers, still bobbing in the water. One by one, they swam the short distance to the *Halsey*.

Boxer turned the conn over to Clemens, and climbed down to the deck to greet each man as he climbed aboard, and shook his hand. Rolly, the first aboard, stood at his side. "Nice work, men."

Boxer stood there for a while with Jones, watching the burning wreck of the *Hezbullah* slip under the sea. "Hellovah job you and your men did, Major. The submarine base is destroyed. The Iranian sub is destroyed. A nice day's work. I hope that we get to work together as a team again."

Rolly Jones smiled. "I'll request that myself. And I take it that the Russian sub is no longer a threat to shipping in the gulf?"

"We caught them red-handed in a hostile action in an area they had no business being. That won't help the world opinion of them. Plus we sank one of their *Alfas*."

Standing there on the deck, Rolly Jones shook Boxer's hand, and smiled. "I guess this calls for a celebration."

Boxer placed an arm on Jones's shoulder, and walked him toward the open hatch. "Good idea, Rolly. Now, let's go home."

A NOTE TO THE READER

Dear Reader,

If you have enjoyed the novel enough to leave a review on **Amazon** and **Goodreads**, then we would be truly grateful.

Sapere Books

Sapere Books is an exciting new publisher of brilliant fiction and popular history.

To find out more about our latest releases and our monthly bargain books visit our website:
saperebooks.com

Printed in Great Britain
by Amazon

36379733R00145